I0667587

ALIEN SOULS

ALIEN SOULS

BY

ACHMED ABDULLAH

Author of "Night Drums,"
"Mating of the Blades," etc.

WILDSIDE PRESS

Copyright 1922 by

THE JAMES A. McCANN COMPANY

All Rights Reserved

TO
PHOEBE FOSTER
"Un Livre Pour Toi"

CONTENTS

FEUD

To-day he lives in Bokhara, in the old quarter of the desert town that the natives call *Bokhara-i-Shereef*. He has a store in a bazaar not far from the Samarkand Gate, where he sells the gold-threaded brocades of Khiva and the striped Bokhariot belts that the caravan-men exchange for brick-pressed tea across the border in Chinese Turkestan, and where, methodically filling his pipe with tobacco from the carved pumpkin-shell at his elbow, he praises the greatness of Russia.

There, at noon every day, his ten-year-old son comes to him, bringing clean and well-spiced food from the market.

"Look at him!" he says often, proudly pinching the supple arms of the lad, and exhibiting him as he would a pedigreed stallion. "Sinews and muscles and a far-seeing eye, and no nerves—none at all. Because of which I give thanks to Allah the Wise-judging, the Opener of the Door of Knowledge with the Key of His Mercy. For one day my son will wear a plaited, green coat and a tall *chugerma* cap of white fur, and serve Russia. He will learn to shoot straight, very straight, and then," he adds, with a meaning smile, if he happens to be speaking to one of the three men whom he trusts,—"then he will desert. But he will return, perhaps,"—rapidly snapping his fingers to ward off misfortunes,—"he will return to his regiment, and he will not be very much punished."

I

A true Russian man he calls himself, and his name, too, has a Russian purring and deep ringing to it—"Pavel Alikhanski." Also there is talk in the town that he is in the pay of that great Bokharan magnate, the *kushbegi,* friend of the Russians, bringing tales to them about his Highness the Ameer, and receiving milled gold for the telling.

But ten years ago, when I called him friend, his name was not Alikhanski. Then he called himself Wazir Ali-Khan Sulaymani, that last name giving clue to his nation and race; for "Sulaymani" means "descendant of King Solomon," and it is known in half the world that the Afghans claim this resplendent Hebrew potentate as their breed's remote sire.

In those days he lived in a certain gray and turbulent city not far from the northeastern foot-hills of the Himalayas, where three great countries link elbows and swap lies and intrigues and occasional murders, and where the Afghan mist falls down like a purple-gray veil. In those days Russia was not on his lips, and he called himself an Herati, an Afghan from Herat, city-bred and city-courteous, but with a strain of maternal blood that linked him to the mountains and the sharp, red feuds of the mountains. But city-bred he was, and as such he lisped Persian, sipped coffee flavored with musk, and gave soft answer to harsh word.

He did not keep shop then, and none knew his business, though we all tried to find out, chiefly I, serving the Ameer of Afghanistan in that far city, and retailing the gossip of the inner bazaars from the border to the rose gardens of Kabul, where the governor sits in state and holds durbar.

But money he had, also breeding, also a certain winsome gentleness of spirit and speech, a soft moving of high-veined hands, well-kept, and finger-nails darkened with henna in an effeminate manner.

He spent many a day in the Khwadja Hills, called poetically Hill A12, C5, K-K67, and so forth, in the Russian and British survey-maps. There he would shoot bighorns and an occasional northern tiger that had drifted down to the wake of the Mongolian snows. This was strange, for an Afghan does not kill for the sake of killing, the sake of sport. He kills only for the sake of food or feud.

Nor could he explain even to himself why three or four times every month he left his comfortable town house and went into the hills, up and down, following the call of the wilderness; through the gut of the deep-cleft Nadakshi Pass; up beyond the table-lands, pleasant with apricot- and mulberry-trees; still farther up to the smoke-dimmed height of the Salt Hills, where he stained his soft, city-bred hands with the dirt of the tent-peg and the oily soot of his rifle.

Once I asked him, and he laughed gently.

"My mother came from the hills," he replied, "and it is perhaps her blood screaming in my veins which makes me take to the hills, to kill bighorn and snow-tiger instead of killing brother Afghans."

"You do not believe in feuds?" I was astonished, for I was young in those days.

Again he laughed.

"I do," he said; "an eye for an eye, and a tooth for a tooth. A true saying, and a wise one. But what worth is there to me in killing my enemy if my enemy's son will kill me in the course of time? An unfinished feud is a useless thing. For, tell me, can even the fleetest horse escape its own tail? Can the naked tear their clothes? Can a dead horse eat grass?"

So month after month he went into the hills, and he came back, his soul filled with the sights he had seen, his spirit peopled with the tales and the memories of the hills. Often I spent the evening with him, and he would digest his experiences in the acrid fumes of his bamboo pipe. He smoked opium in those days.

Then one day he came back from the hills a married man.

She was a hillwoman of the Moustaffa-Khel tribe, and her name was Bibi Halima. She was a distant cousin of his on his mother's side.

Tall, hook-nosed, white-skinned, with gray-black, flashing eyes and the build of a lean she-panther, not unbeautiful, and fit mother for a strong man's sons, I saw her often. For these hillwomen despise the customs of the sheltered towns; they will not cover their bodies with the swathing *farandjés,* nor their faces with the *chasband,* the horsehair veil of the city women.

Ali-Khan loved her. He loved her with that love which comes to fortunate men once in a lifetime—once and not oftener. His spoken love was as his hands, soft and smooth and courtly and slightly scented. He would fill those hands with gifts for her adornment, and he would write poems to her in the Persian manner.

And she? Did she love him?

Assuredly, though she was silent. The women of Afghanistan do not speak of love unless they are courtezans. They bear children,—sons, if Allah wills, —and what else is there for woman in the eyes of woman or of man? Also, since love is sacrifice, can there be greater proof of love than the pain of giving birth?

No, Bibi Halima did not weave words of love, cunning and soft. Perhaps she thought her husband's spoken love-words in keeping with his henna-stained finger-nails, an effeminacy of the city, smacking of soft Persia and softer Stamboul, the famed town of the West.

She did not speak of love, but the time was near when she was about to give answer, lusty, screaming answer. She expected a child.

"May Allah grant it be a man-child," she said to her husband and to her mother, a strong-boned, hooknosed old hag of a hillwoman who had come down into the city to soothe her daughter's pains with her knowledge—"a man-child, broad-bodied and without a blemish!"

"Aye, by God, the Holder of the Scale of Law! A man-child, a twirler of strength, a breaker of stones, a proud stepper in the councils of fighting men!" chimed in the old woman, using a tribal saying of the Moustaffa-Khel.

Ali-Khan, as was his wont, snapped his fingers rapidly to ward off the winds of misfortune. He bent over Bibi Halima's hands, and kissed them very gently, for you must remember that he was a soft man, citybred, very like a Persian.

"Let it be a man-child," he said in his turn, and his voice was as deep and holy as the voice of the muezzin calling the faithful to prayer. "Allah, give me a son, a little son, to complete my house, to give meaning and strength to my life; and to yours, blood of my soul!" he added, again kissing Bibi Halima's hands. "And you, beloved," he continued haltingly, for a great fear was in his heart—"but you, pearl tree of delight—you must live to—"

"Silence, babble-mouth!" the old mother interrupted with a shriek. "Do not speak aloud with naked heart and tongue! You will bring ill luck on your house! Of course she will live. She is my daughter, blood of my blood and bone of my bone. She is of the hills." She laughed. "Seven sons have I borne to my lord, and still I live." And she pushed Ali-Khan toward the door, mumbling bitter words about foolish men of Persian manners sporting with the jinn of misfortune. "Go now!"

"I go," Ali-Khan said submissively; and he returned, half an hour later, bearing many gifts, silk and bracelets and sweetmeats and perfume from Ispahan.

But Bibi Halima waved them aside with a short, impatient gesture. No, no, no, she did not want these man-made things. She wanted him to go to the hills to bring back to her the flowers of the hills, purple rhododendrons, soft-colored mimosas, and wild hibiscus smelling strongly of summer.

"Go to the hills, O pilgrim," added the old woman as she saw his anxious face. "We women need no man around in the hour of trial. Ho!" she spat out her betel through blackened, stumpy teeth, "let women do women's business. Men in the house are as useless as barren spinsters, fit only to break the household pots. Go to the hills, my lord, and bring back the flowers of the hills. On your return, with the help of Allah, there will be a little son strengthening the house."

And so he went to the hills, his rifle in his arm. Up to the high hills he went to pick flowers for his beloved, a song on his lips.

"O Peacock, cry again," I heard his voice as he passed my house.

Early the next morning Ebrahim Asif came to town. He also was of the Moustaffa-Khel, and a first cousin to Bibi Halima, and upon the blue-misted Salt Hills he was known as a brawler and a swashbuckler. A year before he had spoken to her of love, and had been refused. She had married Ali-Khan instead a few months later.

Now he came to her house, and the old mother stood in the doorway.

"Go away!" she shrilled; for being an Afghan herself, she did not trust the Afghan, her sister's son.

Ebrahim Asif laughed.

"I have come to see my cousin and Ali-Khan. See, I have come bringing gifts."

But still the old woman was suspicious.

"Trust a snake before an Afghan," she replied. "Ali-Khan is away to the hills. Go, filthy spawn of much evil!"

"Spawn of your sister's blood, you mean," he replied banteringly; and the old woman laughed, for this was a jest after her own heart. "Let me in!" he continued. "Once your daughter blinded my soul with a glance of her eye. Once the fringe of her eyelids took me into captivity without ransom. But time and distance have set me free from the shackles of my love. It is forgotten. Let me bring these gifts to her."

So the old woman let him into the zenana, where the windows were darkened to shut out the strong Northern sun. Bibi Halima gave him pleasant greeting from where she lay on the couch in the corner of the room.

"Live forever, most excellent cousin!" he said, bowing with clasped hands. "Live in the shadow of happiness!"   He took a step nearer.   "I have brought you presents, dispenser of delights."

Bibi Halima laughed, knowing of old Ebrahim Asif's facility for turning cunning words.   She spoke to her mother.

"Open the blinds, Mother, and let me see what my cousin has brought from the hills."

The old woman drew up the blinds, and Bibi Halima looked.

"See, see, Mother!" she exclaimed, "see the gifts which my cousin has brought me!"

"Aye, Daughter," the old woman replied, "gifts to adorn the house."   And then she added, with the pride of age greedy for grandchildren, "but there will be a gift yet more fit to adorn this house when you lay a man-child into your lord's arms."

Then the terrible rage of the Afghans rose suddenly in Ebrahim Asif's throat. He had come in peace, bearing gifts; but when he heard that the woman whom once he had loved would give birth to a child, the other man's child, he drew his *cheray*.

A slashing, downward thrust, and he was out of the house and off to the hills again.

The blow had struck Bibi Halima's temple with full force. She was half dead, but she forced back her ebbing strength because she wanted to hold a man-child in her arms before she died.

"Stop your crying!" She turned to her mother, who had fallen into a moaning heap at the foot of the couch. "Allah el-Mumit—God the Dispenser of Justice—will not let me die before I have laid a son into my lord's arms. Call a doctor of the English."

So the old woman came to my door, giving word to me of what had occurred. I hurried to the Street of the Mutton Butchers, where the English *hakim* lived, and together we went to the house of Bibi Halima.

He examined her, dressed her wound, and said:

"A child will be born, but the mother will assuredly die."

The old woman broke into a storm of tears, but Bibi Halima silenced her with a gesture.

"It is as God wills," she said, and the doctor marveled at her vitality. "Let but the child be born first, and let that child be a man-child. The rest matters not. And you"—she turned to me—"and you, my friend, go to the hills and fetch me my lord."

I bowed assent, and went to the door.

"Wait!" Her voice was firm despite her loss of blood. "If on the way you should meet Ebrahim Asif, you must not kill him. Let him be safe against my husband's claiming."

"I shall not touch him," I promised, though the sword at my side was whinnying in its scabbard like a Balkh stallion in the riot of young spring.

All that day and the following night, making no halt, I traveled, crossing the Nadakshi Pass at the lifting of dawn, and smelling the clean snow of the higher range the following noon. Here and there, from mountaineers and the Afghan Ameer's rowdy soldiers, I asked if aught had been seen of the two men, both being well known in the land.

Yes, I asked for both men; for while I was hurrying to my friend with the message which was about my heart like a heel-rope of grief, it was also in my soul to keep track of Ebrahim Asif. Kill him I could not, because of the promise I had given to Bibi Halima; but perhaps I could reach Ali-Khan before the other had a chance to make the rock-perched villages of the Moustaffa-Khel, and thus comparative safety.

It was late in the afternoon, with the lights of the camp-fires already twinkling in the gut of the Nadakshi, when I heard the noise of tent-peg speaking to hammer-nose, and the squealing of pack-ponies, free of their burdens, rolling in the snow. It was a caravan of Bokhara *tadjiks* going south to Kabul with wool and salt and embroidered silks, and perhaps a golden bribe for the governor.

They had halted for a day and a night to rest the sore feet of their animals, and the head-man gave me ready answer.

"Yes, pilgrim," he said; "two men passed here this day, both going in the same direction," and he pointed it out to me. "I did not know them, being myself a stranger in these parts; but the first was a courteous man who was singing as he walked. He gave us pleasant greeting, speaking in Persian, and dipped hands in our morning meal. Two hours later, traveling on the trail of the first man, another man passed the *kafilah*, a hillman, with the manners of the hills, and the red lust of killing in his eyes, nosing the ground like a jackal. We did not speak to him, for we do not hold with hillmen and hill-feuds. We be peaceful men, trading into Kabul."

It was clear to me that the hillman intended to forestall just fate by killing Ali-Khan before the latter had heard of what had befallen Bibi Halima. So I thanked the *tadjik*, and redoubled my speed; and late that evening I saw Ebrahim Asif around the bend of a stone spur in the higher Salt Range, walking carefully, using the shelter of each granite boulder, like a man afraid of breech-bolt snicking from ambush.   For a mile I followed him, and he did not see me or hear me.   He knew that his enemy was in front, and he did not look behind.   Again the sword was whinnying at my side.   For Ali-Khan was friend to me, and we of Afghanistan are loyal in living, loyal also in taking life.

But there was my promise to Bibi Halima to keep Ebrahim Asif safe against her husband's claiming.

And I kept him safe, quite safe, by Allah, the holder of the balance of right.   For using a short cut which I knew, having once had a blood-feud in those very hills, I appeared suddenly in front of Ebrahim Asif, covering him with my rifle.

He did not show fight, for no hillman will battle against impossible odds.   Doubtless he thought me a robber; and so, obeying my command, he dropped his rifle and his *cheray,* and he suffered me to bind his hands behind his back with my waistband.

But when I spoke to him, when I pronounced the name of Ali-Khan and Bibi Halima, he turned as yellow as a dead man's bones.   His knees shook.   The fear of death came into his eyes, and also a great cunning; for these Moustaffa-Khel are gray wolves among wolves.

"Walk ahead of me, son of Shaitan and of a she-jackal," I said, gently rubbing his heart with the muzzle of my rifle.   "Together you and I shall visit Ali-Khan.   Walk ahead of me, son of a swine-fed bazaar-woman."

He looked at me mockingly.

"Bitter words," he said casually, "and they, too, will be washed out in blood."

"A dead jackal does not bite," I said, and laughed; "or do you think that perhaps Ali-Khan will show you mercy? Yes, yes," I added, still laughing, "he is a soft man, with the manners of a Persian. Assuredly he will show you mercy."

"Yes," he replied, "perhaps he will show me mercy." Again the cunning look shone in his eyes, and a second later he broke into riotous, high-shrilling laughter.

"Why the laughter?" I asked, astonished.

"Because you shall behold the impossible."

"What?"

"When the impossible happens, it is seen," he answered, using the Sufi saying; "for eyes and ears prove the existence of that which cannot exist: a stone swims in the water; an ape sings a Kabuli love-song—"

"Go on!" I interrupted him impatiently, rubbing his side with my rifle.

So we walked along, and every few seconds he would break into mad laughter, and the look of cunning would shine in his gray eyes. Suddenly he was quiet. Only he breathed noisily through his nostrils, and he rolled his head from side to side like a man who has taken too much *bhang*. And that also was strange, for, with his hands tied behind his back, he could not reach for his opium-box, and I could not make it out at all.

A few minutes later we came in sight of Ali-Khan. He was sitting on a stone ledge near a bend of the road, flowers about him, carefully wrapped in moist, yellow moss so that they would keep fresh for the longing of his beloved, and singing his old song, "O Peacock, cry again—"

Then he saw us, and broke off. Astonishment was in his eyes, and he turned a little pale.

"Ebrahim Asif," he stammered, "what is the meaning of this?" And then to me, who was still covering the hillman with my rifle: "Take away your weapon from Ebrahim! He is blood-cousin to Bibi Halima, distant cousin to me."

"Ho!" Ebrahim's shout cut in as sharp as the point of an Ulwar saber. "Ho! ho! ho!" he shouted again and again. Once more the mad, high-shrilling laughter, and then suddenly he broke into droning chant.

I shivered a little, and so did Ali-Khan. We were both speechless. For it was the epic, impromptu chanting which bubbles to the lips of the Afghan hill-men in moments of too great emotion, the chanting which precedes madness, which in itself is madness— the madness of the she-wolf, heavy with young, which has licked blood.

"Listen to the song of Ebrahim Asif, the Sulaymani, the Moustaffa-Khel," he droned, dancing in front of us with mincing steps, doubly grotesque because his hands were tied behind his back; "listen to the song of Ebrahim Asif, son of Abu Salih Musa, grandson of Abdullah el-Jayli, great-grandson of the Imam Hasan Abu Talib, great-great-grandson of Abd al-Muttalib al-Mahz! I have taken my rifle and my *cheray,* and I have gone into the plains to kill. I descended into the plains like a whirlwind of destruction, leaving behind me desolation and grief. Blood is on my hands, blood of feud justly taken, and therefore I praise Allah, Opener of the Locks of Hearts with His Name, and—"

The words died in his throat, and he threw himself on the ground, mouthing the dirt like a jackal hunting for a buried corpse.

For a moment I stood aghast. Was the man really mad?

But no; I remembered the cunning look which had crept into his eyes when he had said that perhaps Ali-Khan would show him mercy. He was *playing* at being mad. There was no other way of saving his life, for in the hills madmen are considered especially beloved by Allah, and thus sacrosanct.

"Blood has reddened the palms of my hands," came the droning chant as Ebrahim Asif jumped up again from the ground and began again his whirling dance.

"What has happened?" Ali-Khan whispered in my ear. "Has there been killing? Where? When?"

Instead of replying, I pressed my rifle into his hands.

"Shoot him!" I cried.

He looked at me, utterly amazed.

"Why should I shoot him?"

Again the droning chant of Ebrahim rose, swelling and decreasing in turns, dying away in a thin, quavery tremolo, then bursting forth thick and palpable.

"I give thanks to Allah the Just, the Withdrawer of the Veils of Hidden Things, the Raiser of the Flag of Beneficence! For He guided my footsteps! He led me into the plains. And there I took toll, red toll!" There came a shriek of mad laughter, then very softly he chanted: "Once a nightingale warbled in the villages of the Moustaffa-Khel, and now she is dead. The death-gongs are ringing in the city of the plains—"

"Shoot him," I shouted again to Ali-Khan, "or, by

Allah, I myself will shoot him." And I picked up the rifle.

But he put his hand across its muzzle.

"Why, why?" he asked. "He is blood-cousin to Bibi Halima. Also does it seem that reason has departed his mind. He is a madman, a man beloved by Allah. Shall I thus burden my soul with a double sin because of your bidding? Why should I shoot him?" he asked again.

And then, before I found speech, the answer came, stark, crimson, in the hillman's mad chant:

"Bibi Halima was her name, and she mated with a rat of the cities, a rat of an Herati speaking Persian. Now she is dead. I drew my *cheray*, and I struck. The blade is red with the blood of my loved one; the death-gongs are ringing—"

Then Ali-Khan understood.

"Allah!" he shouted. And the long, lean Afghan knife leaped to his hand like a sentient being. "Allah!" he said again, and a deep rattle was in his throat.

The grief in the man's eyes was horrible to see. I put my hand on his arm.

"She is not dead," I said.

"Is that the truth?" he asked; then, pitifully, as I did not reply, "we have spoken together with naked hearts before this. Tell me, is the tale true?"

"The child will be born," I said, quoting the English doctor's words, "but Bibi Halima will assuredly die."

And then—and at the time it seemed to me that the great sorrow had snatched at the reins of his reason—Ali-Khan sheathed his knife, with a little dry metallic click of finality.

"It is even as Allah wills," he said, and he bowed his head. "Even as Allah wills," he repeated. He turned toward the east, spread out his long, narrow hands, and continued with a low voice, speaking to himself, alone in the presence of God, as it were:

"Against the blackness of the night, when it overtaketh me, I betake me for refuge to Allah, the lord of daybreak."

There came a long silence, the hillman again rolling on the ground, mouthing the dirt after the manner of jackals.

Finally I spoke:

"Kill him, my friend. Let us finish this business, so that we may return to the city."

"Kill him?" he asked, and there was in his voice that which resembled laughter. "Kill a madman, a man beloved by Allah the Just?" He walked over to Ebrahim Asif, touching him gently with the point of his shoe. "Kill a madman?" he repeated, and he smiled sweetly at the prostrate hillman, as a mother smiles at a prattling babe.

"The man is not mad," I interrupted roughly; "he is playing at being mad."

"No! no!" Ali-Khan said with an even voice as passionless as fate. "Assuredly the man is mad—mad by the Forty-seven True Saints! For who but a madman would kill a woman? And so you, being my friend, will take this madman to the villages of the Moustaffa-Khel. See him safely home. For it is not good that harm should come to those whom Allah loves. Tell the head-man of the village, tell the priest, tell the elders, tell everybody, that there is no feud. Tell them that Ebrahim Asif can live out his life in peace. Also his sons, and the sons which the future

will bring him. Safe they are in God's keeping because of their father's madness!"

I drew him to one side, and whispered to him:

"What is the meaning of this? What—what—"

He interrupted me with a gesture, speaking close
to my ear:

"Do as I bid you for the sake of our friendship;
for it is said that the mind of a friend is the well of
trust, and the stone of confidence sinks therein and is
no more seen." He was silent for a moment, then
he continued in yet lower voice: "Hold him safe
against my claiming? Assuredly him and his sons—
and—" then suddenly, "O Allah, send me a man-
child!"

And he strode down the hill into the purple dusk,
while I, turning over his last words in my mind, said
to myself that he was a soft man indeed; but that
there is also the softness of forged steel, which bends
to the strength of the sword-arm, and which kills on
the rebound.

So, obeying my friend's command, I went to the
villages of the Moustaffa-Khel. I delivered Ebrahim
Asif safe into the hands of the *jirgahs,* giving them
the message with which Ali-Khan had intrusted
me.

There was a little laughter, a little cutting banter
hard to bear, and some talk of cowards, of city-bred
Heratis turning the other cheek after the manner of
the *feringhees,* of blind men wanting nothing but their
eyes; but I kept my tongue safe between my teeth.
For I remembered the softness of steel; I remembered
Ali-Khan's love for Bibi Halima; and thirdly I remembered that there is no love as deep as hate.

Four days later I knocked at the door of Ali-Khan's

house, and there was the moaning of women, and the ringing of the death-gong.

Ali-Khan was alone in his room, smoking opium.

"A son has been born me, praise Allah!" was his greeting.

"Praise Allah and the Prophet and the Prophet's family, and peace and many blessings on them all!" I laid my left hand against his, palm to palm, and kissed him on both cheeks.

There was no need to ask after Bibi Halima, for still from the inner rooms came the moaning of women and the ringing of the death-gong. But another question was in my heart, and he must have read it. For he turned to me, smiling gently, and said:

"Heart speaks naked to heart, and the head answers for both. And I am an Herati and a soft man."

There was peace in his eyes, at which I wondered, and he continued:

"Once I spoke to you of feud. I said that an unfinished feud is a useless thing, as useless as horns on a cat or flowers of air. For, if I kill my enemy, my enemy's son, knowing my name and race, will kill me, and thus through the many generations. A life for a life, and yet again a life for a life. And where, then, is the balancing of lives? Where, then, is the profit to me and mine? So I have made peace between Ebrahim Asif and myself, cunningly, declaring him a madman, beloved by Allah, thus sacrosanct. And I shall sell my house here, and take my little son and go north to Bokhara. I shall sit under the shadow of Russia, and I shall prosper exceedingly; for I know Central Asia and the intrigues of Central Asia, and I shall sell my knowledge to the Russians. I shall be not without honor."

"Do you, then, love the bear of the North that you are willing to serve him?"

"Love is of the mind and not of the heart,"—he flung out a bare palm,—"unless it be the love of woman. And Bibi Halima is dead."

"Then why serve Russia?" For be it remembered that in those days I served the Ameer of Afghanistan, and that there was talk in the bazaars of a railway being built from Bokhara to Merv, within striking distance of Herat.

Again he smiled.

"Because I said that love is of the mind. What does me weal, that I love and serve. What does me harm, that I hate and fight. See? Years from now, if it be so written, my son, thanks to the honor which shall be mine under the shadow of Russia, will be a soldier of Russia in the north, in Bokhara. He will be trained after the manner of the North, and he will shoot as straight as a hawk's flight. He will be the pride of the regiment, and he will wear the little silver medal on a green ribbon which is given to the best marksman in the army. And one day the young soldier, bearing a Russian name, even as will his father, will desert from his regiment for a week or a month, and the tale will be spread that he has gone north to Moscow because of his young blood's desire to see new sights and kiss strange women. But he will not have gone north at all. No, by the teeth of God and mine own honor! He will have gone south, to these very hills, and there will be no desire in his heart but the desire to kill. He will kill Ebrahim Asif and his sons—may he have as many as there are hairs in my beard!—and also the women, at night, when they go to the brook to fetch water for the evening meal. He will kill from ambush, wasting no shots, being a soldier trained to war. *Ahi!* the carrion of the clan of Ebrahim Asif will feed the kites of the Salt Hills, and for many a day to come the jackals of the Nadakshi will not feel the belly-pinch of hunger. And the family of Ebrahim Asif shall be no more, and thus will the feud be stanched, if God be willing. And then my son will return to the north, to Bokhara. And tracking him will be like tracking the mists of dawn to their home. For what is one soldier more or less in the great land of Russia, where there are thousands and thousands and thousands of them? Also, will not the Government's protection be his, since I, his father, too, will be serving Russia not without honor?"

He left the room and returned, a moment later, holding in his arms a little bundle of silk and linen.

"Look," he said, baring carefully the head of the new-born infant. "See the eagle profile, the hooded brow, the creamy skin, the black, curly hair! An Afghan of Afghans! And see,—he opens his right eye,—has he not the eye of the killer?"

The child twisted and gave a little cry. Ali-Khan took a long, lean knife from the wall, offering its hilt to his son. The tiny hand gripped it, while the blade, point down, shone in the rays of the afternoon sun.

REPRISAL

He *had kept his oath, Hadji Rahmet used to say, for wrong—or for right. He would give to the latter word the emphasis of a slightly lowered voice. For, clear beyond the depths of even subconscious sophistry, he knew that he had done right; and the hills knew it—and perhaps Dost Ali, the Red Chief.*

The happening itself? What did it matter? Nothing mattered except the right and wrong of it. Besides, the last word was not yet said; perhaps never would be. It was bigger than his life; bigger than Dost Ali's life; bigger than the hills themselves.

"The hills!" he would repeat in a voice tinged and mellowed—by distance, as it were. They seemed to play a personal part in the telling; neither in the background nor in the foreground, but hovering enigmatical, fabulous—in a way, naïve. It had an odd effect —his speaking of them, here, in the tainted, brooding heat of India; as if, by speaking of them, he was being carried out of a perplexing present into the austere simplicity of the Himalayas; as if, by leaving them, he had lost some of his own crushing simplicity. Yet, leaving them, he had not been actuated by that complicated emotion called Fear—in spite of Dost Ali's threats, in spite of the leaky tongues of the Kabul market place.

The man did not understand fear. He had gone into the plains to find spiritual release from the memory of the thing. So he had visited the many

*shrines, true to the worship. Assiduously he had re-
peated the ninety-nine excellent attributes of Allah, and
all his thought had been of forgetting, and of devotion
to Him. He had wandered from the Khyber snows to
the sour, sluggish swamps of Ceylon. He had talked
with ascetics of many faiths in that land of many
faiths. He had done bodily penance, gradually subduing his physical Self. But his memory had remained: an inky scrawl across his mind.*

*"For memory," said the hadji, "is of the soul, and
not of the dirt-clouted body. . . ."*

*Also there were the tongues—the tongues which can
crush though they have no bones, the tongues of
Afghan traders who drift through the passes into
Hind. They would babble of the thing, back yonder
in the glitter of the hills. . . .*

It started with the day on which Hadji Rahmet
crossed the Red Chief's path for the first time. Perhaps even—though that is a question for ethnologists
to decide—it had started many centuries earlier, when
one of the hadji's ancestors traveled from Persia
through Seistan into Kabul, there to trade with smooth
silk and flowered Kisbah cloth, to plant the damask
roses of Ispahan, to give a soft philosophical twist to
the harsh lessons of the Koran, and to break his heart
—here—in the stony north; while the Red Chief's
ancestor, driven out of Tatary by squat, flat-nosed
warriors who recognized no God, who fought on horse-
back, and who tore like mastiffs at lumps of raw flesh
and quaffed down curdled milk poured from human
skulls, crossed into Afghanistan from the north. There
he sat himself on a sugarloaf-shaped hill, built a rough
castle, and put his descendants, straight down to Dost

Ali, on a pedestal to represent the power and arrogance of a race that will never grow old, that will never emerge from the sunlight of brazen freedom into the thrall and gloom of civilization.

Symbolic? In a way.

And that Hadji Rahmet should come into the Red Chief's life was also symbolic—and necessary: like the shadow in a light, to emphasize its harsh brightness.

Take the Red Chief up there in his stronghold, the *Mahattah Ghurab*, the Raven's Station, as the hill folk called it.

Above him the jagged, bitter rocks of the higher mountains where scrub oak met pine and where pine— to use the chief's words—met the naked heart of Allah. Still higher up the hard-baked, shimmering snows of the Salt Range, hooded and grim like the gigantic eyebrow of some heathen Pukhtu god, a god mourning the clank and riot of the days before the Arabs pushed into Central Asia and whipped the land into the faith of Islam—alone there with his pride and his clan; clear away from the twitter and cackle of the city marts, from the turrets and bell-shaped domes of Kabul, from the strangling lash of the Ameer's decrees; sloughing his will and his passion as snakes cast their skin; brooking no master but himself and the black mountain thunder.

At his feet a cuplike valley devoured by sunshine; farther up the slopes the lean mountain pasture, smooth and polished with the faint snow haze, and slashing through, straight as a blade, the caravan road which leads to Kabul; the caravan road which, centuries ago, had echoed to the footsteps of Alexander's legions— the caravan road which is as old as strife and older than peace.

Dost Ali was a short, wide-shouldered man, with gray, ironic eyes, high cheek bones, his beard dyed red with henna juice. Like his ancestors, he had always greatly distinguished himself—that's just how he would have considered it—by the cheerful and methodical ferocity of his fighting. He was a man who paid his enemies with the crackle of steel and slaughtered cattle and the red flames licking over hut and byre; a man who had scarred the valley for a week's journey with torch and cord, and whose greatest trust—greater than the fierce desert Prophet by whose name he gave oath —was the Khyber sword, curved like the croup of a stallion.

"I judge by the word of the hand and not by the word of the mouth," he put it in his own epic manner; and so he sat there on his mountain top and watched his breed increase, though they were daughters all but one. For his youngest child was a boy, Akbar Khan, seven years old, short and broad, with a tinge of red in his thick, curly hair—and Dost Ali loved him.

"Thou art a flower in the turban of my soul," he would say, picking up the lad and pressing him to his massive, fur-clad breast, "and my heart is a tasseled floorcloth for thy feet. Ho, thou, my hero!" And then father and son would run through the gray old rooms of the castle, playing like children, frightening the women over their cook pots, screaming and yelling and laughing.

Dost Ali was easily moved to laughter—laughter cold as the hill winds—and he laughed loud and long when early one day, with the valley still waist-high in the clammy morning mist, he saw Hadji Rahmet wander down the slopes, driving a herd of sheep with a crooked staff, and followed by his little son.

He had heard about the hadji a few days earlier.

The blind mullah who ministered to the scant spiritual wants of the Raven's Station had brought word of the stranger: the Kabuli merchant who, after his wife's death, had bidden farewell to the mosques and bazaars of the city and had come to live in the hills—"to forget," as he had told the sneering mullah, "to live mated to the clean simplicity of the hills, to bring up my little son away from the noisy toil of the market places, away from the smoke and strife of the city streets, here in the hills where there is nobody but God."

"God—*and* the Red Chief!" the mullah had croaked through his broken, blackened teeth; and then the hadji had spoken of the faith that was his.

He had spoken of Allah, the God of Peace.

"A new Allah—by Allah!" the mullah had laughed as he repeated it to the Red Chief.

Suddenly his laughter had keyed up to a high, senile scream. For he was a man of stout orthodoxy, to whom a freethinking Sufi was worse than Christian or Jew. "A new Allah! A soft Allah! A sickly Allah wrapped in sweating cotton! An Allah who prates of forgiveness and other leprous innovations. And he—that foul, swine-fed Kabuli—said that he wanted his blood to bear witness to his faith! And I"—again mirth gurgled through the mullah's fury—"I told him that all the faith in the world will not mend his bones when we stone him—as we should—for a blasphemer and a heretic!"

"God's curse on him!" Dost Ali had chimed in—and here he saw the man in the flesh, walking along easily enough for all his city-soft feet, his lean body swinging with the long, tireless pull of a mountain pony, chanting as he walked:

"Peace upon Thee, Apostle of Allah, and the Mercy and the Blessings! Peace upon Thee, O Seal of the Prophets!"—his voice rose and sank in turn, dying away in a thin, quavering tremolo, again bursting forth in palpable fervor, massive, unashamed, sublimely unself-conscious amid the silence of the snows.

"By the Three, the Seven, the Forty-seven True Saints! By the horns of the Angel Israfil! Teach me to see after ignorance!"

The faith in his heart bubbled to his lips—a lonely prayer, but a prayer which was to him a trumpet call of God's eternal laws, a rally clear around the world, a force in his heart to grip the everlasting meannesses of life and strife and smash them against the unchanging portals of peace.

"Peace!" He bit on the word. His lips savored it as a precious thing, then blew it free to lash the cool hill air with the sound of it. A light like a clear flame came into his eyes, illumining his face.

It was not altogether that of an ascetic, in spite of the downward furrows graven deep by long hours of meditation. For the nose beaked out bold and aquiline, with flaring, nervous nostrils, speaking of courage— unconscious, racial courage—scotched, it is true, by his Persian ancestry, by breeding and training and deliberate modes of thought, but always there, dark-smoldering, ready to leap.

Even Dost Ali read the signs, though he had never had cause to learn the kind of mental stenography known as character reading and psycology, preferring to judge men by the work of their hands and the venom of their tongues. But he had known fighters—fighters of many races—and this—

"Peace, O Opener of the Locks of Grief!" droned

the hadji's chant, with a trembling, throaty note of religious hysteria.

He had left the hard grist of worldly ambition behind him in Kabul, in the stench of bazaar and mart, in the burnished dome of the Chutter Mahal, the Audience Hall, where once he had sat at the right hand of the governor, giving of his stored wisdom to help rule the turbulent Afghan nation. Wealth and honor and fame he had flung behind him, like a limp, worn-out turban cloth, to bring peace to this land of strife, from village to village.

Peace! With the thought he forgot the grim, jagged rocks frowning above his head. He forgot the bastioned castle which blotched the snow blur of the slopes. He forgot the lank, rime-ringed pines which silhouetted against the sky like sentinels of ill omen. He even forgot the waddling sheep which gave him his simple living.

They turned and stared at him out of their flat, stupid eyes, helpless without the point of the staff to marshal their feeding.

"Peace!" came the word again—a strange word here, and to Dost Ali it seemed an affront—an affront to the sweep of the hills, an affront to his own free breed, to the Raven's Station which had always garnered strife and fed on strife. Yes, an affront, and the Red Chief stepped square into the hadji's path and shot forth his hatred and contempt in a few sharp-ringing words: "Ho! Abuser of the Salt!"

The deadly insult slashed clear through the other's voice and thoughts. He looked up. Automatically—for there had been years of hot blood before the message of peace had come to him—his hand leaped to his side, fingering for the blade.

Dost Ali smiled at the gesture. Thank Allah, he thought, this babbling heretic was a man after all. He would not eat dirt. He would fight.

"Good!" he breathed the word, and his own sword flashed free. But the next moment the hadji's hand dropped—dropped like a wilted, useless thing; and the Red Chief smiled again—a different smile, slow, cruel —and again he spoke.

He chose his words carefully, each a killing insult, and he spoke in an even, passionless voice to let their venom trickle deep. Moreover, such is the Afghan code with its strange niceties of honor and prejudice, that unless he who is insulted respond immediately with the point of the dagger, the consciousness of moral rectitude rests with him who insults; and so Dost Ali was shocked, morally as well as ethically, when the hadji stood there and smiled; in spite of the fact that he had called him a beggar, a cut-off one, the son of a, burnt father, a foreigner, and a Yahudi; though he had wished that his hands be withered and his fingers palsied; though he had compared him to the basest kinky-haired one that ever hammered tent peg, and to one cold of countenance; though he had assured him—"*ay wall'ahi!*" the Red Chief reënforced the statement, "by the teeth of God and mine own honor!"—that his head was as full of unclean thoughts as a Kabuli's coat is of lice, and that he himself, though an impatient man, would rather hunt for pimples on the back of a cock-roach than for manliness and decency in the heart of such a one—"as thou, O son of a hornless and especially illegitimate cow!"

And still the hadji was silent, passive, his sword hand twisting the wooden beads of his rosary, only the slow red which mantled his cheeks telling that he had heard.

Dost Ali looked at him, open-eyed, puzzled. It was beyond his comprehension. If the other had thrown himself at his feet, imploring protection and mercy, or if he had run away, he would have understood. He would even have understood a sort of caustic placidity —a silent, minatory contempt which would presently leap into flame.

But—why—this man stood his ground. He stood his ground without fighting, with no answering flow of abuse, and only a throaty "Peace! Peace!" uttered automatically, like the response in a litany, followed by an admonition to the mountaineer not to be impatient —"indeed thou seest through the whirling mists of passion, brother!"—and finally a few stammering, ragged words drawn across his helplessness when the Red Chief burst into another flood of invective.

Dost Ali was a simple man. He could not sift the hadji's heart. He did not see the waves of passion which were lapping beneath the other's smiling countenance and soft words. He did not understand how the hadji, slowly, painfully, had purged his heart of lust and hatred—how even now, with the terrible insults ringing in his consciousness, he was forcing his faith in God and Peace to buffet a road straight through the black wrath which was consuming him; how he was struggling with himself, finally doffing his worldly pride like a dirty garment.

A coward? Only in so far as he did not want realities to brush him too close. And here reality was bulking big—reality as expressed in the Red Chief's squat mightiness, in his screaming abuse, the half-

drawn sword flickering like a cresset of all the evil
passions which he loathed and which he had set out to
combat.

"Peace, brother!" he said again. His voice was
steady; and then, even in Dost Ali's slow-grinding
mind, rose the conviction that this man—this man who
suffered the most deadly insults without fight or flight
—was not a coward. And his hatred grew apace. For
he did not understand.

A man who fought—yes! Also, a man who feared
and fled. He had met both sorts, had handled both
sorts. But here was a man who neither feared nor
fled. It was a new experience to the mountaineer's
naïve brutality—a new experience to crush which he
would have to devise new means. What means? He
wondered. He jerked back his head as a racing
stallion slugs above the bit.

He stood there, squat, wide-shouldered, his red beard
flopping in the wind like a bat wing, looking with
puckered, puzzled eyes toward the east where the
farther fog banks were melting and rolling into noth-
ingness and where a scarlet flush was shooting up in
fantastic spikes—as if the east could give answer.

Should he kill—outright?

A sob of steel, a gurgle, blood caking on the ground
—he knew the tale of it, oft repeated—and the fire of
his hatred would be out; the heat thereof would be
spent.

But to what profit?

Where was the satisfaction in killing a man who
did not resist, who did not answer steel with the song
of steel, flash for flash, and strength for strength? It
would leave the mystery still unsolved, the riddle un-
read, the grape unpressed. The fact that the hadji had

once lived and, living, had been as he had been, would remain—like dregs; as salt as pain. Also, Dost Ali was a superstitious man. He could imagine the hadji's ghost, after the death of the body, squatting on a mountain top like a lean, red-necked vulture, looking down at the Raven's Station with flat, gray, indifferent eyes—perhaps smiling, perhaps still croaking about Peace.

Should he rob him? And what was there to rob? A muslin shirt, a rough khilat, a sheepskin coat, a pair of grass sandals—not enough to satisfy the greed of the meanest dancing girl from the south.

"Ho! man of great feet and small head!" he began again, then was silent. For the other had dropped on his knees.

"May the Lamp of Peace clear my path from hearthstone to byre," he was praying, oblivious of man-made passion and man-made words; and the Red Chief trembled with rage. What—by the blood of God!—what was the use of a talker when there were no listeners; when nobody heard except the lank pines and the cursed, blinking, waddling sheep, and—*ahi!*—the hadji's little son?

There he stood, looking on with wondering eyes, munching a wheaten cake with the solemn satisfaction of childhood; strong, good-looking with his father's hawklike profile and deep-set eyes.

The hadji was still droning his prayer of peace, and the Red Chief laughed. The answer? The answer to the riddle of his hatred? He had it. It lay in the strength of his arms, the clouting strength of his will. It was the hills' way—his own way.

He would pour the black brewage of fear down this stranger's throat till it choked him and he squealed for mercy. He would drive him into the shadow of his love and cause him to whimper like a beaten dog—like a dog well beaten with thorn sticks.

This babbler of meekness had no fear of the Red Chief, no fear of the hills, but—"Pray!" laughed Dost Ali, "pray to me, a man of strife, O thou fool of peace! Pray, or thou shalt moan like the Bird of the Tamarisk which moaneth like the childless mother!" And with a quick gesture of his great hands he picked up the hadji's little son by the waist shawl.

He held him high—the child was rigid with fear— he walked over to the edge of the precipice where, deep down, the lower mountains lay coiled and massive, offering their immense stillness to the fiery face of the sun. Still farther down the cataract of the Kabul River fluffed like some waxen, blatant tropical flower.

"Father!" screamed the child.

The hadji turned and at the moment of seeing he seemed to be struck blind. The second before, straight through the fervor of his prayers, he had vaguely realized the world about him—the peaks and the sunlight and the cold glitter of the snows.

Now, suddenly, a nothing—black.

All that was bright and light and good seemed to have leaped back. There was nothing—just a scream in the dark: "Father!" and the chief's harsh bellow as he swung the lad by the twisted waist shawl around his head, with that savage, hairy strength of his.

A moment later vision returned to the hadji's eyes. He saw everything. Absurdly, incongruously, the first thing he saw, the first impressions which his eyes graved on his brain, were the details, the petty, contemptible details of inanimate nature: the eastern sky, serenely cloudless, running from milky white into gold-flecked crimson with a purple-nicked edge near the horizon's rim; farther south the sun rays racing in a river of fire and melting into the snows with a sort of rainbow-colored foam. He saw it. He understood it.

Often, in after years, he would speak of it. He would say that his first glimpse of his son, helpless in the mountaineer's grip, at the verge of death, had seemed but another detail; a strange detail; a sudden, evil jest which he could not grasp.

He used to say that even after he had begun to comprehend the reality of it his immediate thoughts had not been of his son's life, but of the waist shawl. He had remembered when he had bought it: in Kabul, in the Bazaar of the Silk Weavers. His son had liked the pattern and the bright blending of colors. So he had bought it, and—

Words had come to him. "Don't! Don't!"—just those words: weak, meaningless, foolish. But he spoke them solemnly, as if he had found a powerful formula, and then his little son gave a frantic, straining kick.

He jerked. His head shot down and his feet up, shifting the weight of the sturdy young body. The waist shawl snapped. Quite distinctly, for the fraction of a second, the hadji saw the broken silk strands. He saw their feathered ends ripping through the pattern, brushing up, then down in the wind which sucked from the precipice—and his son's body fell away from the Red Chief's grip.

It turned a somersault. It plunged into space. Came a dull thud, from far down. Silence.

Dost Ali stood motionless. By the Prophet, he had not willed this—this thing. He had only meant to sport after the manner of the hills; and he had taken a child's life—like a snake or a Hindu.

He must atone, somehow, according to the code of the hills.

But how? Blood money? Of course. But a life was a life, and a son was a son—and there was his own little son running and playing through the gray rooms of the Raven's Station.

The hadji had fallen on the ground, his hands stretched out, clutching the short-stemmed, tufted grass, his body jerking and twitching.

"Hadji!" said the Red Chief. "Hadji!"—and, as the other did not reply, did not hear, "by Allah, I did not will—this!"

He was silent. His lips twisted oddly, and had the hadji looked up he would have seen a tear in the mountaineer's beady, puckered eyes—a tear which, strangely, seemed to lift what was abominable into something not altogether unworthy; to overshadow, somehow, the drab, cruel, sinister fact of the broken body down there by the cataract of the Kabul River.

"Hadji!" the mountaineer called again. Then, as the other did not look up, did not reply, hardly seemed to breathe, he walked away, shrugging his broad shoulders. What was done was done, he thought, and he would pay blood money as the Koran demands it. Also, he would give the hadji a wife from among his own people, and there would yet be another little boy, with hawklike profile and deep-set eyes, to prate about Peace.

And he took the road to the Raven's Station, where he gave a sound beating to the blind mullah—who, according to the Red Chief's simple logic, had been the cause of the whole trouble—while the hadji was knitting his riven soul to hold the pain in his heart.

"Yes," the hadji would say years later as he was wandering through the sun-stained plains of India, from shrine to carved shrine, searching for release from the memory of the thing—"yes, the Red Chief had prophesied right. Indeed I crept into the shadow of my fallen love, and I whimpered like a dog that has been beaten with thorn sticks!" And, with a flat, tortured laugh, he would add that God seemed to have answered his prayer for peace—"I had asked for Peace, don't you see, and He sent me the final peace—the peace of death, the peace of a hawk's claw and a snake's fang and a hill-bred's heart."

An hour later, at the edge of the cataract, he found his son. Instinctively he folded his feet under his haunches, squatting by the side of the broken body, and his heart's remembrance followed the little crushed life—followed it, followed it back through the narrow span of years, back to the day when the old Yusufzai nurse had come from the couch of his wife and had laid a tiny bundle into his arms—"a son, my lord, may life be wide to him!"

He remembered the first cry of that tiny, white, warm bundle. It had been like the morning cry of a wild bird.

He remembered his son's last cry—strangled, frantic —"Father! Father!" drowned in the Red Chief's harsh bellow. He would never forget it.

And the hadji sat there until the sun died in a sickly haze of coppery brown—decayed, it seemed to him, like the sun on the Day of Judgment—and the moon came up, stabbed on the outer horns of the world, dispassionate, calm, indifferent to the heart of man.

He sat there silent and stony, while some friendly hillmen carried his son's body away, decently wrapped in a white fringed death shroud, a kindly old woman's blue turquoise beads forced between the rigid little fingers so that the hand of Ali, which had not protected his body during life, might protect his fluttering soul after death.

He sat there till the wind came driving the dusk toward the East; till the sky flushed with the green of the tropics, like a curved slab of thick, opaque jade; till the afternoon sun glared hot and golden; till once more the mists of evening rose and coiled. The mists of the hills—the mists in his soul! They echoed this day to the scream and toll of the death gongs, and from his heart there beat up a sob which all his faith could not still.

He sat the next night through and watched the hiving stars swarm and swirl past the horizon. He watched them die one by one. He watched the young sun shoot up, racing along the rim of the world in a sea of fire, with shafts of purple light that put out the paling moon. He watched a long streamer of northbound birds, wild parrots tumbled out of their southern home by the moist sweep of the Punjab monsoon; they flopped about the lank pines, screeching dismally, their motley finery of feather bedraggled with the snow chill of the Himalayas.

A scout bird detached itself, flew down, then up, flanking the packed crowd of its comrades in long, graceful evolutions, finally leading them toward the Raven's Station, which etched the sky line, peaked and hooded, jeering like a face, extending its somber, scarred walls like a grim jest hewn out of stone, evilly infinite, like the very stronghold of the night and the hills, like a sooty smudge on the crimson and gold blaze of day—and Hadji Rahmet's thoughts whirred on the parrot's wings: up to the Raven's Station.

Up there was the patter of little hard feet tapping the stone flags; a curly head, tinged with red; a sturdy little nut-brown body: Akbar Khan, the Red Chief's son, blood of his blood and bone of his bone.

Up there was childish laughter, as the old women whispered Persian fairy tales—of the flea who tried to lighten the camel's load, of Oguun, the god of little babes, whose fingers and toes are made of sugar cane and whose heart is a monstrous ball of pink sweetmeat that was baked in far China.

A child's laughter!

The thought tore the hadji's heart, ragged, paining, like a dull knife.

"O Lord!" the prayer came automatic and meaningless, "pardon and pity and pass over what Thou knowest, for Thou art the most dear and the most generous—" He was silent. He bent his head as if listening. At his feet the cataract gurgled away to the darkness of the deep-cleft passes—*lap-lap-lap*—mocking.

"And then," the hadji would say afterward, "the dagger of grief pricked the bubble of my faith." And a great turmoil surged in his heart, beyond control, beyond prayer even; running into something molten, finally emerging into the solid fact of his hatred, his desire for revenge.

It seemed to bring up from his heart and brain unexpected, rather forgotten qualities, as a storm-whipped wave brings up mud and gravel from the ground bed of the shore. . . .

That night Hadji Rahmet turned thief. He stole a tiny trotting bullock belonging to Ram Chander Dass, the Hindu who picked up a scant living by lending badly chipped silver rupees to the hillmen and, as the mullah said, by praying every night for the swag-bellied and bestial god of the Hindus, which same god is the guardian angel of Compound Interest.

He stole the bullock. For he had decided to kill the Red Chief's son, and he knew that, while sharp eyes would detect a stranger wandering up the slopes to the Raven's Station, none would bother about a bullock—in a land where bullocks mean money and food and clothes—nor would sharp eyes, looking from above, see a man clinging to the bullock's shaggy belly, his hands buried in the thick pelt of the wabbly hump.

His long, lean body tortured into a grotesque angle and now and then bumping against the sharp stones of the rock path, the hadji hung on precariously while the bullock lashed out right and left, lowering its head, snorting, bellowing, stamping, whisking its tufted tail, dancing about as if stung by a bramra beetle in its efforts to shake off the strange burden that clung to its nether side; at last settling into a resigned, bovine trot and reaching the horses' paddock which stretched beyond the Red Chief's sheep corral just after daybreak.

Already, down in the valley, the night mists were twisting into baroque spirals, tearing into gauzelike arabesques that burned like the plumage of a gigantic peacock in every mysterious blend of green and purple and blue.

Once in the paddock, the hadji dropped to the ground while the bullock trotted away to join its mates that were dipping their ungainly noses into a stone bin half buried beneath the crimson, feathery foliage of a squat

manna bush. There was nobody about the inner court-
yards this time of early day. The watchmen were pac-
ing above, on the crenelated, winglike battlements that
flushed out sharp and challenging under the rays of the
young sun, farther on, where the sun had not yet pene-
trated, melting into the great pine woods that poured
down the steep slopes and running together into a single
sheet of purplish black, stippled white here and there
with a sudden glisten of snow.

The hadji stood still and listened. There was no
sound except the occasional *click-clank-click* of a metal
scabbard tip dragged along the stones of the battlements or the creaking of a grounded rifle butt.

The watchmen were looking across the valley. It
was there that, a week earlier, the Red Chief had lifted
the slate-blue, mottled Kabuli stallion belonging to
Jehan Tugluk Khan, the great naib of the Uzbek Khel;
it was thence that the Uzbek Lances might pour toward
the Raven's Station to take toll. The sentinels had seen
the bullock dance up the paddock, stamping and lash-
ing and roaring. But what harm was there in a bullock,
mad with spring fever?

Hadji Rahmet looked about him. To the left, separated from the paddock by a stone wall, was a garden,
transplanted painfully tree for tree and shrub for shrub
from the Persian lowlands, and challenging the eternal
snows in an incongruous, stunted, scraggly maze of
crotons and mangoes, teak and Mellingtonia, poin-
settias and begonia creepers—all frozen, homesick, out
of place. The Red Chief had slaughtered a hundred
head of cattle and sold their hides to pay for the exotic
plants on the day when his little son had first repeated
after him the words of the *Pukhtunwali,* the ancient
Afghan code of honor and conduct: "As to him who

does me harm, may I be permitted a full measure of revenge. May I cause his hands to drop away, and his feet. May his life pass into the dark like a sheet of foam. . . ."

Beyond the garden, a little higher up, stretched the gray stone stables of the blooded horses. The hadji could hear the strangely human cry of a mare heavy with foal, a stallion's answering whinny.

He crossed the paddock toward the castle itself. It towered in massive outlines over a hundred feet high, built of rough granite and shiny quartz blocks set in concrete, swinging out in a great semicircle, its flanks resting upon the naked rock of the hills. Directly in front of him he saw a door, doubtless stolen generations ago during a raid into India. For it was made of a single, solid, age-darkened, adz-hewn teak slab, with dowels that fitted into a fretted ivory frame. No Afghan hand—clumsy except with martingale and tempered steel—had carved this door. No Afghan hand had fashioned the bossed, jewel-crusted silver plaque set in the center. But it was Afghan carelessness which had let the door warp, which had caused the delicate bayonet lock to crack away from the wood, leaving room for a narrow, nervous hand to slip inside and finger the bolt.

The hadji sucked in his breath. His fingers moved noiselessly. Another short jerk and the bolt would slide from its groove—

He stood quite still, his heart beating like a hammer.

Faint, from the other side of the door, came a rustle of silken garments, the noise of bare feet pattering away. The zenana, the women's quarter, doubtless, he thought; and there would be an old nurse about, with sharp ears and shrill, lusty tongue.

He shut his teeth with a little dry click. His heart felt swollen, as if he had washed it in brackish water, and he asked God—it seemed a personal issue between him and God—if he should be cheated of his revenge because an old woman, thin of sleep, was rummaging about the zenana in search of charcoal and hubble-bubble and Latakia tobacco spiced with rose water and grains of musk.

And, steadily, as he waited, his finger immobile on the bolt of the door, undecided what to do, the sun was rising, striking the jagged cliffs with dusted gold, tumbling broken-rayed into the courtyard and drinking the newly thawed snow. Already the east was flushing with pink and orange as the mists drifted through the valley, shearing a glittering crimson slice from the morning sun. Already, looking nervously over his shoulder, he saw down the path one of the Red Chief's peasants carrying a rough, iron-tipped milking yoke across his shoulders. Still he stood, undecided, ears and eyes tense.

The thousand noises of the waking day were about him. Somewhere a tiny koel bird was gurgling and twittering. A little furry bat cheeped dismally. A peacock-blue butterfly flopped quick—quick as the shadow of a leaf through summer dusk. A mousing owl rustled in the byre thatch.

The stallions whinnied. There was a metallic buzzing of flies around a gnarled siris tree.

Then, through the drowsy canticle of waking day, straight through the cheeping and rustling and whinnying and buzzing, the hadji heard another sound—a cry —faint, then louder, decreasing, then stabbing out sharp and distinct: "Father!"

A human cry, calling for human help; rising to an

intolerable note of appeal, half choked, accompanied by a rattling and crackling of steel, a crunching and stamping and snorting—curious, flat, dragging noise—and for a moment the hadji's heart was as still as freezing water. "Father!" came the cry again, and again: "Fa——" cut off in mid-air. Like his son's last cry, the cry of a dead soul trying to span the gulf of consciousness to the living heart!

Then once more the snorting and stamping, the steely jar, coming from the stables of the blooded horses.

The hadji gulped his fear and looked.

Beyond the stunted garden he saw a little curly, red-tinged bullethead peep above the wall, a small brown leg stretching up, the heel, helpless, foolish, trying to find hold on the smooth stone coping. Once more the cry, agonized—the little head jerking, the little heel slipping—a soft thud . . . and the hadji, the hair on his neck bristling as though Death had whispered in his ear, ran across courtyard and garden. He cleared the stone wall at a jump.

Inside, at the open door of the stables, he saw the Red Chief's son, a small, huddled bundle, the neck strangely twisted, the hands grasped clawlike about the left front fetlock of a slate-blue, mottled stallion. It was clear to the hadji what had happened.

The boy had sneaked out, very early, to take a look at the Kabuli stallion which his father had lifted from Jehan Tugluk Khan. He had tried to undo the steel chain by which the horse was fastened. The animal had become frightened, had reared and plunged and kicked; the boy had become entangled in the steel halter, had tried to jerk himself free; the stallion had become more frightened than ever.

"Patience, little Moslem. Patience, little brother!"

said the hadji. He approached the stallion sidewise, hand held high and open to show that he carried neither bit nor martingale, soothing with soft voice, then with cunning palm, rubbing the high, peaked withers, the soft, quivering muzzle, the tufted ears, leaning forward and blowing warm into the dilated nostrils, finally loosing the steel halter chain.

The headstall dropped. The stallion jumped back, and the little boy fell on the ground, flopping grotesquely—and something reached out and touched the hadji's soul, leaving the chill of an undescribable uneasiness.

He bent to pick the boy up. The little body lay still, lifeless.

He looked. He saw a blue mark across the lad's windpipe where the steel chain had pressed—and he thought that his own son was dead, and that dead was the Red Chief's son. He thought that the hand of man had killed the former, the hand of God the latter, thus evening the score.

But—was the score even?

For a full minute he considered.

His mind resisted from the spontaneous passivity bred by long-continued meditations on Peace. But his hand surrendered to the brain's subconscious, driving will. His hand acted.

He drew the dagger from the waist shawl. He cut across the blue mark which the steel chain had graved on the boy's windpipe, obliterating it with torn flesh and a rush of blood. He left the dagger sticking in the wound. His name was cut in the ebony hilt. The Red Chief would find, and read, and—yes!—thus the score would be even!

The hadji never knew how he reached safety. He

had a vague memory of a sentinel challenging him, of a bullet whistling above his head, of how he went down the path scudding on his belly like a jackal to the reek of carrion. He remembered how, as he reached the valley, the western tower of the Raven's Station seemed like a spire away on the world's rim—a spire of hope and lost hope. He remembered the sudden gusts of snow coming down like hissing spears, with the moon reeling above him through the clouds like a great, blinding ball of light and with a lonely southern peak pointing at the mute stars like a gigantic icicle, frozen, austere, desolate.

He remembered vaguely how he traveled day and night, day and night, and it was only gradually, slowly, as his mind jerked free from fleshly thrall and buffeted its road back through the mists of passion to God's Peace, that there came to him knowledge of why he was fleeing from that thing in the glitter of the hills as from a thing accursed.

It was not fear of the Red Chief. Nor was it remorse that he had mutilated the dead body. For the hadji was an Afghan, and there was no worth nor dignity to him in a lifeless thing.

What weighed on his soul, like a sodden blanket, was the doubt of what he would have done had he found the Red Chief's son alive.

He had gone to the Raven's Station to kill. But would he have killed? Would he have broken God's covenant of Peace—and, killing, would he have done right or wrong?

The doubt was on his soul like a stinging brand; and so the hadji took stick and wooden bowl and lived on alms and went through the scorched Indian plains, from shrine to shrine, seeking release from doubt, release from memory.

He did bodily penance, gradually subduing his physical Self. He submitted to the ordeal of fire, walking barefoot through the white-hot charcoal, uncovering his shaven head to the burning fire bath. And he felt not the pain of the body. Only his soul trembled to the whip of doubt.

Then he met a Holy Man from Gujrat who told him that to clear his vision and fatten the glebe of understanding he must do penance with his head hanging downward. True, the other was a Hindu infidel whose gods were a monkey and a flower. But he himself was a Sufi, an esoteric Moslem, taking the best of all creeds and despising none, and he did as the fakir told him.

He swung with his head to the ground and shut his eyes. When he opened them again he saw all upside down, and the sight was marvelous beyond words. The blue hills had lost their struggling height and were a deep, swallowing, mysterious void. Against them the sky stood out, bold, sharp, intense, immeasurably distant; and the fringe of clouds at the base of the sky seemed a lake of molten amber with billows of tossing sacrificial fire.

He gazed. He gazed himself into stupefaction. But his memory remained: an inky scrawl across his soul.

"For memory," said the hadji, "is not of the body, but of the soul!"

THE HOME-COMING

YAR KHAN was off to his own country in the Month of Pilgrimages. He broke the long journey at Bokhara, to buy a horse for the trip South, to exchange his Egyptian money for a rupee draft on a Hindu banker in Afghanistan, and to buy sweets and silks for the many cousins in his native village.

He had left there sixteen years before, a child of seven, when his father, a poor man, but eager for gain, and sensing no chance for barter and profit in the crumbling basalt ridges of the foot-hills, had gone West—to Cairo. There he and his father—the mother had died in giving him birth—had lived all these years; all these years he had spent in that city of smoky purple and dull orange, but never had he been of Cairo. The tang of the home land had not left him; always his heart had called back to the sweep and snow of the hills, and he had fed his love with gossamer memories and with the brave tales which his father, Ali Khan, told him when the homesickness was in his nostrils and when the bazaar gold of Cairo seemed gray and useless dross.

Of gold there had come plenty. Ali Khan had prospered, and in his tight little shop in the *Gamalyieh,* the Quarter of the Camel-Drivers, he had held his own with the Red Sea traders who meet there, and cheat and fight and give one another the full-flavored abuse of near-by Asia.

Yar Khan had lived the haphazard life of Eastern childhood, with no lessons but those of the crowded, crooked streets and an occasional word of prosy Koranic wisdom from some graybeard among his father's customers. When he had reached his fifteenth year, manhood had come—sudden and a little cruel as it comes to Asians. On that day, his father had taken him into the shop, and, with a great gesture of his lean arms, had pointed at the dusty confusion of his stock-in-trade; at the mattings full of yellow Persian tobacco, the pipe bowls of red clay, the palm-leaf bags containing coffee and coarse brown sugar, the flat green boxes filled with arsenic and rhubarb and antimony and *tafl* and sal-ammoniac.

"He of great head becomes a chief, and he of great feet a shepherd," Ali Khan had said, ridiculing Fate after the manner of the hill-bred. "Thou art blood of my blood. From this day on, thou wilt be a trader, and thou wilt prosper. Gold will come to thy hands—unasked, like a courtezan."

Ali Khan had been right. Together, father and son had prospered. They had heaped gold on clinking gold, and of gold, too, had been the father's endless talk, praising the cold metal at yawning length, dwelling, as it were, on the outer husk of things; and when Yar Khan's softer mind rebelled at the hard philosophy Ali Khan would laugh and say: "Thou art right, little son. Gold is the breath of a thief. Gold is a djinn. Gold is an infidel sect. But—"with a shrewd wink—"give gold to a mangy dog—and the people will call him Sir Dog. For gold is strength!"

It was only in the evenings, when they had put up the heavy wooden shutters of their shop and were returning to their tiny whitewashed living-house in the

Suk-en-Nahassim, that often something like a veil of discontent would fall over the older man's shrill greed.

"Gold buys this—and that—and this," he would say, in a hushed voice, pointing at some rich Pasha's silent, extravagant house, with its projecting cornices, its bulbous balconies of fretted woodwork supported by gigantic corbels and brackets, and the dim oil lamp glimmering above the carved gate—"gold buys this—and no more!"—and when a woman of the Egyptians —a woman swathed from head to foot, with only the eyes showing—crossed his path, he would cry, "They do not wear veils, at home, in the hills."

Then, quite suddenly, he would break into harsh laughter and add, "But veils cost gold, Yar Khan, and we sell veils . . . thou and I— in the *Gamalyieh!*"

Yar Khan understood that his father was homesick. But when he begged him to return to the hills Ali Khan would reply with the proverb which says that the cock leaves home for four days only—and returns a peacock. He would add, with a crooked smile: "Of what use the peacock's green tail on the dung-hills? Of what use the gold of Egypt on the barren rocks?"— and then again the talk would be of seasons and of the gold which comes with the shifting seasons' swing.

But Yar Khan would not understand why his father did not return to the hills, why he preferred to live in Cairo—between the dusty shop and the tiny white-washed living-house—up and down, up and down, like a buffalo putting his shaggy back to the water-wheel— heavy and slow and blind. He only knew that his father was eating out his heart with longing for the chill, dark pines; and his own homesickness—though his memories were vague—would be upon his shoulder like a stinging brand.

Now his father was dead. There was no lack of gold; and once more the thought of home had come to Yar Khan like a sudden inrush of light after a long, leaden, unlifting day. He was off to his own country in the Month of Pilgrimages.

The old priest whom he met at Bokhara—mumbling his prayers and clicking his rosary beads in front of the little pink mosque of *Bala-i-Hava*—told him that there was a certain significance to the date—told him, too, after the thin, pretentious manner of Moslem hierarchy, that he did not know if the omen be bad or good—"For," he added, "there is no power nor strength save in Allah the Most High!" and Yar Khan, who had lost most of his respect for holy men in the blue, slippery mud of the Nile, snapped his fingers with gentle derision, threw the whining gray-beard a handful of chipped copper coins, and turned to the bazaars to buy presents for his cousins.

He bought and bought—embroidered silks from Khiva and from far Moscow, pink and green sweetmeats from across the Chinese border, and Persian silver filigree for the young girls. He paid royally, without bargaining; for to-day he was master—buying, not selling—and the smooth touch of the gold pieces as he took them from his twisted waistband and clinked them down on the counter was pleasant. It was like prophecy: of conquest and, in a way, of freedom. He swung the furry goat-skin bag which held his purchases over his supple shoulders and turned toward the open market-place to buy a horse.

Rapidly he passed through the bunched crowds—crowds of all Asia—solemn, impassive-looking Bokharans, gently ambling along on gayly caparisoned mules; straight-backed gipsies, swaggering with the

beggars' arrogance of their race; melancholy Turko-
mans in immense fur-caps and plaited duffle coats;
Greeks, cunning-faced and sleek and odiously hand-
some; green-turbaned, wide-stepping *shareefs,* the
aristocracy of Islam; anxious-eyed, tawdry Armenians;
Sarts bristling with weapons and impudence; here and
there a bearded official of the Ameer's household, with
his air of steely assurance, superb self-satisfaction
hooded under his sharply curved eyelids—and once in
a while a woman, in white from head to foot, a restful
relief to the blaze of colors all around.

Yar Khan looked, but he felt no desire to linger.
For him there was no fragrance in the blossom-bur-
dened gardens, no music in the song of the *koil* bird,
no beckoning in the life of the streets—motley and
shrill and busy—with shaggy Northern dromedaries
dragging along their loads and looming against the
sky-line like a gigantic scrawl of Asian handwriting,
with the hundreds of tiny donkeys tripping daintily
under their burdens of charcoal and fiery-colored vegetables, with numbers of two-wheeled *arbas* creaking
in their heavy joints—with all the utter, riotous meaning of trade and barter and gold. He bought a horse,
a dun stallion with high, peaked withers, and rode out
of the Southern Gate without turning around. Down
the long south trail he rode—toward the little steel-
gray village perched on a flat, circular mountain top
which is called *The Hoof of the Wild Goat* in the
Afghan tongue.

He pulled into Balkh, white as a leper with the
dust of the road, traded his stallion for a lean racing
camel, which had a profusion of blue ribbons plaited
into the bridle as protection against the djinns and
ghouls of the desert—a superstition of his native land

at which he smiled, quite without malice—filled his saddle-bags with slabs of grayish wheaten bread and with little hard, golden apricots, and was off again, crossing the Great River at the shock of dawn. He watched it for a long time; for, springing up in the Hindu Kush, storming through the granite gorges of the lower ranges, it was to him a messenger of the home he had dreamt of and longed for these many years. So he watched the impetuous, green-blue flood bearing down to the soft Persian lowlands with a shout and a roar, dashing against the bank as though trying to sweep it away bodily, then swirling by in two foaming streams on either side. And from the cool waters there rose a flavor of that utter, sharp freedom which was to him the breath, the reason, the soul of the hills as he remembered them.

Yar Khan gave a deep, throaty laugh of sheer joy. "Home—and the salt of the home winds!" he thought, and he thought the words in the Afghan tongue, the harsh tongue of his childhood which he had nearly forgotten in the gliding, purring gutturals of the Cairo streets. Impatience overtook him.

"Home, lean daughter of unthinkable begetting!" he shouted at the snarling camel; he tickled its soft muzzle with the point of his dagger, urging it on to greater speed; and on the fifteenth day out of Bokhara, the thirtieth out of Cairo, he found himself in the valley below *The Hoof of the Wild Goat*.

He opened wide his lungs and filled them with the snow-sharp air, as though to cleanse himself from the shackling abominations of that far Egypt where he had lived the years of his youth. Already night had dropped down from the higher peaks; and in the purple depths of the cloudless sky hung a froth of stars that sparkled with the cold-white gleam of diamonds.

He jerked the camel to its knees and dismounted. But that night he did not stop to make camp, nor did he sit long at his meal.

For above him, like a dream of freedom, stretched the rock-perched village of his birth, and every minute spent here in the valley was like another wasted year. So he sat down, picked up a handful of mulberries and ate them; and when a shaggy, skulking Afridi came wandering into the valley, a wire-bound Snider in his arms, and doubtless out to take a late shot at a blood-enemy, Yar Khan stopped him with a shouted friendly greeting and offered him the camel as a present. For he was anxious to tread the jagged rocks of *The Hoof of the Wild Goat,* and he knew that no plains-bred animal could find foothold on the narrow, winding path which led to the mountain top. Often his father had described the path to him, every foot of it—too, savoring every foot of it in the telling.

The price of the camel? *"Masha, illah!"* he thought, "my father bartered the years of his manhood for a waistbandful of coined gold; let me then throw away a handful for a minute of home!" and he put the bridle in the Afridi's eager hand, crooking two fingers in sign of a free present.

"Manda na bash—May your feet never be weary!" the grateful Afridi shouted after Yar Khan, who was already speeding up the dark path, the heavy goat-skin bag punctuating each step, the joy in his heart as keen as a new-ground sword.

The night was a pall of deep brown, and the road twisted and dipped and turned. But he walked along steadily and sure-footed, though he had not seen the hills, except in dreams, since he was a lisping babe riding astride his nurse's stout hips. It seemed to him as if the flame in his heart was lighting up the uncharted night, as if the thought of home was serving him for an unerring beacon among the slippery timber-falls and the hidden, crumbling rock-slides; on he pushed, toward the higher peaks cooled with the wailing Northern thunder, and, just before the break of day, turning a massive rock crowned with a stunted lone pine, he came upon the village which huddled, dwarfed and shapeless, among the jagged granite bowlders—stretching on toward the North like a smudge of sooty gray below the glimmering band of the eternal snows.

"O Allah!" he mumbled, softly. "O Thou Raiser of the flags of increase to those who persevere in thanking Thee—I praise Thee and I bless and salute our Lord Mohammed, the excelling in dignity!" and again, with rising, high-pitched voice, "O Allah!"— letting loose all his long-throttled love and longing in one great cry.

Then quite suddenly he was silent. He drew back a step. He listened intently. There was a faint stir of dry leaves, a soft crackling of steel and, the next moment, a squat form robed in sheep-skins loomed up from a clump of thorn-trees; a wide-mouthed smooth-bore was pressed against Yar Khan's chest, and a raucous voice bade him state his name, the names of his father and grandfather, his race, his clan, his destination and his reasons for coming by night, unasked and unheralded, to *The Hoof of the Wild Goat*.

"Speak quick, cow maiming-jackal spawn!" commanded the Afghan, with the ready abuse of the hills, and Yar Khan laughed delightedly. This was what he had expected, what he had hoped for, this greeting out of the wilderness; this savage, free call of his own people, his own blood—cousin and cousin again through frequent intermarriage.

Smiling, he looked at the face of his cousin—for cousin he must be—which was like a bearded smear of gold-flecked red in the dim light of the rising sun. He stated whence he came and why and whereto, winding up by saying, "I am Yar Khan, the son of Ali Khan, grandson of Abderrahman Khan—the Afghan—the Usbek-Khel," and, unknown to himself, a note of savage pride had crept into the telling of name and pedigree.

The other eyed him suspiciously, undecided what to do. He had heard of Ali Khan, the man who had left the hills and who had gone South, in search of gold. And this—he clutched his rifle with steady hands—this smooth-faced, leaky-tongued stranger claimed to be his son. But perhaps this night-prowler was a spy sent by the Governor of Kabul to look into the matter of certain bullocks that had strayed away from the valley. Still, Ali Khan had had a son—and—

Suddenly he gave a shrill, kitelike whistle, and, a moment later, a second sentinel dropped from a rock crest. Came a whispered colloquy between the two villagers, another rigorous cross-examination as to Yar Khan's pedigree and antecedents, and finally the new-comer declared himself satisfied.

He walked up to Yar Khan, his right hand raised high in sign of peace.

"I am Jehan Hydar," he said, "the son of Shujah Ahmet, and I give thee peace—" and with a slight laugh he added, "O Egyptian!"

A great rage rose in Yar Khan's throat. Often,

in the past, people had called him Egyptian. There was that gray-haired Englishwoman who had come to his father's shop, year after year during the cool season, in search of scarabs and damaskeened brass; always had she addressed him as "my little Egyptian," and he had not minded it. But this was different, somehow. Rash, bitter words crowded on his lips, but he suppressed them. He was home—home!—and he would not mar the first day with the whish and crackle of naked steel. Better far to turn away ridicule with a clear, true word.

"I am not an Egyptian, Jehan Hydar," he replied, "but an Afghan and cousin to thee—cousin to all this!"—making a great gesture which cut through the still air like a dramatic shadow and which took in the frowning gray hills, the huddled squat houses, and the deep-cleft valley at his feet; and as the other grudgingly admitted the relationship, he swung his goatskin bag from his shoulders, opened it, and groped among the presents he had bought in the bazaars of Bokhara. For his heart seemed suddenly filled to overflowing with the fine, impulsive generosity of youth.

"Here, cousin mine," he laughed, "see what I have brought thee from—"

"Peace, peace!" interrupted the other, impatiently; "the night is for the sleep of the sleepers, not for the babble of the babblers," and, motioning Yar Khan to follow, he led him to a low stone hut and bade him enter.

In the middle of the room flickered a charcoal fire in an open brazier, and there was no furniture except a water jar and an earthen platform covered with coarse rugs and sheepskins. Jehan Hydar pointed to it without a word and left the hut, the tip of his steel scabbard bumping smartly against the hard ground.

Such was the home-coming of Yar Khan, the son of Ali Khan; and, as he stretched himself on the earthen platform and gathered the covers about him, he was conscious of a faint flavor of disappointment. They had accepted him, those two, but there had been no joy in the accepting, no generosity, no quick, warm-hearted friendship; and they were his cousins, blood of his blood and bone of his bone—and he had longed for them so!

For their sake he had left Cairo and the smooth gold of Cairo; for their sake he had traveled the many miles, riding till his spurs were red and his hands galled with the pull of the reins and his saddle broken across the tree.

And they—Jehan Hydar and the other? Why, they had accepted him as a man accepts salt to his meat, and they had sneered—a little.

He drew himself up on his elbow and looked out of the tiny window which was set low into the wall. A stark black pine stood spectrally in the haggard, indifferent light of the young day. He shivered.

But again the impulsive magnanimity of youth came to his rescue, and he said to himself that these men were his cousins, hill-bred, their whole life a rough fact reduced to rougher order. And he? He was home, and nothing else mattered. Henceforth he, too, would be a hill-man, free and unshackled. The weaver of his own life he would be, running the woof and warp of it as he willed, away from whee-dling barter, away from the crowded, fetid bazaars and the shrill trade cries of the market-place. To-morrow he would greet his clan, his family, and they would ask him about his dead father, about Cairo, and—yes—they would ask him about himself and give him a fair measure of honor. For he was coming among them, not as a beggar asking for asylum and bread because of kinship, but as a rich man bearing gifts bought with the red gold of Egypt.

"Home—Allah be praised!" he thought as he dropped into the dreamless sleep of youth.

"Ho, cousin mine! Ho, great lord out of Egypt!" . . .

The voice seemed to come from a far distance, and Yar Khan thought that he was dreaming, perhaps of his cousin, Jehan Hydar—he who had addressed him as "Egyptian"; so he stretched his body luxuriously for a second sleep—and then he felt a hand touch his shoulder and shake him gently.

At once he was wide awake. It was high day, with the cool golden mountain sun already in the upper arc of the heavens and weaving a lacy, ever-shifting pattern into the drab emptiness of the little hut.

"Ho, cousin mine!" again came the voice from the head of the bed. Slowly he raised himself upright. He turned and he—saw. A young girl was standing there, looking down at him with a smile, her narrow hand on his shoulder. And Yar Khan blushed and closed his eyes.

For be it remembered that all his life he had lived in Egypt and that, while he had seen foreign women walk about unveiled as well as old Moslem hags who were considered too old to spread the soft scent of temptation, he had never seen a young girl of his own race and faith without a veil. Nor had he ever spoken to such a one. He had dreamt of it—as boys dream—

and there had been his father's tales of hill customs.
Dreams and tales! And now he had seen—

For a moment he felt oddly checked and baffled.
He did not know what to say, and what bereft him
of speech was not embarrassment, but this new fact
of different customs and manners slowly awakening in
his consciousness. Quite suddenly it seemed to him
that his great yearning for the hills had grown out
of a far deeper foundation than he had yet thought
of; subconsciously he felt that this young girl was at
the root of it, and, with the thought, with the gather-
ing conviction of it, he opened wide his eyes and looked
at her.

She was tall and lean, with black hair which fell
in heavy braids over either shoulder, a low white forehead, the reddest of lips, and huge gray eyes set deep
below boldly curved brows. She was not beautiful.
But there was about her something best described as
a deep, luminous vivacity—something like an open,
clashing response to the free life, the wild life, the
clean life—the hills. And she was his cousin?

He formed the last thought into a wondering question, and her reply held both confirmation and, somehow, the flavor of prophecy. "Yes," she said, "I am
Kumar Jan, the daughter of Rahmet Ullah, chief of
The Hoof of the Wild Goat—I am cousin to thee.
Thus were our fathers cousins and our grandfathers
and our grandfathers' fathers—cousin aye mating with
cousin, according to the rules of the hills."

As he still stared at her, wide-eyed, unwinking, she
asked him why he looked at her. "Am I then a dancing girl of the South or," she added, mockingly, "hast
thou never seen a girl in all thy life?"

And when Yar Khan replied truthfully that he had

not, she was out of the hut with a silvery laugh and
the parting advice to make haste and rise—"For thy
clan is waiting for thee in full durbar!"

A few minutes later he left the hut and stepped out
into the village street, his goatskin bag over his shoulder.   A snow-bitten wind was drifting down from the
higher peaks, and the harried sun shivered and hid
among the clouds.

But Yar Khan, South-bred though he was, did not
feel the sleety, grained mountain chill; his heart seemed
flushed with a hot June prime, and he raised his right
hand with an exuberant gesture as he stepped into the
council of the villagers who were squatting around a
flickering camp-fire—behind every man his wife, unveiled, proudly erect, her hand on her lord's shoulder,
and everywhere the sturdy children of the hills: boys
of twelve and thirteen who were already trying to
emulate the fierce, sullen swagger of their sires, little
bold-eyed girls, fondling crude dolls made of stones
and bits of string and wood, and wee babes, like tiny
gold-colored puff-balls, playing about their fathers'
knees or munching wheaten cakes with the solemn satisfaction of childhood.

"I have come—" began Yar Khan, and then he was
silent and his heart sagged like a leaden weight.   For
no sound of greeting rose from the villagers, and the
bearded faces which were turned toward him seemed
impassive and cruel and slightly mocking.

Yar Khan felt like an intruder; there was something like a crash in his brain, and suddenly he realized
that he was longing for Cairo, for the busy, motley
crowds, the gay cries of bazaar and market-place, and
the dancing, red-flecking sunlight of the Southern sky.

He stood still, embarrassed, undecided what to do;

and then a clear voice called to him. "Ho, cousin!"—
it was the voice of Kumar Jan.

He looked.

She was standing behind a massive, white-bearded
man who was squatting at the head of the durbar,
evidently her father, Rahmet Ullah, chief of the tribe;
and Yar Khan's flagging spirits rose, and he walked
up to Rahmet Ullah, kissing the hem of his robe in
sign of fealty.

Then—and often in his thoughts, since he had rid-
den out of Bokhara, had he enacted the scene—he
threw the goatskin bag at the feet of the chief so that
the gifts which he had brought tumbled out on the
barren gray ground.

"Presents for all of you, my cousins," he cried;
"silks from Bokhara and sweetmeats from China . . ."
—suddenly he was silent. A hot red flushed his
cheeks.

For the uncomfortable thought came to him that he
was praising the gifts as he had praised bartered wares
across his father's dusty counter in the *Gamalyieh;*
and there was a tense pause while some of the men
and women stooped leisurely and fingered the presents,
with now and then a short grunt of wonder at the
touch of the glittering Northern silks, but with never a
word to him—of thanks or joy or pleasure.

Even Kumar Jan, to whom he had given a fine
Khivan shawl with his own hands, took the offering
in a matter-of-fact way. She threw it about her shoulders without a word, and Yar Khan was hurt and sad-
dened; his soul seemed charged to the brim with an
overpowering loneliness, and terror came to his heart—
the terror of the mountains, of the far places which
he did not understand.

His lips quivered.   He was about to turn, to leave
The Hoof of the Wild Goat, to rush down the steep
path and to take the trail—the long trail, to Bokhara,
to Cairo—when the voice of Rahmet Ullah cut sharply
into his reverie.

The chief welcomed him into the tribe with a few
simple words, and, indicating the whole assembly, he
added: "These be thy cousins, Yar Khan, son of Ali
Khan!   Their laws be thy laws, their customs thy customs, their weal thy weal, their woes thy woes, their
feuds thy feuds!   Thou art blood of our blood and
bone of our bone!   Whatever is ours is thine!"—and,
one after the other, the villagers rose and walked up
to him.

They greeted him, pressing palm against palm,
coldly, impassively, with short, rasping *"Salaam
Alekhum's"* and now and then a graybeard's querulous
reflection as to manners learned among foreigners and
infidels—reflections spiced and sharpened with Afghan
proverbs.

"If a man be ugly what can the mirror do?" croaked
a battle-scarred grandfather who walked heavily with
the aid of a straight-bladed British cavalry saber doubtless stolen during a raid across the Indian border; another chimed in with the even, passionless statement
that the cock went to learn the walk of the goose and
forgot his own, while a third—gaunt old warrior with
the bilious complexion of the hashish-smoker—inquired of the world at large why it was that in the
estimation of some people the strings of their cotton
drawers rivaled in splendor the Ameer's silken
breeches.

The girls and the children tittered at the last remark; and when the younger tribesmen came up to

salute their cousin there were open sneers, and finally a loud, insulting question from Jehan Hydar who asked Yar Khan, pointing at his peach-colored Cairene waistcoat, if he had ever considered what a pig could do with a rose-bottle.

Yar Khan flushed an angry purple. This—he thought—was the fair measure of honor which he had expected, this the home-coming—and he had traveled the many weary miles, he had bought presents for them purchased with the bitter gold of exile, he had given them of his best in loyalty and desire and free-handed generosity!

He was silent. He felt Kumar Jan's eyes resting upon him, wonderingly, expectantly—and what *could* she expect? He had gone to the hills in search of freedom, and now he was forfeit to the customs of the hills. He had gathered the swords of humiliation under his armpits, and the feeling of it was bitter and vain.

He looked up. Jehan Hydar was still standing in front of him, a mocking smile playing about his thin lips and in his oblique eyes a light like a high-eddying flame.

"Cousin," he drawled, and the simple word held the soft thud of a hidden, deadly insult, "cousin to me, to all of us! Yet do I declare by the teeth of Allah," here his eyes sought those of Kumar Jan, who stood close by, her whole attitude one of tense expectancy, "yes! I declare by mine own honor that thou seemest more like an Egyptian, a foreigner, an eater of fish from the South—of stinking fish, belike," he added as an insulting after-thought; and there was mocking laughter all around, high-pitched, cruel, rasping; but clearest and sharpest rose the laughter from Kumar Jan's red lips.

It was then that Yar Khan's good-humor suddenly broke into a hundred splintering pieces. His rage surged in deadly crimson waves. He forgot that these men were his blood-kin. He forgot the yearning of the swinging years. He only saw the sneer which cleft Jehan Hydar's bold face; he only heard the laughter which bubbled from Kumar Jan's lips, and he stepped up close to the other.

"Better dried fish in the South," he cried, "than a naked dagger in the hills," and his knife leaped out with a soft *whit-whit*. But he had no time to strike, to stain his soul with the blood of kin; for, even as he spoke, even as the knife left the scabbard, a dozen stout arms were about him, hugging him close—and there were laughter and frantic shouts of joy. Bearded faces touched his; the children crowded about him and hailed him with shrill cries; the women bowed before him with a clank and jingle of silver ornaments; and again, clearest, sharpest, rose Kumar Jan's laughter—but this time it was not the laughter of derision.

Suddenly, Yar Khan understood. They had tested his manhood after the manner of the hills and they had not found him wanting; and so, when he walked away from the camp-fire with Kumar Jan by his side, the hard, pent rage which had bitten into his heart disappeared like chaff in the meeting of winds.

He was home, home!

He said to himself that these men were his kin, that their woes were his woes, their laws his laws, their feuds his feuds—and he knew why there had been no thanks when he had emptied his goatskin bag at the feet of the chief. Yes! Whatever was his was theirs—thus the law of the hills—and then something in his heart seemed to flame upward.

He looked at Kumar Jan.

She, too, had spoken of the law of the hills—the law which says that cousin shall aye mate with cousin; and she—she was his cousin.

And then, thinking epically as hillmen do in moments of great emotion—he said to himself that the stroke and slash of his dagger were hers, that hers was his brain, hers the eloquence of his tongue, hers the strength of his body and the golden dreams of his soul.

He gripped her hand—and he knew that he had come home.

THE DANCE ON THE HILL

Behind him the Koh Haji-Lal, the "Mountains of the Red Pilgrim," closed like a ragged tide. In front of him the snowy peaks of the Gul Koh pointed to the skies in an abandon of frozen, lacy spires, while ten miles the other side Ghuzni dipped to the green of the valley with an avalanche of flat, white roof-tops, huddled close together beneath the chill of the Himalayas. The English doctor lived there, mixing his drugs and scolding his patients in the little house at the end of the perfume-sellers' bazaar, in the shadow of the great bronze Mogul gun which both Afghans and Lohani Sikhs called the Zubba-zung.

Mortazu Khan thought of him as he came down the mountain-side, his rough sheepskin coat folded across the small of his back to give free play to his lungs; his short, hairy arms, sleeves rolled to the elbows, moving up and down like propeller-blades. He walked with the suspicious step of the hill-bred who reckons with inequalities of ground, lifting his rope-soled sandals gingerly over timberfalls and crumbling granite slides, putting on extra speed when he crossed a wide spread of rust-brown bracken that covered the summer hue of the slope like a scarf, again warily slowing as he forded a swift little stream bordered with scented wild peppermint and chini stalks and gray, spiky wormwood.

But straight through he kept up a steady clip, averaging well over five miles an hour, up-hill or down.

There was peace with the Suni Pathans who squatted on the upland pastures and so he had left his rifle at home, carrying only a broad-bladed dagger. He was glad of it, for a rifle meant weight, weight in the hills meant lack of speed, and speed was essential. All last night his wife had moaned terribly, and the village wise-woman, at the end of her remedies, had told him that he needed the English *hakim's* skill before the day was out if he wanted his wife to live: his wife, and the little son—he hoped it would be a son—whom she was bringing into the world with such anguish.

Three hours he figured to Ghuzni. Three back. Rather a little more, since the foreigner was not hill-bred. Thus he would safely reach his village before the sun had raced to the west; and by night his wife would hold another little son in her arms.

Of course there would be a wrangle with the *hakim*, Mortazu Khan thought—and smiled at the thought.

First was spoken the ceremonious Afghan greeting, cut short by the Englishman's impatient, "Why haven't you come sooner?" and his reply that his wife was a stout hill woman who had borne children before this; also that he had called in the wise-woman.

"What did she do?"

"She gave her fish sherbet to cool her blood. She put leeches on her chest. She wrote a Koran verse on a piece of paper, lit it, and held it smoking under Azeena's nose—"

And then the *hakim's* furious bellow: "Of all the damned—! Good God! man, let's hurry, or your wife'll go out before we get there!"

At the end of the imagined scene Mortazu Khan's

smile twisted to a lop-sided frown. The doctor would be rightly angry. He should have gone to him yesterday. He should not have called in the wise-woman. He had given her five rupees— He shrugged his shoulders. To-morrow he would make her eat stick and force her to give back the money—

He increased his speed as he reached the edge of the slope where it flattened to a rock-studded plateau, with here and there little gentians peeping from granite splits and opening their stiff, azure stars. He bent and picked one to put in his turban for good luck, and as he straightened up again he smelled a familiar odor and saw two small, reddish eyes glaring at him from a clump of thorny wild acacia.

He stood quite still. Instinctively he fingered across his left shoulder for the rifle—which was not there. Then he walked on. At this time of the year the blue-gray, bristly haired mountain bears were not dangerous. They were busy filling their sagging bellies with prangus leaves and mulberries against the lean season. He would leave the bear alone, he decided, and the bear would leave him alone.

But when a moment later he heard the animal give tongue—a low, flat rumble growing steadily into a sustained roar, then stabbing out in a squeaky high note that sounded ridiculously inadequate, given the brute's size—Mortazu Khan, without looking over his shoulder, jumped sideways like a cat, cleared a heap of dry twigs, and made straight for a stout fir-tree that towered in lanky loneliness a dozen yards away. He reached it and jumped behind it. His hands gripped the rough, warty bark.

"Some cursed fool of a foreigner must have burned her pelt with a bullet of pain." He spoke aloud, after the manner of hillmen. "And now Bibi Bear has a grouch—"

He completed the sentence just as the bear tore out of the acacia clump and made after him with a huge, plumping, clumsy bound and a whickering, whinnying roar.

"Allah be thanked because He gave me nimble feet!" ejaculated Mortazu Khan. "And praise to Him furthermore because He made this tree and caused it to grow thick!" He finished his impromptu prayer as he slid rapidly to the west side of the fir while the bear lunged, big flat paws clawing, gaping mouth showing the crimson throat, the chalk-white teeth, the lolling, slobbering tongue, ears flat on the narrow head—like the head of a great snake.

The bear missed the hillman by half a yard and, carried away by her weight and impetus, she landed, paws sprawling, head down, on a bed of ochre moss studded with needle-sharp granite splinters. Her pointed muzzle bumped smartly against the ground, was torn by the ragged stone edges, and plowed a painful furrow through the moss so that it rose to either side in a velvety cloud.

She bellowed her disappointment and fury, sat on her hunkers, slid back half a dozen yards, using her fat hams with the speed and precision of roller-skates, then returned to the attack, launching her blue-gray bulk straight for the west side of the tree.

"*Ahi!* Pig, and Parent of Piglings!" shouted Mortazu Khan, as he rapidly made the half-circle around the tree to the opposite side.

"*Waughrrrr-yi-yi!*" said the bear, very low in her throat and with a certain hurt, childish intonation.

"Pig!" repeated the hillman, wiping the sweat from

his forehead, while the bear, who had again landed head down on the ground, wrinkled her ugly, thin-skinned nose where the warm blood was trickling down into her open mouth.

Mortazu Khan watched carefully. He knew that he was safe as long as he kept the tree between him-self and the brute, knew, too, that he was the more agile of the two.

Not that the bear was slow, but her body was longer, her bulk larger. She could not make short turns in a whizzing, flying half-circle like the hillman. She could charge—with a thousand pounds of bunched muscle and brutal meat—but when she missed, the best she could do was to use her nose and forepaws as brakes, bump back, twist in a sharp angle right or left, according to what side of the tree Mortazu Khan had slid—and return to the charge. And always the man, keeping tight to the fir, got ahead of her, while the bear, squealing like an angry boar, landed on the ground, hurting her delicate nose and clawing with her paws till the moss was shredded to rags and the sand beneath seemed to look up with scared, yellow eyes.

Little stones clattered mockingly. Twigs crackled and whined. Somewhere from the higher branches a noise trembled—a gurgling, throaty noise. Doubt-less the cry of a *buzra kurra*, a black tree grouse, thought the hillman, cursing the bird because of its place of security, cursing the bear because of her wickedness.

"Dog! Jew! Drunkard! Illegitimate cow!" he yelled as he danced around the tree, left and right and left again, his fingers scraping the bark and the bark scraping his fingers—"Away! away!"—Bibi Bear after him, roaring, fuming, and always missing her aim.

The bear's little, narrow-lidded eyes glowed like charcoal balls. The hair along her back was thick and taut, her ears flat. There was something ludicrous in her appearance, too—something which spoke of iron, sinister resolution.

Plump! Down on her nose, paws furrowing the ground! Twist and squat and twist.

She tried to learn from Mortazu Khan, tried to whiz her bulk in shorter circles, to charge straight at her foe. But always she missed. Always she had to brake with head and paws and make sharp angles while the man danced away.

"Infidel! Parent of naughty daughters!" shouted Mortazu Khan as the bear missed him by less than a foot.

His hands were hot and raw. His heart was cold with fear. For back across the hills was the mother of his sons—and then he cursed again the little bird which gurgled in the branches. He could not see it. But the gurgle was becoming loud, insistent, blending curiously and malignantly with the bear's wicked bellow.

Underneath his duffle shirt sweat rolled in little icy balls. His feet hurt. Moss had been around the base of the tree, but he had worn great holes in it, then long furrows and grooves. Now the whole cover of moss was trampled away, and he was dancing on the naked ground. One of his sandals had split the heel-rope and had flown away and out, while he had stepped through the other so that it was around his ankles. His toes were bleeding—

And Azeena waited!

But what could he do with his bare hands, without his rifle? The dagger? He could throw it—yes! And what then? One does not kill a mountain bear with a single thrust of steel. So he kept whizzing around the tree, and his thoughts whizzed along, his fears, his hopes—and then, quite suddenly, the bear changed her tactics.

"*Airrrh—whoof—airrh!*" she said with low, rumbling dignity.

"*Wheet-wheet!*" came the echo from the branches of the tree where the cursed, feathery thing was roosting in safety.

And Bibi Bear rose on her hind feet, fir needles and moss sticking to her pelt, belly sagging loosely, perspiration rising from her nostrils in a gray flag of steam. Straight toward the tree she walked, forepaws wide extended as if to embrace the fir and the miserable being who was clinging to it for dear life.

Something like a slobbering grin curled the brute's black, leathery lips, and Mortazu Khan watched. His skin seemed to shrink. Blue wheels whirled in front of his eyes. A hammer beat at the base of his skull.

Ahi! There was Azeena—who would not live out the day unless. . . .

"Allah!" he said. "It is not I who shall be a widower to-night, but Azeena who shall be a widow!" —and his knife flashed free while the bear came on, slow, ponderous, thinking in her ugly, twisted brain that all would be over in two crimson minutes if she could only tear the man away from the protecting tree.

Mortazu Khan knew it, too. "Assassin!" he cried. "Base-born and lean bastard!"

"*Waughree!*" replied the bear.

She came on without haste, leaned smack against

the tree, and tried to reach around it, right and left, with her murderous claws. But the tree was too stout, and for the moment the hillman was safe.

He smiled. Then he frowned. For the sun was rising higher, and he had to reach Ghuzni—the doctor—and back yonder Azeena was dying . . .

"Unclean spawn of filth!" he cried. "Large and stinking devil!"—and quite suddenly, watching his chance, he flashed his dagger to the left. He brought down the point with speed and ferocity, straight into the brute's right eye.

Something warm and sticky squirted up his arm. The bear, crazed with pain, jumped high in the air like a rubber ball, came down again, roaring, squealing, bellowing, slid lumberingly to the left, and again Mortazu Khan resumed his dance .

But this time it was another dance. This time the bear had no sharp angles to make. Both man and beast were close against the tree, circling, circling—

The sun rose and dipped. Far on the edge of the horizon the peaks of the Gul Koh flushed gold and lavender.

"*Waughrrr!*" snorted the bear, stamping her clumsy paws.

"*Wheet-wheet!*" chirped the echo from the uppermost branches of the fir, silly, mocking—and safe! And back beyond the bracken-clad slope, Azeena was dying hard, and his son was dying—dying before he was born—because Bibi Bear had broken the truce of the fat season.

Mortazu Khan trembled with rage and fear. But—away!—circling the tree, escaping the murderous claws!

He did not jump. No longer did he dance. He seemed to stream, to flow, like a liquid wave, his body scrunched into a curve while his lungs pumped the breath with staccato thumps. Only his hand was steady, taking crimson toll again and again, and the bear followed, roaring like forked mountain thunder. The blood on her huge body was caked with dirt and moss until the wounds looked like gray patches on a fur jacket.

A shimmering thread of sun-gold wove through the branches and dipped low to see what was happening. Far in the east a crane-pheasant called to its mate. The wind soared lonely and chilly.

They were out of breath, man and beast. Momentarily they stopped in their mad circling, the bear leaning against one side of the tree, a deep sob gurgling in her hairy throat, the blood coming through her wounds like black-red whips, while the man was huddled against the opposite side as tight and small as he could. He was tired and sleepy. His right hand felt paralyzed, but still it gripped the dagger. He knew that the end was near, knew that he himself must hasten it, that he must face Bibi Bear—face her in the open—and kill or be killed. For back yonder was Azeena, and the minutes were slipping by like water.

He raked together the dying embers of his strength. "Allah!" he mumbled. "Do thou give me help!"— And then he heard again the cry of the cursed, feathery thing:

"*Wheet-wheet!*"

But it seemed less mocking than before, more insistent, as if the bird, too, had lost its sense of security, had begun to fear the shaggy murderer below.

Mortazu Khan looked up. Then he saw it. It had dropped to a branch lower down, and it was not a bird— It was round and toddling and fluffy and blue-gray. A little, fat bear cub it was; and then Mortazu Khan knew why Bibi Bear had broken the truce of the fat season, and a certain pity and understanding came to the hillman's simple heart.

Here he was fighting for his wife, his unborn son, and he said to himself that the bear, too, was fighting for the young of her body, for the thing which gave meaning to life. And it was without hatred—with respect, rather, and a feeling of comradeship—that Mortazu Khan stepped away from the protecting tree, deliberately to give battle in the open.

The bear followed, growling. And so the two stood there, confronting each other, both breathing hard. ready to leap, ready to finish the fight.

It was the man who leaped first. For the fraction of a second he balanced himself, his bleeding toes gripping the ground. Then he went straight into the bear's embrace, the point of his dagger ahead of him like a guidon. His lips were crinkly and pale, his tongue like dry saddle leather, his eyes cold and gleaming. But straight he jumped, and straight stabbed the knife, finding the brute's pumping, clamorous heart, while the claws met across his shoulder-blades and tore a furrow down his back.

Straight to the heart! With every ounce of bunched strength and despair, and as the bear, in mortal agony, realized her steely grip, he struck again and again and again. But there was no hatred in the blows.

"*Ahi!*" he sobbed, as the bear toppled sideways and

'fell, curling up like a sleeping dog. *"Ahi!* Poor Bibi Bear! Brave Bibi Bear!"

His back bled and hurt. But he jerked the pain away with a shrug of his massive shoulder. The English *hakim* would have two patients instead of one, he told himself, and, dizzy, a little depressed, he turned to resume his walk across the plateau.

But something seemed to float down upon his consciousness, imperceptibly, like the shadow of a leaf through summer dusk, and he stopped and returned to the fir-tree. Standing on his toes, he reached up and caught the toddling, fluffy cub which was trying hard to back up, to regain the security of the higher branches.

"Come, little Sheik Bear!" he crooned as he might to a frightened child. "Come! There is room for thee in the house of Mortazu Khan! Room and food and water—and soon, if Allah be willing and the *hakim's* medicine strong, a little man-child to play with thee!"

And, the cub nuzzling his heaving chest with a little grunt of satisfaction, Mortazu Khan walked toward the flat roofs of Ghuzni, leaving behind him a thin trail of blood, but hurrying, hurrying.

THE RIVER OF HATE

"THE Wrath of the Thunder Gods," the Kafiri hill-men called the river that dropped to the western plains of Afghanistan and over into soft Persia in a succession of overlapping falls like the feathers on the breast of a pouter pigeon, while the Afghan nobles who, armed with the great, carved seal of the Governor of Kabul, came there to levy the quota of young men for the Ameer's army, called it the "River of Hate."

And Kafiri, as well as Afghans, spoke the truth.

For, during three months of the year, the North wind was riding a wracked sky and met the shock of the racing, roaring river, and the thunder crashed from the high ranges, splintering the young pines, occasionally taking toll of human life; and it was hate, even more than the swirling breadth of the river, which divided the villages that squatted on either bank.

South of the river, the Red Village lay spotted and threatening, like a tiger asleep in the sun, while North the flat-roofed houses of the White Village seemed snow flakes dropped on slabs of sullen granite—as sullen as the temper of the people when they looked across and saw the men of the Red Village sweep the whirlpool of the Black Rock with crude, effective net traps made of jungly rattan and hempen ropes; when they saw the catch of fat, blue-scaled, red-eyed *khirli* fish drawn up on the bank and flopping in the quivering light like dusky flecks of sunshine.

The Black Rock was the fortune of the Red Village.

Forming the end and pinnacle of a chain of ragged, slippery stones that spanned three-fourths of the river's breadth and rose and fell to the rise and fall of the water, it was within fifteen feet of the southern bank, and in winter, when rain had been heavy in the mountains and the River of Hate surged up a man's height in a couple of hours, it acted like a natural dam.

But in summer, when, freed from snow, the higher range limned ghostly out of the purple-gray distance and drouth shrunk the river, the Black Rock peaked to a height of thirty feet and caused the water to drop into a great whirlpool, not far from the Red Village, where it blossomed like a gigantic waxen flower.

Too, it is in summer that the *khirli* fish, obeying their ancient tribal customs, come from their spawning, and when they return down the River of Hate on their way to the Persian Gulf, they are tired and weary with the many miles. So they lie down to rest in the bottom of the whirlpool of the Black Rock where the fishing rights, by immemorial law, antedating the law of the Koran, belong to the people of the Red Village; and the villagers catch them and feast, while the men of the White Village bemoan their fate and take the name of Allah and—if the Afghan priests be not listening—the names of various heathen gods decidedly in vain.

But they do not fight the people of the Red Village, except with an occasional stone or stick hurled from ambush and not meant to kill. For a law is a law.

When, after seven years' service in the Ameer's army—during which he had learned to shoot straight, to substitute a tall black fur cap, worn rakishly over the right ear, for the greasy shawl turban of the Kafiri, to embroider his rough hill diction with flowery Persian metaphor, and to ogle the women in the bazaars—Ebrahim Asif received word that his father, Sabihhudin Achmat, had died, and that he was now chief of the White Village, he went straight to the Governor of Kabul and asked to be released from service.

"My people are clamoring for me," he added in a lordly manner.

The Governor saw before him a young man, not over twenty-five, of a supple sweep of shoulders, a great, crunching reach of arms, a massive chest, and a dead-white, hawkish face that rose up from a black, pointed beard like a sardonic Chinese vignette. He thought to himself that here was a Kafiri, a turbulent pagan hillman indeed; but that seven years in Kabul must have put the Afghan brand upon his soul, and that he might be a valuable ally if ever his lawless tribesmen should give trouble—perhaps, only Allah knew! as a raiding vanguard accompanying an invading British or Russian column, as the little, sniveling, dirt-nosing jackals accompany the tiger.

"Your prayer is granted, Ebrahim Asif," the Governor said. "Return to your own people—a chief. And—" he smiled, "also remember that you are an Afghan, and no longer a lousy hillman!"

"Yes, Excellency!" said Ebrahim Asif.

On the second day out of Kabul he was back over the borders of his own country. On the third, he saw the faint, silvery gray mountain, flung like a cloud against the sky, that marked the western limit of the White Village.

On the morning of the fourth, he was sitting on a

raised earthen platform in the communal council hut
of the village where his ancestors had been hereditary
rulers since before the shining adventure of Shikandar
Khan, he whom the Christians call Alexander the Mace-
donian, his rifle across his knees, and a naked, pot-
bellied boy of ten fanning him with a silver-handled
yak tail, stolen during some raid into Tibet. He was
holding a perfumed, daintily embroidered handkerchief
to his nose.

On the bare mud floor, below the platform, squatted
the men of the village, some thirty in number, in a
confused heap of sun-and-dirt-browned arms, legs and
patched multi-colored garments.

Ebrahim Asif, remembering the days of his childhood when his father had occupied the seat of chief
which to-day was his, turned slightly to the left.

Directly in front of him squatted an old man whose
name was Jarullah. His face was like a gnarled bit
of deodar wood beneath a thatch of bristly, reddish
hair.

Ebrahim Asif pointed at him.

"Jarullah," he said, "you are the oldest. Let me
hear what wisdom, if any, the many years have
brought you."

"It is not money we want," muttered Jarullah.

Then, embarrassed he knew not why, he checked
himself. His roving eyes sought his knees and he
coughed apologetically, until a young man, lean, red-
haired, with pock-marked vulpine features and bold
gray eyes, stepped forward, pushed Jarullah uncere-
moniously aside, and squatted down in his place.

Over his shoulder, he pointed through the doorway,
at the River of Hate, and the hissing whirlpool of the
Black Rock, and beyond, at the Red Village, that

seemed stiff and motionless in the quivering heat as if forged out of metal. Only at the bank were signs of life—the men pulling in the nets sagging with their shimmering load. Occasionally, a high-pitched, exultant yell drifted thinly across.

"Our bellies are empty, Chief," the young man whose name was Babar, said sulkily, "while they—" he spat—"the people of the Red Village—"

Ebrahim Asif rose, picked up his rifle by the shoulder strap, and walked toward the door.

"The old feud, eh?" he asked. "The feud over a potful of stinking *khirli* fish? By the teeth of the Prophet—on whom peace—I shall spice their mid-day meal with a couple of bullets and a rich sluicing of blood!"

But Jarullah stepped into his path and laid a trembling hand on his shoulder.

"There is the law, Chief!" he cried in a cracked, excited whine. "The fishing rights of the southern bank belong to the Red Village. Remember the law of the Kafiri!"

"There is no law for Afghans," smiled Ebrahim Asif.

"Right!" shrieked the old man. "There is indeed no law for Afghans! But you are a Kafiri, Chief. You must keep sacred the ancient law of the tribes—" and an angry, clucking chorus rose from the squatting clansmen.

"The ancient law! The ancient law!"

Ebrahim Asif was utterly astonished.

Quite instinctively he had picked up his rifle. Quite instinctively he had decided to send a few bullets whizzing to the opposite shore. It would be perfectly safe. For the only firearms that ever came into Kafiristan

were those of the Ameer's ruffianly soldiers, soldiers
either on active duty or, like himself, released from
service, and he knew that for many years past no man
of the Red Village had been drafted into the army.

Thus he was perfectly safe in announcing his presence to them with a charge of lead and, later on, of
coming to terms: a fair half of the *khirli* catch to his
own village—otherwise bullets and blood.

It was simple—as sublimely simple, as sublimely
brutal as his whole philosophy of life.

But they had spoken about the law—the ancient
law—

The young man with the pock-marked, vulpine face
—Babar—had seemed the most manly of them all.

"What do you say, Babar?" he asked, and the other
mumbled piously, "It is the law. The fishing rights
of the southern bank belong to the Red Village."

Ebrahim Asif shook his head. He stalked through
the doorway, while the villagers looked after him,
stolid, sullen. He walked up to the River of Hate.

The men of the Red Village were still fishing, peaceful, undisturbed, serenely safe. One looked up,
squinted against the light with sharp, puckered eyes,
and seemed to see the rifle in Ebrahim Asif's hand.
But he paid no attention to it. To him, too, there
was the ancient law.

And, suddenly, out of the nowhere, a heavy weight
dropped on Ebrahim Asif's soul.

"Yes," he murmured, "there is the law—for us
Kafiri—" and he tossed the rifle into the swirling,
foaming water.

Late that night, as he sat alone in his father's hut,
which was now his, scraps of memory came to him.
Piece by piece he put them together.

He remembered how, years ago, when he had been a naked, sun-burned child with a red turban cloth wound about his shaven poll, his father, Sabihhudin Achmat, had been guide to a Kashmere rajah who had come North to hunt the thick-pelted, broad-headed tigers that drift into Kafiristan in the wake of the Mongolian snows. The rajah had brought a large retine of servants, and one evening they and their master and his father had whispered together.

They had set to work, under the rajah's guidance. All night they had worked, with little Ebrahim looking on open-mouthed, using odd bits of steel and wire taken from the rajah's voluminous baggage, and wood and stones and spliced ropes and rattan.

About midnight they had sneaked out of the house and through the sleeping village, to the bank of the River of Hate, carrying between them a strange contrivance that seemed round and heavy. Hours later, his father had returned, drenched to the skin, but triumphant.

Today, Ebrahim Asif knew that the strange contrivance the Kashmere men had fashioned that night and which his father had put in a hole of the Black Rock, below the surface, was a water wheel to change the main current of the whirlpool, for since then he had seen many such wheels.

And when the next drouth had shrunk the river and the *khirli* fish had returned from their spawning, when the people of the Red Village had swept the whirlpool of the Black Rock, day after day, they had caught no more than a lean handful of skinny, smelly dagger-fish, while the men of the White Village, wondering, yet obeying their chief's command, had gone down to the northern bank where the fishing rights were theirs and had set to work with improvised gear.

The catch had been huge; and for weeks, they had eaten their fill of *khirli* spiced with turmeric and sesame, while the people on the opposite shore had bemoaned their fate and had rubbed empty wrinkled stomachs.

Only the hereditary chief of the Red Village, Yar Zaddiq, a shrewd, elderly man, over six feet in height, with gray hair that had once been reddish-brown, a biting tongue and doubting, deep set eyes, had suspected the hand of man and, late one night, when the water was very low, had swum over to the Black Rock at the risk of his life and had investigated.

He had called for help. The wheel had been torn out, and a few days later, four miles up the river, accompanied by several of his clansmen, he had chanced upon Sabihhudin Achmat and had beaten him terribly.

After that, there had been no more catching of *khirli* fish on the northern bank, and the old hate of White Village against Red had grown a thousandfold.

The days that followed were drab and listless.

Ebrahim Asif stalked through the village in his best, most braggart Kabuli manner.

But, for the first time in his life, he was aware of a strange sensation which, had he been a westerner, he would have correctly analyzed as self-consciousness.

He said to himself that these were his people, that they had put their grievances before his feet trusting to his wisdom and strength—and their greatest grievance was the matter of the *khirli* fish, the matter of the River of Hate. Willing and ready he had been to help them, he continued his thoughts angrily, but they had tied his hands with their babble about the ancient tribal laws; he had tossed his rifle into the water—and—what did they want him to do?

They supplied him with food and tobacco and *bhang* as was his right, since he was their chief. But it was all done grudgingly, as a drab matter of duty.

Yet there was little open complaint; just an undercurrent of muttering and whining. Only the young man, Babar, put it into words one day.

"You are the Chief," he said. "You must help us!"

Simple enough words. But, somehow, they seemed to Ebrahim the final, unbearable stigma.

"Do you want me to attempt the impossible, O Abuser of the Salt, O Son of a Burnt Father?" he cried. "Do you want me to make noises with my ears and catch the wind of heaven with my bare hands, O Cold of Countenance?"—and he beat Babar with the flat of his saber till the blood came.

After that, the people of the village, his own people, trembled when he passed. And in all Kafiristan there was no man more lonely than he.

Thus he took to roaming the hills up and down the River of Hate, climbing to the higher range where, caught in crevices, the snow lay clean and stainless beneath the crisp air, down abrupt precipices, and into thick forests of spruce and beach where the dry leaves lay in intricate, wind-tossed, fox-red patterns fretted with delicate green shadows; and one day, returning past the natural bridge that marked the line between the two villages and where, years earlier, his father had been beaten by Yar Zaddiq, he saw a young girl standing there, poised lightly upon narrow, sandaled feet, and looking out upon the foaming River of Hate.

She turned as she heard his approach and stared at him fearlessly, and he stood still and stared back.

She was sixteen years of age. Her small slender body, just budding into the promise of womanhood beneath the thin, fringed, brown and gray striped fustian robe that covered her from her neck to just below her knees, was perfect in every line. Her parted, braided hair was light brown and as smooth as oil, her eyes were gray with intensely black pupils, and her nose straight and short. There was a sweet curve to her upper lip and a quick, smiling lift at the corners.

The smile rippled into low, gurgling laughter when she saw Ebrahim Asif bow deeply before her with clasped hands, as she had seen the men of her village salaam to the Ameer's swashbuckling emissaries.

He straightened up. With unconsciously graceful ease he put his hand on the heavy, carved silver hilt of his sword and looked at her squarely.

And his words, too, were square and clear, yet tinged with a certain reckless, boisterous good humor, a certain swaggering bravado.

"Your name, Crusher of Hearts!"

Again the girl laughed.

"I am Kurjan," she said. "I am the daughter of Yar Zaddiq, Chief of the Red Village, who, it is told, once gave your father a sound beating."

"Then—you know my name?" he rejoined, flushing darkly.

"Evidently, Ebrahim Asif!" came her mocking reply. "The fame of your splendor has traveled many miles, also the tale of how wisely you rule your own people, how you fill their stomachs with *khirli* fish—how they love you, O great Afghan—"

But, suddenly, she checked the flow of words and turned to go when she saw the man's insolent, black eyes fixed upon her with a calm, uncontrolled expression of admiration and desire, and instinctively she drew in her breath and clasped her right hand against her heart, as unhurryingly, he stepped up to her.

"Kurjan, daughter of Yar Zaddiq," he said very gently, "I am not an Afghan, though my dress is that of the Kabuli and though my lips have forgotten the proper twist and click of my native tongue in the many years I have spent away from home. I am a Kafiri, a hillman of hillmen and—" suddenly his voice peaked up to a high, throaty note, like the cry of an eagle circling above a frightened, fluttering song bird—"I love like a Kafiri!"

And, before she had time to run or defend herself, his great arms were about her, crushing her against his massive chest so that the long braids of her hair swept the ground behind her.

Very slowly, as if reluctantly, he released her.

"Go back to your father," he continued as she stood there, panting, a rush of unknown sensations, shyness, mixed with fear and a strange, tremulous, paining delight, surging through her body. "Tell him that a man has come to the River of Hate. Tell him that to-night I shall come to his house to demand you as my wife. And—as to you, Crusher of Hearts— tell yourself when you lie on your couch, that I love you—that there is a sweetness and strength in my soul which is known to your soul only!"

And he walked away, his saber clanking behind him; and he did not turn once to look back at her.

Kurjan did not know if it was the strange, sweet shyness which had come to her so abruptly, or fear of her father's terrible, raging temper which sealed her lips. At all events, she did not say a word of what had happened to her when she reached home. Courteously she bowed to her father who was resting his huge old gnarled body on the earthen platform, and stepped through the curtain into the back part of the house where the women crouched over the crimson charcoal balls of the cooking fire.

Thus, hours later, when night had dropped as it does in the hills, quickly, like a black-winged bird, and when Ebrahim Asif had gone up the river, crossed the natural bridge, and passed through the silent Red Village to the house of Yar Zaddiq, he found the latter unprepared for his coming.

But his first words explained the purpose of his visit. "I am Ebrahim Asif, the son of Sabihhudin Achmat, Chief of the White Village," he said with nonchalant dignity. "I have decided that your daughter shall be the mother of my sons. Hasten the wedding, old Chief. For I am an impatient man who does not brook denial or contradiction, and my young blood is sultry with passion."

And, calmly, he squatted down and helped himself to the other's supply of finely shaved *bhang*, conscious, by the rustle of the curtain that shut off the back part of the house, that Kurjan was looking at him.

She was standing very still, her heart thumping violently. Quickly, imperceptibly, the knowledge floated down upon her that she loved him. Anxiously, she waited for her father's reply.

When Yar Zaddiq looked up his words dropped smooth and even, as stones drop down a glacier.

"So you are Ebrahim Asif—" his lips curled in a crooked smile, exposing the toothless gums stained with opium and tobacco—"the son of him whom once I beat grievously with sticks—as a dog is beaten with thorn sticks—?"

"You—*and* your tribesmen! A dozen against one!"

"I could have killed him with my bare hands. I, alone! I was stronger than he!"

"But to-day you are old—and I am young. Your body is withered, while my body is bossed with muscles as the night sky is with stars," Ebrahim Asif said in a gentle voice, while his fingers toyed with the crimson cord of his sword, an action the significance of which was not lost on the older man.

And so he smiled.

"It is thus," he asked, "your wish to marry my daughter?"

"Yes."

"But—there is the ancient enmity between Red Village and White—"

"Over a potful of stinking *khirli* fish. I know." Ebrahim Asif waved a great, hairy hand. "But there will be no more babbling and jabbering and foolish quarreling after I have married your daughter. I am my late father's only son, and she—" negligently, with his thumb on which shone a star sapphire set in crude silver, he pointed at the curtain where she stood—"she is your only child. Let peace be the dowry of our wedding, peace between your village and mine, a forgetting of ancient hatreds, a splitting of future profits. Let us put aside the old enmities as a clean man puts aside soiled linen. In the future we shall divide the *khirli* catch evenly between your people and mine."

Yar Zaddiq laughed in his throat.

"*Ahee!*" he cried. "It is I who gives all the dowry. And what will you give, young Chief?"

"I?" Ebrahim Asif raised an eyebrow. "Where hate has died, no room is needed to wield a sword. Where strength goes to the making of peace, no vio-

lence is needed to strike a dagger blow. Where quarrel is buried, no fertilizer is needed with which to
grow friendship. But—I am an honest man! I shall
make the bargain even, so that nobody may complain
and that none of your people may say that you are
unwise. Your daughter shall be mine! Half the *khirli*
catch shall be my people's. And I, on my part, shall
lend to your people the help of wisdom which I learned
amongst the Afghans. And after your death—which
Allah grant be not for many years—I shall rule both
villages."

He rose and bowed with grave courtesy.

"I am an impatient man," he went on. "My heart
plays with my passion. Let the wedding be the next
time I set foot in the Red Village. Come. Give oath."

He stood still and looked at Yar Zaddiq who, too,
had risen. For several seconds, the older man did
not speak. His stubborn resolve that never, as long
as he was alive, should Ebrahim Asif marry his daughter, that never, until the end of time, should his people
cede to the White Village one tenth, not one hundredth
part of the fishing rights which were theirs according
to the ancient law, stood firm; but his opponent's equal
resolve hacked at his faith like a dagger.

"Give oath!" repeated the other, touching the hilt
of his sword, and then Yar Zaddiq spoke.

"You shall wed my daughter the next time you set
foot in the Red Village," he said solemnly. "I swear
it upon the Koran!"

But Ebrahim grinned boyishly.

"And yet I have heard," he said very gently, "that
you men of the older generation, converted to Islam at
the point of the sword, are not the stout Moslems you
claim to be. Thus—swear by the gods of our people,

our own people! Swear by the ancient gods of the Kafiri!"

And again he toyed with his sword, and again the old chief, a great bitterness bubbling in his words—for the Moslem oath meant nothing to him—swore that the next time Ebrahim set foot in the Red Village, he should wed Kurjan. By Ogun, god of sunshine, he gave oath, and by the three thunder gods; by Woggun, the god of the mid-week, and by Khanli, the grim god on whose forehead is an ivory horn from which hangs the fates of men; and finally by Gagabudh, the jeweled god of the mountain glens who, alone of all the gods, is immortal and whom even Time cannot slay.

And Ebrahim Asif, well satisfied, went out into the night, courteously avoiding speech with Kurjan though, during the last words, she had stepped fully into the room.

She looked after him. "I shall follow him," she said in a low voice. "I love him. He is brave and arrogant and cruel. There is passion in his heart and strength in his arms. I love him. He is brave."

Quite suddenly, Yar Zaddiq laughed.

"Yes, little daughter," he said. "He is brave. But—" he burst into high-pitched, senile cackle, "it is not wisdom he has learned amongst the Afghans! Not wisdom!"

"Except the wisdom of love!" murmured Kurjan as she left the house and looked into the dark. "The wisdom of love—which is simplicity—and arrogance—and strength!"

Love had come to her. She knew the lore of the Red Village and of the White, the old feud, the bitter, sullen enmity; but, somehow, Ebrahim Asif was neither of the Red Village nor of the White. He seemed to her the very spirit of the land, serenely brutal, resolutely pagan to the core of him, but a man!

"A man of men!" she said to him one whirling, golden afternoon when she met him amongst the frayed basalt ridges of the farther hills and lay panting in his crushing embrace. "A man of men—with the bowels of compassion of a striped tiger!"

"You have spoken true words, Dispenser of Delights," Ebrahim Asif agreed naïvely. "I am indeed a man such as with whom any other chief would be proud to have a quarrel."

"And such as any other woman might—" she slurred and stopped; and he held her close.

"That, too, is the truth, little musk rose," he said calmly. "Often have I dragged my crackling sword through the bazaars of Kabul, and black eyes of Afghan women and maids stared at me through close-meshed veils—and, perhaps, there may have been hooded eyelids raised quickly in sign of promise—and hope—and—*ahee!*—reward. But—" and with a great gesture he dismissed the past as if it had never existed—"they passed into the dark, like gray djinns of evil. They left no trace, no heartache. There is only you in all the world, heart of my heart, and my soul is a carpet for your little feet. Step on it. Step on it with all your strength! For I am strong, strong!"

"My father, too, is strong. And he hates you. He speaks of you to me—though I do not reply. He curses you—"

"Allah!" Ebrahim Asif laughed and snapped his fingers. "Your father is a barren mule, bragging about the horse, his father. He is a toothless she-wolf—and presently I shall set foot on the soil of the Red Village and claim you."

"When, heart o' me?" she whispered.

And the answer came low and triumphant. "To-morrow, Crusher of Hearts!"

And, the next day, in the White Village, the conches brayed and the gongs were beaten; the young men danced over crossed daggers, and the unmarried girls drowned their heads with the dowers of the hillside and the forest.

For that morning, Ebrahim Asif had called the villagers to full durbar and had given them the good news. There had been uncouth rejoicing.

Only Jarullah had struck a discordant note.

"Beware, young Chief," he had said, following Ebrahim from the council hut. "Yar Zaddiq has a forked tongue. His father was a hyena, and his mother a she-devil," so he warned.

"Possibly," the other had laughed. "But, whatever his ancestry, his curse has not descended to his daughter. She is a precious casket filled with the arts of coquetry. Too, she is strong and well turned of hip and breast. She will bear me stout men-children."

And now he was in his house, adorning himself as becomes a bridegroom; for he had decided that he would wed Kurjan that very night.

He curled and oiled his beard; he drew broad lines of antimony down his eyelids; he heightened the color of his lips by chewing betel; he stained his finger tips crimson with henna; he wound an enormous green muslin turban around his fur cap; he arranged well the folds of his waistband; he perfumed his body from head to toes with pungent oil of geranium, a small bottle of which had cost him a year's pay to Kabul.

Then he threw a peach-colored silk khalat, embroidered with cunning Persian designs in gold thread, over his broad supple shoulders, picked up his sword, and stepped out on the threshold where Jarullah was squatting.

"Jarullah," he said, "to-morrow morning I bring home the bride. See that a feast is being prepared. I myself shall bring some fat *khirli* fish, the pick of the catch. As to you, have the women roast a sheep, well stuffed and seasoned with condiments. In there, amongst the boxes I brought from Kabul, you will find many things, spices of India and the far countries, strange sauces, and exquisite Chinese confections compounded of rose leaves and honey. Let the feast be worthy of the bride—and do not steal too much."

Jarullah overlooked the laughing insult of the young chief's last words. He clutched the hem of Ebrahim's khalat. He was terribly in earnest.

"Take care, young master," he whined, "lest evil befall you. You are brave, and trusting. But neither with bravery nor with trust can you knit the riven, lying tongue of such a one as Yar Zaddiq. Take along a dozen stout fighting men. Do not go alone."

Ebrahim smiled as he might at a babbling child.

"What avail is a rotten plow to a sound ox?" he asked casually. "What shall talkers do when there are no listeners? What is the good of lies when truth is the greatest lie?"

With which thoroughly mystifying words, he walked away in the direction of the natural bridge that linked the two villages. Evening was dropping.

Steadily Ebrahim Asif kept on his way, along the northern bank of the river, well within sight of the southern, so that his peach-colored khalat flashed like a flame in the rays of the dying sun; and he laughed softly to himself at the thought that, doubtless, sharp eyes in the Red Village were watching his progress from bowlders and trees.

Half a mile below the natural bridge, he disappeared behind the shoulder of a basalt ledge that jutted out from the river and entered a thick clump of dwarf acacia.

Five minutes later, the watchers of the Red Village saw once more the braggard sheen of peach-colored silk—and Yar Zaddiq whispered a last word to the Kafiri who crowded at his heels as jungle wolves to the tiger's kill.

Another ten minutes. The sun was hissing out in a sea of blood. The heavens were melting into a quiet night of glowing dark-violet with a pale moon peaking its lonely horn in the North, and up at the natural bridge where the two villages met, there was the sudden yelling of war cries, the rattle of stones, the throwing of thorn sticks,—and, above the noise, Yar Zaddiq's voice stabbed out as, flanked by the pick of his fighting men, he hurled himself upon the peach-colored khalat before its wearer had had time to cross the bridge.

"When you set foot in the Red Village, Ebrahim Asif! I swore it! By the Koran did I give oath, and by the ancient gods of the Kafiri! When you set foot in the Red Village! True I am to the double oath!"— and his stick came down, tearing a great gash in the bridegroom's silken finery, brought from far Kabul.

The men of the Red Village closed in, with exultant, savage shouts.

Night had dropped, suddenly, completely, as it does in the tropics, with a burnous of black velvet.

Nothing was visible except the shadowy, fantastic outline of a dozen human bodies balled together into a tight knot, heaving, straining, wrestling, pulling down their lonely opponent as hounds pull down a stag.

But the lonely man fought well. Time and again he jerked himself loose. Time and again his sword flashed free and tasted blood.

Time and again he drove his assailants before him towards the boundary of the Red Village.

But always, rallied by Yar Zaddiq's warring shouts, they hurled themselves back at him before he had a chance to cross the line.

And then came the end.

A jagged rock crashed on his head and he fell down, unconscious, bleeding from a dozen flesh wounds, curled up like a sleeping dog, his right hand across his forehead as if to ward off the blows of Fate.

Yar Zaddiq bent over him.

"You are a brave man, Ebrahim Asif," he said quite gently, "and doubtless you were a swashbuckler and a brawler in the tumult of the packed Kabul bazaars! Doubtless the gods have dowered your heart with stanch courage and your body with the strength of bunched muscles! But there is no wisdom in your soul, young Chief. *Ahee!* Your caution is as uncertain as a Tartar's beard, as rare as wings upon a cat!"

He laughed.

But, with utter, dramatic suddenness, just as the moon stabbed down with a sharp wedge of silvery light that brought the features of the unconscious man into crass relief, his laugh changed to a howl of disappointment and rage, cracked, high-pitched and ludicrous.

He kicked the prostrate form with all his might, turned, and rushed back across the bridge as fast as his gnarled old legs would let him, while his clansmen, wondering, astonished, cluttered after him.

Stumbling, falling, cursing, he ran through the night. His withered lungs beat like a hammer. But he kept on, along the southern bank, towards his house that sprang out at him with warm, golden lights.

With his last ounce of strength he hurtled across the threshold—and there, by the side of Kurjan, one arm around her waist, the other gesturing some flowery words of love he was whispering in her ear, sat Ebrahim Asif, in the ragged clothes of Babar, drenched to the skin, but happy, serene, supremely sure of himself.

Languidly he looked up and greeted the old man who was speechless with rage and fatigue.

"Have the women prepare me a meal," he said, "a *khirli* fish, carefully boned, and spiced with tumeric, also a goblet of tea, steaming hot. For it was cold swimming the River of Hate above the whirlpool of the Black Rock, and it is not right that the bridegroom should sit shivering at the wedding."

Then, casually, he asked:

"Did you by any chance kill that youth of my village —ah—Babar—who changed clothes with me in the acacia clump below the bridge?"

"No—no—" stammered Yar Zaddiq; and Ebrahim Asif sighed contentedly.

"Good, by Allah and by Allah!" he said. "There are the makings of a man in that youth—once I shall have taught him the shining wisdom I learned at Kabul—"

And, dreamily, with Kurjan's head on his shoulder, he looked through the open door where the night was draping the River of Hate in her trailing cloak of purple and black.

THE SOUL OF A TURK

THAT night, with no hatred in his heart but with a Moslem's implacable logic guiding his hand, he killed the Prussian drill sergeant who, scarlet tarbush on yellow-curled, flat-backed skull, was breveted as major to his regiment, the Seventeenth Turkish Infantry.

His comrades saw him creep into the tattered, bell-shaped tent where the Prussian was sleeping the sleep of utter exhaustion. They heard the tragic crack of the shot, and saw him come out again smoking revolver in his right hand. Calmly squatting on their haunches, they watched him go to the commissary, help himself to slabs of spongy, gray bread, dried apricot paste, and a bundle of yellow Latakia tobacco leaves, fill his water canteen, and take the road toward the giant breast of the Anatolian mountains, studded here and there with small, bistre-red farms, like brooches clasping a greenish-black garment.

"Allah's Peace on you, brother Moslems!" he said piously, turning, the fingers of his left hand opening like the sticks of a fan, then closing them again, to show the inevitability of what he had done.

"And on you Peace, Mehmet el-Touati!" came their mumbled reply, tainted by just a shade of envy, because they told themselves that soon Mehmet el-Touati would be in his own country while their homes were far in the South and West, and they did not know the roads.

They were neither astonished, nor shocked. They understood him, as he understood them.

For, like himself, they were simple Turkish peasants, bearded, middle-aged, patient, slightly rheumy, who had been drafted into the army and thrown into the frothy, blood-stained cauldron of European history in the making, by the time honored process of a green-turbaned priest rising one Friday morning in the mosque pulpit and declaring with melodious unction that the Russian was clamoring at the outer door of the Osmanli house, and that Islam was in danger.

The Russian—by Allah and by Allah, but they knew him of old!

He would ride over their fields, over the sown and the fallow. He would cut down the peach trees. He would pollute their mosques, their harems, and their wells. He would stable his horses in their cypress-shaded graveyards. He would enslave the women, kill the little children, and send the red flame licking over byre and barn thatch.

Therefore:

Jehad!—Holy War! Kill for the Faith and the blessed Messenger Mohammed!

Thus, uncomplaining, ox-eyed, they had pressed their wives and their children to hairy, massive chests, had adjusted the rawhide straps of their sandals, had trooped to district military headquarters, had been fitted into nondescript, chafing, buckram-stiffened uniforms, had been given excellent German rifles, wretched food, brackish water; and had trudged along the tilting roads of stony, bleak Anatolia.

Moslems, peasants, pawns—they had gone forth,

leaving their all behind, stabbed on the horns of Fate; with no Red Cross, no doctors, no ambulances, to look after their wounded or to ease the last agonies of their dying; with sleek, furtive-eyed Levantine government clerks stealing the pittance which the war office allowed for the sustenance of the women and children and feeble old men who tilled the fields and garnered meagre crops with their puny arms while the strong, the lusty, the bearded, were away battling for the Faith; with none to praise their patriotism or sing epic pæans to the glory of their matter-of-fact courage; with neither flags waving nor brasses blaring; with no printed or spoken public opinion to tell them that they were doing right, that they were heroes; with nobody back home to send them encouragement or comforts or pitiful little luxuries.

They had gone forth, unimaginative, unenthusiastic, to kill—as a matter of duty, a sending of Kismet.

For Islam was in danger. The Russian was clamoring at the outer gate, beyond Erzeroum.

Turks, they. Cannon fodder. Bloody dung to mulch the fields of ambition.

Had come long months of fighting and marching and fighting again. Victories, soberly accepted. More marching, through a hot, sad land speckled with purple shadows.

And they had wondered a little, and one day Mehmet el-Touati, as spokesman of his company, had asked a question of his colonel, Moustaffa Sheffket Bey, who, in time of peace, was the civilian Pasha of his native district.

The colonel had smiled through white, even teeth.

"Yes, Mehmet el-Touati," he had replied. "We are going South."

"But Russia is in the North, Effendina, beyond the snow range."

"I know. But—have you ever hunted?"

"Often, Effendina."

"Good. You stalk deer against the wind, don't you, so that it may not scent you and bolt?"

"Yes, Effendina."

"It is the same with warfare, with hunting men. We are traveling South—for a while. We do not want the Russian to smell the Turkish scent."

"But—" Mehmet el-Touati had pointed at a corpse that lay curled up in the middle of the road, like a dog asleep in the sun. "These people are not—"

"No. They are not Russians. They are the Armenian jackals who accompany the Russian lion in search of carrion. They are the Russian's allies. They, too, are the enemies of the Faith. Kill them. Kill the jackals first. Presently, with the help of Allah, the All-Merciful, we shall nail the lion's pelt to the door of our house."

"Alhamdulillah!"

He, and the others, had accepted the explanation. They had marched—South. They had fallen on the Armenian villages with torch and rope and scimitar. They had killed.

It was an order.

Many of his regiment died. Others took their places, Turkish peasants like himself, middle aged, bearded, solemn—but from districts farther South and West.

They, too, had heard that Islam was in danger, that the Russian was at the door.

Came more fighting, through many, weary months. Then a defeat, a rout, a debacle; the ground littered

with their dead and dying, amongst them the colonel
of the Seventeenth, Moustaffa Sheffket Bey; and talk
of treason in exalted places, of a renegade Saloniki
Jew by the name of Enver Bey throttling the ancient
Osmanli Empire and handing it over, tied hand and
foot, to a Potsdam usurper.

Greeks and Syrians and Druses had spread the
hushed, bitter tale through the ranks of the retreating
army. But the grave Turkish peasant soldiers had
slowly shaken their heads.

Leaky-tongued babble, that!

They had never heard of either Enver Bey or the
Potsdam usurper. Their very names were unknown
to them. They were fighting because Islam was in
danger.

Had not the green-turbaned priests told them so?

They had been defeated. What of it? That, too,
was Fate—Fate, which comes out of the dark, like a
blind camel, with no warning, no jingling of bells.

At first they had won, and presently they would win
again. They would conquer as of old. It was so
written.

They would return to their quiet, sleepy villages and
once more till the fields. Once more they would
harrow on the strips of fallow, shouting to their
clumsy, humped oxen. Once more they would hear
the creaking song of the water wheels, the chant of
the mullahs calling the Faithful to prayer, and the
drowsy zumming of the honey bees. Once more, on
Friday, the day of rest of all God's creatures, they
would stroll out with their women and children into
the sloping hills and smoke their pipes and eat their
food and sip their coffee and licorice water beneath
the twinkling of the golden crab apples that clustered

high up in the hedges and the greenish elderberries on
their thick, purple-blue stalks.

Meanwhile more fighting, marching, suffering.

Torch and rope and scimitar had done the work.
The Armenians had died by the thousands.

The land was a reeking shambles.

And—what of the Russian?

With the Armenians strung up in front of their
own houses, or buried in shallow graves, there was
only the Russian left to fight.

And he did fight, with long-range guns and massed
machine-gun fire and airplanes and blazing white shells
that screamed death from afar.

Daily he took toll, gave toll.

"But," said Mehmet el-Touati, voicing the sluggish, gray doubts of the Seventeenth Infantry which,
in its turn, voiced the doubts of the army—"why is
the Russian here, in the South? How did he come
down from behind the snow ramparts of the Caucasus
and is facing us here, in the flat lands, the yellow
lands, the fertile lands? Also, I fought the Russian,
twenty, thirty years ago, when I was a youth, with
no gray in my hair and never a crack in my heart.
Then the Russian was heavy and bearded and dressed
in green. Now he is tall and lithe and slim and ruddy
of skin and—" he pointed at an English prisoner—
"dressed in khaki brown. I cannot understand it. Is
there then truth in the bazaar babble that treason has
crept into the Osmanli house on silent, unclean feet?"

Thus he spoke to the new colonel of the Seventeenth,
Yakub Lahada Bey.

The latter was a monocled, mustached dandy from
Stamboul, who had learned how to ogle and speak

German and misquote Nietzsche and drink beer in the
Berlin academy of war. Too, he had learned, nor
badly, certain rudiments of strategy and tactics. But
he had paid a bitter price for his lessons. For he had
forgotten the simple, naïve decencies of his native
land, the one eternal wisdom of the Koran which
says that all Moslems are brothers, equal.

He dropped his eyeglass, twirled his mustache,
and turned on Mehmet et-Touati with a snarl.

"Shut up, son of a dog with a dog's heart," he
cried. "Get back—or—"

He lifted his riding crop significantly, and Mehmet
el-Touati salaamed and walked away. He shrugged
his shoulders. A beating from a master and a step in
the mud, he said to himself, were not things one should
consider in times of stress. Nor did he mind the killing, the dying, the wounds, the bleeding toes, the
wretched food.

But what of Islam? What of the Russian? What
of—treason?

Still, the priests had told them that Islam was in
danger, that they must fight. And they did. Though
not as well as before.

For doubt had entered their hearts.

Came another defeat; another retreat; another dis-
grace hushed up, followed by hectic clamorings from
Stamboul, the seat of the Caliph, the Commander of
the Faithful, and thunderous, choleric, dragooning orders zumming South from Berlin along the telegraph
wires.

Then, one day, a red-faced, blue-eyed, white-mus-
tached, spectacled giant, eagle-topped silver helmet on
bullet head, stout chest ablaze with medals and ribbons,
rode into headquarters camp and addressed the sol-

diers, who were lined up for parade review, in halting
Turkish with a strange, guttural accent.

Mehmet el-Touati did not understand the whole of
the harangue. But he caught a word here and there:
about Islam being in danger, and the Russian at the
door; too, something about a great Emperor in the
North, Wilhelm by name, who, like themselves, was a
good Moslem and coming to their rescue.

Thus Mehmet el-Touati cheered until he was hoarse.
So did the others. And hereafter foreigners—Prussians, they called themselves—took the places of the
Osmanlis as officers and drill sergeants in many of
the regiments, including the Seventeenth. They said
that they were Moslems—which was odd, considering
that their habits and customs were different from
those of the Turks. But—said the priests—they belonged to a different sect, and what did that matter in
the eyes of Allah, the All-Knowing?

On and away, then!

Kill, kill for the Faith!

For days at a time they were loaded on flat, stinking cattle cars pulled by wheezy, rickety, sooty engines, until they lost all ideas as to direction and time
and distance. East they were shipped—and fought,
losing half their effectives, quickly replaced by raw
village levies, until the Seventeenth was like a kaleido-
scope of all the many provinces of the Turkish
Empire, with Mehmet el-Touati the last surviving
soldier of the Anatolian mountain district in his company.

Again they were loaded on flat cars, then unloaded,
rushed into battle, bled white. Back on the cars once
more—South, East, North, West!

The Russian—Mehmet el-Touati wondered—was he

then all around them? Was he attacking the house of the Osmanli from all sides?

Hard, hard Fate! But—fight for the Faith! Islam was in danger—and on, on, along the never-ending road of suffering and death!

Followed days of comparative quiet while the engines rushed their armed freight to the North; and Mehmet el-Touati, who had not complained when the food was wormy and the water thick with greenish slime, who had not complained when bits of shrapnel had lacerated his left arm and when a brutal German student-doctor had treated the wound, with no anesthetics, no drugs, with just his dirty fingers and dirtier scalpel—Mehmet el-Touati complained to the Prussian officer in charge of his company while they were camping on both sides of the railroad track.

"*Bimbashi!*" he said, salaaming with outstretched hands. "We are clean men, being Moslems. There is no water with which to make our proper ablutions before prayer."

"*Schnauze halten, verdammter Schweinehund!*" came the reply, accompanied by the supreme Teutonic argument: kicks and cuffs; and a detailed account in halting, guttural Turkish of what he, himself, brevet-major Gottlieb Krüger, thought of the Moslem religion, including its ablutions and prayers.

"Go and make your ablutions in—"

Then a frightful, brutal obscenity, and the soldiers who had accompanied Mehmet el-Touati drew back a little. They questioned each other with their eyes. They were like savage beasts of prey, about to leap.

"*Bashi byouk, begh; ayaghi byouk, tchobar—*" purred one of them, in soft, feline, minatory Turkish.

A knife flashed free.

The Prussian paled beneath his tan. . . .

A tight, tense moment of danger. A little moment, the result of a deed—brutal, though insignificant, except in the final analysis of national psychology—that might have spread into gigantic, fuliginous conflagration, that might have sent the whole German-Turkish card house into a pitful, smoldering heap of ruins!

But a Turkish staff officer, fat, pompous, good natured, his eyes red and swollen with too much hasheesh smoking, played the part of the *deus ex machina*. He stepped quickly between the Prussian and the Turks and talked to them in a gentle, soothing singsong, winding up with the old slogan, the old fetish, the old lie:

"Patience, brother Moslems! Patience and a stout heart! For Islam is in danger! The Russian is at the door!"

Yet, deep in the heart of Mehmet el-Touati, deep in the hearts of the simple peasant soldiers, doubt grew, and a terrible feeling of insecurity.

It was not alone that the Russian seemed to have many allies—Armenians yesterday, to-day Arabs and Syrians, to-morrow Greeks and Druses and Persians. All that could be explained, was explained, by the green-turbaned priests who accompanied the army. But they had been told that the Emperor of the North who was coming to their rescue was a Moslem, like themselves. Why then did these Prussian officers— for the case of brevet-major Gottlieb Krüger was not an isolated one—kick and curse their brother Moslems, the Turks? Why did they spit on Islam, the ancient Faith, their own Faith?

Mehmet el-Touati shrugged his shoulders resignedly.

The Russians must be beaten. Nothing else mattered. So, half an hour later, with his company, he was entrained once more and under way, toward the East this time, until one day the railroad tracks ended suddenly in a disconsolate, pathetic mixture of red-hot sand, twisted steel, and crumbling concrete.

They marched, horse, foot, and the guns, North, Northwest.

"Where to?" ran the question from regiment to regiment.

Then the answer:

"To Russia!"

And cheers. For, while they had heard vaguely of England and France and America, Russia alone expressed to them all they hated and feared; and, gradually, their doubts and misgivings disappeared as time and again they passed long columns of prisoners in the familiar bottle-green of the Tsar's soldiery, and as day after day the road tilted higher and the sharp scent of the foot hills boomed down on the wings of the morning wind and the ragged crags of Anatolia limned ghostly out of the purplish-gray welter.

Mehmet el-Touati was kept busy explaining to the men in his company, Southern and Western Turks all but himself.

"It's the North," he said. "It's my own country. Russia is over yonder—" sweeping a hairy, brown hand toward the hills that rolled down in immense, overlapping planes, blue and orchid and olive green, while the high horizon was etched with the lacy finials of spruce and fir and dwarf oak.

"My own country," he went on. "I can smell it, feel it. My heart is heavy with longing."

A terrible nostalgia was in his soul. Too, day after

day, as the weeks of fighting had grown into the drab, sad cycle of years, he felt more old and lonely and tired. There was something ludicrously pathetic, something almost tragic, in the picture of this middle aged, bearded, rheumy peasant shouldering a musket and fighting and killing.

But he did not complain, not even in his own heart. He marched on, patient, stolid. First there must be a victory. The Russian must be vanquished, the house of the Osmanli made safe.

Then peace—and the creaking of the water wheels, the chant of the mullahs, the happy laughter of the little children playing in the sun.

By this time, since the roads were narrow, mere trails made by stray cattle and wild beasts, the army corps had split into a number of columns, each composed of a half company with its complement of light mountain guns, taken into pieces and carried on the backs of small, mouse-colored mules; and the half company to which Mehmet el-Touati belonged was the rearmost column, winding along hot, jagged roads where occasional thickets threw fleeting moments of shade, up steep hillsides where thick, purplish-gold sun shafts cleft the black rags of the fir trees, through valleys sweating with brassy, merciless heat, past fields of young corn that spread beneath the pigeon-blue sky like dull, sultry summer dreams.

On, while their feet chafed and bled, while the knapsacks cut their shoulders, and the rifles felt like hundredweights!

A few of the Seventeenth, Kurdish tribesmen mostly, nomads drafted on the way from amongst the black felt tents, had tried to desert.

Why fight any more, had been their sneering com-
ment, since their pockets were lined with Syrian and
Armenian gold and they had their fill of Syrian and
Armenian blood?

So they had snapped their fingers derisively and had
glided into the night shadows like ghosts, relying on
the hereditary, kindly negligence of their Osmanli
overlord.   But they had reckoned without the fact that
the latter was no longer master in his own house—
that the brevet-major of the company was a Prussian
drill sergeant, reared and trained with the Prussian
ramrod, the Prussian code.

"*Rücksichtslos*—inconsiderate of everything except
duty!" was his watchword, and his slogan was:

"I shall make an example—for the sake of discipline!"

He had halted the marching column—he drove them
afterwards to make up for the time he had lost—
until the deserters, one by one, had been recaptured,
courtmartialed, sentenced to death.

The melancholy Turkish staff officer who was attached to the Seventeenth to act as a sort of philo-
sophic, good-natured yeast, had tried to argue the
point, to reason; had said that Brevet-Major Krüger
was making a slight error, that he did not know these
people.

"They are like homing birds, these tribesmen," he
had said. "If a few of them want to go, let them. We
can always get more, and you cannot catch the winds
of heaven with your bare hands. These deserters are
Kurds, nomads, unreliable cattle, while the bulk of
the army is Turkish. You know yourself that the real
Turk is patient and obedient."

"Makes no difference! *Schlechte Beispiele verder-*

ben gute Sitten—bad examples spoil good morals! If we let the Kurds do what they please, some day, when we least expect it, these stolid Turks of yours will take the bit between their teeth, and then there'll be the devil to pay! No! I am a Prussian. I will have discipline. Discipline is going to win this war. I shall make an example of these fellows!"

Then a firing squad. Blood stippling the dusty ground.

And Gottlieb Krüger was right. Perhaps, as the months dragged along on weary, bleeding feet and there was no end to suffering and dying, it was his slogan of discipline—with its obbligato accompaniment of courtmartial and death—which kept the Seventeenth as a fighting unit fully as much as the ancient fear and hatred of the Russian.

Then, one day, Mehmet el-Touati overheard a few words not meant for his ear; and, with a suddenness that to a Westerner would have seemed dramatic, even providential, but that to him, Turk, Moslem, was merely a prosy sending of Kismet to be accepted as such and used, a veil slipped from his eyes and slowly, in his grinding, bovine mind, he dovetailed what he overheard into relationship with himself, his own life, his past and present and future.

It was late in the afternoon and the company was camping in a little grove, spotted with purple lilac trees and walled in with the glowing pink of the horse-chestnut. The soldiers had loosened the collars of their tunics and lay stretched in the checkered, pleasant shade, sipping quickly brewed coffee, smoking acrid Latakia tobacco, talking of home, and Mehmet el-Touati, on the way to a little spring to fill his water canteen, happened to pass the tent where the

THE SOUL OF A TURK

Prussian brevet-major was sharing the contents of his brandy flask with the Turkish staff officer.

As he passed, a few words drifted through the tent flap, flew out on the pinions of Fate, buffeted against the stolid mind of Mehmet el-Touati with almost physical impact—caused him to tremble a little, then to drop to the ground, to creep close, to listen, tensely, with breath sucked in, lungs beating like trip hammers.

"Russia is smashed!" the Prussian was saying in his halting, guttural Turkish. "The Russians have signed a peace treaty with us, with Austria, with Bulgaria, with your country—Turkey. There'll be a little desultory border fighting—but all danger is past. The Russian is out of the running."

"You are sure of that?" asked the other.

"Absolutely. Remember the despatches I received this morning?"

"Yes."

"They were from headquarters. The peace treaty at Brest-Litovsk had been signed. Russia is out of the running—as harmless as a bear with his teeth and claws drawn. And now—"

"And now?" breathed the staff officer.

"And now?" came the silent echo in Mehmet el-Touati's heart, as he glued his ear against the tent.

"And now you Turks are going to see some real fighting. Of course I am only guessing. But I lay you long odds that your crack troops—like this regiment, the Seventeenth—are going to be sent to the Western front, brigaded with Prussians—and used against the French and British. Or perhaps they'll be sent to Albania to fight with the Austrians against the Italians, or to Macedonia to stiffen the Bulgarians a little."

"You mean to say the war is not over—with the Russian beaten?" asked the Turkish staff officer.

"Your war? Yes. It is over. But *our* war is not! And you are going to fight for us, my friend—and you are going to toe the mark and fight well. For—" he laughed unpleasantly, "remember our Prussian slogan—Discipline! Discipline!"

Mehmet el-Touati crept away, into the shadow of a horse-chestnut tree, to think. But he did not have to think long.

Only one fact stood out: the Russian was beaten; Islam was safe—and the house of the Osmanli.

Nothing else mattered.

The West front? Albania? Macedonia?

The French and British and Italians?

No, no! He shook his head. He knew nothing about them. They were not in his life, his world. Russia was beaten. Islam was safe, and he had done his duty, and now he must go home and look after his fields and his wife and his children. They had been neglected so long.

He must go soon. To-day. This very night. For here he was in the foot hills of his own country, where he knew the roads.

But—how?

He remembered the Kurds who had tried to desert, who had been caught, courtmartialed, shot, by orders of—

Yes! By orders of the Prussian, the foreigner!

The Turkish staff officer would not care. He would argue that one man more or less in the company was not worth the trouble of halting the column, of searching the surrounding valleys and mountains with a fine-tooth comb.

Thus—there was just one way—

And so, that night, with no hatred in his heart but with a Moslem's implacable logic guiding his hand, Mehmet el-Touati killed the Prussian officer and took the road toward his own country.

MORITURI

(An Episode of the Balkan War)

DRAMATIS PERSONÆ

CAPTAIN BORIS PLOTKINE, Third Bulgarian Infantry.

CAPTAIN MEMET ABDERRAMANN TOUATI, First Turkish Cavalry.

LANCE-CORPORAL NADJ HANIECH, Second Battery Turkish Horse Gunners.

SCENE:—*Represents a battlefield in Macedonia. It is the early dawn of morning. The sky is pink and silver and orange, and as far as the eye can see, there are the shadowy, grim outlines of dead soldiers, Turks and Bulgarians, dead horses, broken wheels and dismounted gun-limbers. A thick, humid haze rises from the slimy ground, and there is the acrid smell of battle, —blood and powder and putrescence and dirt. In the far distance are heard the crunching wheels of commissariat wagons, the heavy grumble of artillery, and once in a while the sharp hissing of musketry fire.*

TIME:—November, 1912.

DISCOVERED:—*Plotkine and Touati, both badly wounded.*

PLOTKINE (*writhing on the ground; moaning*)
Oh, Holy Kyrill and all the dear Saints—this is insufferable. I can't stand it.

TOUATI (*Slowly and painfully turning his head in the direction of Plotkine*)
You'll *have* to stand it, comrade.

PLOTKINE
Who's there?—a friend?

TOUATI
No. I am of the First Turkish Cavalry. I am Captain—but never mind my name. I do not suppose a ceremonious introduction is necessary under the circumstances.

PLOTKINE
Come over and give a chap a bit of help, will you?

TOUATI
I am awfully sorry, but . . .

PLOTKINE (*interrupting*)
Oh, you're wounded yourself, are you?—Can you move?

TOUATI
Not as much as I'd like to. A piece of shrapnel struck me, and one of my legs is shattered—it's only just making a bluff at hanging together by a shred of skin.

PLOTKINE
I got mine through the chest—right chest. (*Short pause.*) You talk jolly good Bulgarian. (*Another pause.*) I say, comrade, there must be a Turkish ambulance corps kicking about here somewhere. I can't

speak a word of Turkish—and talking hurts me so—
my chest—you know. Don't you think you could call
them?

TOUATI

Quite unnecessary, captain. There's nobody here,
nobody who could help us. The column marched away
long ago. You see, we two are lying in a sort of hole
in the ground. That's why they didn't notice us. Oh,
well—Allah's will—

PLOTKINE (*with sudden, helpless fury*)

God's curse on it,—so we are lost—what?—helpless?

TOUATI

Yes, captain. You're perfectly right.

PLOTKINE (*after a short pause*)

But couldn't we help each other?—somehow?

TOUATI

I don't think I can do a thing. I am very weak,
you know. I've lost so much blood. You see, it took
me nearly all night to crawl six feet—a little bit away
from my brother—

PLOTKINE

From your brother?

TOUATI (*passionless*)

Yes. He's dead, too. He was such a nice, brave
young lad. But you see, this confounded heat—and
then this wretched humidity—and so he's been getting
rather smelly. Nothing against him, you know, nothing against him. But I had to move—and you see, it
took me all night—crawling—crawling—

PLOTKINE

And I can't move at all, not at all. Even when I try to breathe hard, the air whistles through my lungs as if there's a draft somewhere in my chest. And a ton of rock seems to lie on my legs. I can't turn my head. I can't see you. Can you see me?

TOUATI

Oh, yes. I am looking at you.

PLOTKINE

Then tell me: how far distant are we from each other?

TOUATI

I should judge about three yards. But for all it would help you or me it might as well be three thousand miles.

(Both are silent for several minutes; Plotkine sighs.)

PLOTKINE

I am hungry. Got anything to eat about you?

TOUATI

Yes. A few dried dates. Here, look out. I'll throw them over so that you can reach them with your left hand. *(He throws over a handful of dried dates to Plotkine, who takes them and eats.)*

PLOTKINE *(between bites)*

Thanks awfully. *(Laughs.)* You aim better than did your artillery at the Tschataldja lines.

TOUATI *(very stiffly)*

I beg your pardon.
(Long silence.)

Plotkine
So you think there's no hope for us, captain.

Touati
Only a miracle would help us.

Plotkine
I shall pray to my Patron Saint.

Touati
Well—if it gives you any pleasure—
(*Plotkine prays fervently for a few minutes. Then there is complete silence. They do not exchange a word for over half an hour.*)

Plotkine (*suddenly*)
Ho there, comrade! Are you dead already?

Touati
No, not yet.

Plotkine
It must be getting on towards noon.

Touati
I think you're mistaken. It's hardly half an hour since I had the pleasure of making your acquaintance —and that was early in the morning.

Plotkine
Which one of us is going to cash in first, do you think?

Touati
I think I'll go out first. You see, the chances are that I'll get gangrene very soon now.

PLOTKINE (*after a short silence*)

I say, captain. You speak very excellent Bulgarian. Where did you learn it?

TOUATI

I?—Oh, I lived in Sofia for two years—studied there at the Polytechnicon.

PLOTKINE (*excited*)

You don't say so! Then you must know Professor Nyachnioff?

TOUATI

I certainly do.

PLOTKINE

Isn't that odd? You know, I married his daughter —little Lisaveta.

TOUATI

Oh, I remember her. I saw her once when I called on her father. She was a very charming girl.

PLOTKINE

Yes, isn't she? She is an angel, I tell you. And how she loves me—you've no idea, captain. If she knew that I'm lying here, dying—why, the poor little kiddie—she'd cry her eyes out—I tell you, she'd kill herself.

TOUATI (*a little doubtful*)

You think so?

PLOTKINE (*angry*)

Don't you believe it? I tell you she'll kill herself when she reads my name in the list of those killed in battle. You'll see.

TOUATI (*with a laugh*)

Pardon, comrade, but I don't think I'll see. Also, I don't think we'll be in the list of casualties. We'll be amongst those who are reported missing; don't you think so?

PLOTKINE

God! that's right. The poor little girl—that'll make it worse for her. There she'll go on hoping for months and months. (*He cries.*)

TOUATI

Did that relieve your feelings, captain?

PLOTKINE

Oh, my body just feels paralyzed. I tell you, I can't even move my fingers any more. Damn this war! What are we fighting about, anyway? Just because you confounded Turks insist on having Macedonia.

TOUATI

No—because you are trying to steal it from us.

PLOTKINE

Yes—as you wish. Makes no difference now. It's all the same. Gracious Heavens, Tsar Ferdinand had enough territory, God knows. What does he want this infernal desert for? I tell you, when I was a child, hopping and playing about the ryefields, I had no idea I'd have to die here, in this desert. And poor little Lisaveta will also die—she loves me so much, the dear little girl. (*Pause.*) Why, there is no sense in all this—this fighting—this dying— Tell me, where is the sense of all this?

TOUATI

You Christians are forever asking questions, and then you either get no answer at all, or you get several answers to the same question—which is worse. We have war—well—and we are soldiers—and so of course we die. What's there extraordinary about that?

PLOTKINE

Yes—but we die because of this confounded Macedonia—this damned desert—where nothing grows—

TOUATI (grimly)

Well, captain, even a desert will grow wheat if you give it enough manure—and just look about you; look at yourself and at me—smell our dead comrades. Oh, there'll be enough manure, enough stinking dung for a good, rich crop. (Laughs.) Everything for which one dies is good. And then, there are so many human beings in this world. What do we count, you and I? Just think how many millions will come after us.

PLOTKINE

I have no children. And what possible good is it to Bulgaria if I die here? The priests will babble as before, the tschinovniks will steal as before—and the comrades who return home will brag about their heroic deeds and their decorations. Nobody will think of me. My parents are dead—and Lisaveta will kill herself—

TOUATI

Yes, yes, she'll kill herself. But, captain, now's your time to think of your former life, to think of all life meant to you, of all you've accomplished—

PLOTKINE *(with a grim laugh)*

What?—I should think of what my life meant to
me? Of my advancement in the army, I suppose,
what?—new uniforms—parties given for Lisaveta—
an accolade by Tsar Ferdinand. Why, it's all over,
man—and when I think of it, it seems all so horribly
prosy, so horribly cheap and indifferent. Does it con-
sole you to think about your old life?

TOUATI

Yes. I think that I've always done my duty, in
life and in death. Also I've obeyed my Faith. That's
enough.

PLOTKINE *(sneering)*

All for Turkey. All for the Crescent, what?

TOUATI *(quietly)*

No. All for myself. If I learned anything, it was
for myself. If I achieved anything, it was for myself. And thus it was for Turkey and for my Faith,
even thus. What more could I do?

PLOTKINE

And—your wife?

TOUATI

The day I left for this war, I asked her to buy her
widow-dress.

PLOTKINE

Do you think she'll kill herself—like Lisaveta?

TOUATI

No. She'll marry again. You see, we have no
children. And now so many of us Turks died in this
war—so we need more children, more sons—to fight

again—a few years hence—to die again—perhaps to win—

PLOTKINE

Oh, you wish to reconquer what you have lost?

TOUATI

Of course.

PLOTKINE

Yes, I see; you love your country. And I love mine. But must we die on the battlefield to prove our love?

TOUATI

It's the best proof.

PLOTKINE

No. It's the last proof.

TOUATI

The last proof only for ourselves. There are others will come after us.

PLOTKINE *(suddenly, with a loud, gurgling voice)*
Oh, Mary, Mother of Jesus, pray— *(He dies.)*

TOUATI *(calls)*

Oh, captain, captain— *(Pause.)* Oh, he's dead. I knew when he asked me, that he'd go out before I would. A shot through the chest—of course. But why should I have told him? *(Smiles.)* And I don't think Lisaveta will kill herself. *(Pause.)* After all, it's quite indifferent one way or the other. *(Laughs.)* Queer people, these Christians—
(Lance-Corporal Nadj Haniech appears from the distance; Touati hears his footsteps, and calls to him.)

TOUATI

Ho, there!—

HANIECH *(running toward him)*

Coming, coming—

TOUATI *(looking up at him)*

No use trying to get me to the hospital, corporal. But I am suffering. I also would like to smoke—got a cigarette about you?

HANIECH

Yes, captain. *(He gives a cigarette to Touati and lights it.)*

TOUATI *(smoking)*

Just wait until I've finished my smoke and then— *(points to Haniech's revolver)*—you don't mind, do you? You see, I am suffering—and I can't be saved—

(Haniech nods his head, squats on his heels near Touati, and loads his revolver, while Touati finishes his cigarette.)

CURTAIN

THE JESTER

FATE wrote the first chapter of this tale before either Zado Krelekian or Mohammed Yar came to New York; long before the transatlantic steamship lines, seeing their European immigration business dwindle, thanks to improved wage conditions, began to invade Asiatic Turkey with agents who spoke the many languages of that motley and illy patched empire, who gave untold promises and were guilty of untold lies, who plastered ancient walls, tumbledown mosques, and battered, crumbling bazaars with garish six-sheet posters that pictured the New World as an immense block of real estate, entirely paved with minted gold and especially protected by the blessed hand of Ali.

Fate wrote the tragedy of this tale when, shortly after Creation itself, it made a compromise with Al-Shaitan the Stoned, the Father of Lies, by planting the seed of hatred in two races, Armenian and Kurd, the first Christian, the second Moslem; a curse which in the swing of the centuries stretched beyond the western vilayets of the Ottoman Empire, across the ragged, frayed basalt frontiers into the Caucasus and Southern Russia, the plains of soft, lisping Persia, west into the yellow, purple-blotched glare of Egypt, and west again . . . even beyond the sea, following the churned lane of Cunarder and White Star boat,

into New York, there to abut in the maze and reek
and riot of half a dozen tired, melancholy old streets
that, a few blocks away from the greasy drab of the
river, cluster toward the Rector Street Elevated station, toward the pride of the Wall Street mart, as far
even as busy, bartering, negligent Broadway.

Smelly, wheezy, threadbare old streets.

Gray, flat, dull. Powdered here and there with the
mottled brick-red of a once patrician house, a stable
or a garage that generations earlier had been a stately
residence. Streets branching west, north, and south,
in an irregular pattern of rays; rays of wretched,
lumpy cobblestone and wretcheder gutters; rays par-
alleled by rickety frame dwellings that bring you
straight back to the days when square-rigged clippers
rode the waters and when men imported their liquor
from Holland and called it genever.

Tragic streets, fit background for a tragic tale.

Not that this tale is entirely tragic.

For both tragedy and comedy are a matter of view-
point, perhaps of race and faith and prejudice (a wise
Arab once said that prejudice is but another name for
race and faith) ; and if your sense of humor be slightly
crooked, slightly acrid, in other words Oriental, you
will laugh at the thought of Zado Krelekian cooped
up in the back room of his house, with windows nailed
down and curtains and shutters tightly closed both
summer and winter, the doors hermetically sealed, with
fear forever stewing in his brain, in his very ears and
eyes, as he imagines he can see or hear the approach
of those whom he dreads, praying at times so as to
be on the safe side of ultimate salvation, praying quite
fervently to the God and the many saints of his ancient
Armenian church, in whom he does not really believe.

You will also laugh at the picture of Aziza watering the starved geraniums in her window-box and looking from her balcony across Washington Street for the return of her lover; with her braided bluish-black hair that looks as if cigarette smoke had been blown through it, her immense, opaque eyes, her narrow, pleasurable hands, her tiny feet, the soles stained crimson with henna, the big toes and the ankles ablaze with gold and precious stones.

And finally you may smile tolerantly at the thought of Mohammed Yar, once a ragged, thin-mouthed, hook-nosed Kurd tribesman, but dressed to-day in swagger tweeds that bear the Fifth Avenue label, his brown, predatory fingers encircled by rings of great value, his shirt of silk and embroidered over the heart with an extravagant monogram in lavender and pale green, his shoes handstitched and bench-made; lording it gloriously and arrogantly over Krelekian's Armenian clerks, spending Krelekian's money, and at times kissing Aziza, Krelekian's wife.

"There is no power nor strength save in Allah, the One!" he says with typical Moslem hypocrisy every time he kisses her pouting lips. Always he smiles when he kisses her. Always he snaps his fingers derisively in the direction of the closed shutters behind which Zado Krelekian shivers and prays.

Thus he had laughed and snapped his fingers that day, half a year earlier, when he had walked down the length of Washington Street, supple shoulders thrown back, great, hairy hands swinging up and down like flails, elbowing out of his path Armenian and Syrian as if he were back in his native Turkish village of Khinis, up in the hills, between Erzerum and Biltis.

There was angry murmuring at his back; curses;

occasionally a fist furtively clenched. But none challenged his insolent progress. For the man was lean and thin-mouthed and hook-nosed: a Kurd of Kurds; and a dozen years of American freedom cannot wipe out the livid fear of the centuries.

"Out of my way, sons of burnt fathers!" snarled Mohammed Yar, studying the sign-boards above the stores, Armenian all, Kabulian and Jamjotchian and Nasakian, and what-not, advertising all the world's shopworn goods at a shopworn discount; and then, taking a sallow, raven-haired youth by the neck and twirling him like a top: "Where does Krelekian live —Zado Krelekian?"

The evening before, the youth had learned in the Washington Street Night School about all men's being born free and equal, and so he mumbled something hectic and nervous as to this being a free country, and what did the other mean by—

"Answer me, dog!" came the Kurd's even, passionless voice. "Where is the house of Zado Krelekian?" He tightened his grip.

The Armenian looked up and down the street, but no policeman was in sight. He decided to fence for time, since he did not trust the stranger's intention.

"What do you want with Zado Krelekian?" he asked.

Mohammed Yar slowly closed one eye.

"I want words with him. Honeyed words, brother of inquisitiveness. Words smooth as silk, straight as a lance, soft as a virgin's kiss. Krelekian is a friend of mine, much beloved."

"A friend of yours? *Ahi!*" sighed the Armenian, in memory of past happenings in his native vilayet.

"Was there ever friendship between your race and mine?"

"Indeed, there was not, goat of a smell most goat-ish!" came the pleasant rejoinder. "But this is America. A free land, say you! A land of brothers, say I! Therefore, tell me, or"—with a significant back sweep of his right hand—"I may think too much of this being a land of brothers, and, being older than you, may feel morally forced to chasten your reckless spirit with many and painful beatings, as becomes an elder and loving brother solicitous of his younger brother's welfare. *Do you get me?*" he wound up disconcertingly in plain American English.

"Yes, yes, yes! . . . Zado Krelekian lives at 84 West Street."

"Is he rich?"

"Yes, yes!"

"Is he happy and honored and contented?"

"Yes. None more so."

"Good! Good! And—is his wife still with him?"

"Yes." The young Armenian essayed a lopsided smile. "She is with him, and she is beautiful and—"

"Silence, dog! Do not besmirch a woman with foul praise, or—"

But the Armenian twisted quickly away from his grip and ran down the street, rubbing his shoulder, while Mohammed Yar turned into West Street, looking at the numbers of the houses until he reached Eighty-Four.

Eighty-Four was a shop, swollen and bulbous with merchandise that tumbled across the counter and through the open door, spilling into the street itself in a motley, crazy avalanche. There were bolts of silk and linen and wool; wooden boxes filled with Syrian and Greek sweets; figs and dates, raisins from the isles of Greece, and brittle, yellow Persian tobacco tied up in bundles; pyramids of strange, high-colored vegetables; slippers of flimsy red and orange leather. Dried fish there was, and incense in crystals; oil of rose and jessamine and geranium in slim bottles picked out with leaf gold; carved walking-sticks from Smyrna; inlaid metal work from Damascus; black and white veils heavy with twisted silver and gold, rugs from many lands, coffee and tea and what-not.

The whole seemed prosperous, and prosperous, too, seemed the youngish, stout Armenian merchant—about a year Mohammed Yar's junior—who stood in the doorway, hands in pockets, contentedly puffing at a fat, crimson-and-gold-banded cigar.

Peaceful he looked, and rosy, and well fed; pleased with himself, his neighbors, and the world in general. And then, quite suddenly, his knees began to tremble. An ashen pallor overspread his features. He dropped his cigar. Up went his right eyebrow and his upper lip in a curling, nervous twitch, and with a rapidity that belied his solid bulk he tried to rush into his shop.

But he was not quick enough.

For Mohammed Yar's hairy hand fell on his shoulder, and he heard the Kurd's raucous voice:

"Good morning, friend!"

"Go-goo—go-ood morning," stammered Krelekian, feebly trying to twist away; and the Kurd broke into low laughter.

"Allah!" he said. "Is this the way in which you welcome the man who has traveled many miles for the pleasure of shaking your honest hand, of feasting his eyes on your honest face? Shame on you, Zado of

my heart!"—and he slipped his arm through that of
the other and begged him to lead the way where they
could sip their coffee and smoke their pipes in
peace . . . "and speak of our home in Turkey, of the
olden days when you and I were even as twin brothers
rocked in the same cradle!"

Krelekian sighed.   He looked to right and left, at
his clerks who were behind the counter attending to
the wants of the half-dozen customers.   But not a
word did he utter in protest.   He walked along by
the side of the Kurd; for beneath the man's ragged,
shabby, hand-me-down coat he could feel the sharp
angle of the crooked dagger-handle pressing into his
side—like a message.

"Ah!" gently breathed Mohammed Yar as he sat
down on a carved, inlaid Syrian chair in the back
room of the shop, facing his host, who was still as
livid as a dead man's bones, still furtive-eyed, shaking in every limb.   "This is good!   Good, by mine
own honor!   It is as if we were back in our home
village, in Khinis of the hills, friend of me!"

He made a great gesture with his hairy, high-veined
hand, that cut through the clustered shadows of the
little room like a dramatic incident, that brushed
through the sudden, clogged stillness like a conjurer's
wand, sweeping away the drab grime and riot of West
Street, and conjuring up the glare, the acrid sweetness, the booming, dropping snow chill of the little
hill village where both had lived—and loved.

Clear across Zado Krelekian's livid realization of
the present slashed the picture of the little town,
Khinis, on the way to Erzerum, and what had happened there between him, not then a well-fed, rosy,

prosperous New York shop-keeper, Mohammed Yar, not then dressed in the slops of the New York water-front, and Aziza, the blue-haired girl with the henna-stained feet and the anklets that tinkled, tinkled mockingly.

Three years ago. And one day. And he had tried to forget that day!

Three years rolled back like a curtain. And the happenings of that one day, popping back again into the cells of his remembrance, sitting in a solemn, graven row, and jeering at him because of the pitiful futility of it!

A cold, raw hill day it had been, with cottony snow-flakes thudding softly and with the old mosque of Hajji Ali the Sweetmeat-Seller raised on its broad marble steps as on a base, lifting the apex of its wide horseshoe gate forty feet up in the air, and the gate-way—how well he remembered it all, here in the flat, melancholy drab of West Street!—covered with arabesques of mosaic faïence in green and peacock blue and deep rose and bearing its holy message in conventionalized *mushakil* Arabic characters.

"In the name of Allah, the One, the All-Merciful, the All-Knowing, the King of the Day of Judgment!" read the inscription, and always he had feared it, he and the others of his race, like something terribly pious and terribly ironic, since it expressed the arrogant, harsh faith of the Kurd masters who ruled them, and beat them, and robbed them, and at times killed them because of the sport of it.

Well he remembered how he had trembled—even as he was trembling now—when Mohammed Yar, dressed in sweeping woolen cloak, leather sandals, and tall, rakish fur cap, had come out of the mosque of Hajji the Sweetmeat-Seller, had whispered a rapid word to him, and had walked on by his side, towards the coffee-house of Malakian, where they had sat down.

He remembered his own brazen words.

Yes. Brazen.

For, careful man, he had taken with him that day Musa Lahada, the lean, sardonic Turkish Jew who was attached as dragoman to the British Consulate and thus protected by the Union Jack.

"I saw and heard the whole thing, Mohammed Yar," he had said. "I was passing through Nahassim Street, and I heard the quarrel, the insults. I saw the blow—"

"He insulted me first!" the Kurd had cried. "That cursed Frankish infidel! He struck the first blow!"

"True; but you drew steel and killed. I saw it. I know where you hid the corpse—back of the camel stables in Farid Khan's Gully. And I have witnesses."

"Armenian witnesses! Fathers of pigs, and sons of pigs! Liars—"

"Armenians? Yes! Fathers of pigs, and sons of pigs? Perhaps! But not liars, Mohammed Yar. They saw the thing which is true, and they will swear to it. And Armenians or not, pigs or not, they will be believed by the British consul. For the man whom you killed was an Englishman, and—"

"And—?" Mohammed Yar had asked with a side-long glance.

"Death is bitter—bitter as the fruit which grows near the *Bahretlut!*"

"But—must there be death?"

"No, Mohammed Yar. I am willing to stuff my mouth with silence for a consideration, supplemented by an oath."

"Name the oath first," the Kurd had laughed. "It is cheaper than the consideration—when dealing with an Armenian, O Father of Compound Interest!"

"Possibly cheaper." Krelekian had inclined his head. "Here it is, for you to take or leave, according to how you prefer life or death. You must swear on the Koran, by your own salvation and that of your parents, by the honor of your mother and your sisters, by the blood of the Prophet and the horns of the Archangel Gabriel—you must swear a most sacred oath that, as long as you live, there shall be no killing nor beating in revenge of what I shall ask of you, that never for what is happening to-day between you and me will you take toll with steel or bullet or whip or fist—with blood—nor with pain—neither you nor your tribesmen nor your friends! My life must be sacred to you, and inviolate."

"Good! I swear it. Yes, yes, yes"—as the Armenian had insisted on the exact phraseology. "Never shall I take toll, neither I nor my friends nor my tribesmen, neither with steel nor bullet nor whip nor fist. I swear it on the Koran, by my own and my parents' salvation, by the honor of my mother and my sisters, by the blood of the Prophet and the horns of the Archangel Gabriel! May my right hand dry on my body—may I eat dirt—may God strike me dumb and deaf and blind—if I break this solemn oath! And now—what is the consideration for your silence in that little killing matter?"

"It is simple, Mohammed Yar. Only a woman whom you love and whom I love, but who, being a gypsy, loves neither you nor me, but only gold and silver and jewels and sweets and laughter."

"Aziza?" the Kurd had whispered, the blood mounting to his high cheek bones.

"Yes; Aziza."

Aziza! The gypsy!

Up there on the second floor above his shop, glistening among the heaped green cushions of her couch like an exotic beetle in a nest of fresh leaves; with her tiny oval of a face that through the meshes of her bluish-black hair looked like the face of a golden statue with living eyes—and the expression in those eyes, hard, keen, narrow, like the curling shimmer of moon-rays on forged steel . . .

For he had married Aziza after the Kurd, confronted by the inevitable, had given in. He had taken her to New York with him. For love of her he had outwitted his brother Armenians. He had outgeneraled them, outbargained them, and—if the truth be told—outcheated them . . . yes . . . because he loved her.

And now—?

"Mohammed Yar!" he stammered. "Remember the oath you gave!"

"I do remember," smiled the other, with a flash of even, white teeth, "and I shall keep it. Do not be afraid, Zado. And now—a cup of coffee, a few figs, a handful of dates. Give me welcome!"

Zado gave a relieved laugh. The color came back to his cheeks. He clapped his hands, summoning a clerk, and ordered coffee and figs and pipes to be brought, and for the next hour he sat facing his guest, chattering gayly.

Finally the Kurd rose.

"I shall call again if I may," he said.

"Please do." Krelekian accompanied him to the door. "Call again. I shall make you welcome. What are you doing in New York? Where are you staying? How long have you been here?"

"I came with an Arab doctor whom I met in Smyrna," replied the Kurd. "We live—oh, a ways north, near the University. He is taking a special course in the medicine of the Americans, and he teaches me in payment for my services. Some day I shall be a doctor myself." He took the other's hand, shook it, then, just as he was about to release it, raised it close up to his eyes and studied it. "Zado!" he went on, giving his words the emphasis of a low-ered voice. "What is the matter with you?"

"Why—nothing."

Again the Kurd studied the other's pudgy, flabby hand.

"Well"—he shrugged his shoulders—"perhaps I am mistaken. Never mind."

And he walked away, while the Armenian looked after him, smiling, happy once more, and saying to his chief clerk that indeed America was a great and won-derful country.

"It teaches decency and kindliness and forgiving even to a Kurd," he wound up, and he went upstairs to kiss the red lips of Aziza.

She yawned.

Mohammed Yar had not lied when he had told Zado Krelekian about his relations with the Arab doctor. The latter, a graduate of the University of Paris, had come to New York to take a special course under Professor Clinton McGarra, the great skin specialist, and had picked up the Kurd in Smyrna. For Mohammed Yar had left his native village shortly after Krelekian and Aziza had departed for America, drifting on the trail of the Armenian with the instinct of a wild animal, serene in his belief that presently Fate would send him across the other's path.

The Arab, being an Arab, thus an ironic observer of living things, had taken an interest in the savage tribesman, who took him completely into his confidence, telling him about Zado—and Aziza.

"Come with me to America," El-Touati, the Arab, had said. "You say he has gone there. It will not be hard to find him. Armenians are a clannish folk, herding together like sheep."

And thus Mohammed Yar became cook, bottle-washer, valet, and half a dozen other useful things to the smiling, bearded Arab, receiving in exchange a small wage and certain lessons in medicine—certain lessons which, when first mentioned, had sent both the Arab and the Kurd into fits of high-pitched, throaty laughter.

El-Touati laughed now as Mohammed Yar came into the room, returned from his morning's expedition to West Street.

"Did you find him?" he asked.

"Yes, Haakim."

"Did you bridle your tongue and your temper?"

"Yes. I spoke honeyed words, sweet words, glib words."

"And," pursued the Arab, "did you speak forked words, twisted words, words filled with guile and worry?"

"Yes. I planted the seed of worry, Haakim."

The Arab raised his thin, brown hands in a pious gesture.

"Is-subr miftah il-faraj!" ("Patience is the key of relief!") he muttered. And then Kurd and Arab smiled at each other through half-closed eyes, and the latter turned to the former and asked him to come with him to the next room, his little private laboratory. "I shall give you another lesson, my savage friend. Hand me down that leather case with the crystal-tipped needles—and the little box filled with the tiny green vials. Listen . . ."

And the Kurd inclined his great head, listening to the other's smooth, rapid words, occasionally asking a question when his primitive mind could not grasp the technical and scientific details, but sturdily bent on his task, until El-Touati declared himself satisfied.

"There is no danger?" asked Mohammed Yar. "You know, Haakim, I gave a most solemn oath."

"There is no danger. None whatsoever. Except"—he smiled—"to Aziza. For she may change the gentle hand of Zado for—"

"I shall beat her," said Mohammed Yar. "Then I shall kiss her red lips until they hurt. Then I shall beat her again. She will love me very much. She is a gypsy. . . ."

"And you—a Kurd!" laughed El-Touati, closing the little leather case, but not before the other had dipped a furtive hand into its contents.

The next day, and again the next, and every day the following week, Mohammed Yar called on Zado Krelekian. Moslem, thus believing in the sacredness and proprieties of married relations, he never inquired after Aziza, never as much as mentioned her name to her husband, and it was not his fault that on his fourth visit the gypsy was looking from the narrow balcony where she was watering her starved, dusty geraniums. It was not his fault that suddenly her eyes opened wide—and that one of the flowers fell at his feet.

Gradually the Armenian looked forward with real pleasure to the Kurd's coming. For not only was it a link with his little native Turkish village, but also the fact of his being on such good terms with a Kurd, a hereditary master, served to heighten his importance and social standing among his countrymen.

There was only one thing to which he took exception, namely the Kurd's habit of inquiring after his health.

It was not the usual, flowery Oriental way, but a detailed inquiry: "How did you sleep? Did you perspire last night? Have you a headache? Does your body itch? Have you fever?" And always Mohammed Yar would study his hand intently, then release it with a flat, sympathetic sigh, until Krelekian one day lost his temper and made an ill-natured remark that the Kurd's association with the Arab doctor seemed to have developed in him a positively ghoulish instinct.

"You are like some cursed, toothless Syrian midwife," he exclaimed, "forever smelling out sickness and death—sniffing about like some carrion-eating jackal of the desert!"

Mohammed Yar spread his hairy paws in a massive gesture.

"I am sorry, my friend," he replied. "I meant only to— Never mind . . ."

Krelekian's nerves trembled like piano wires under the hammer of the keys.

"Never mind—what?" he cried in a cracked voice; and the Kurd, like one making a sudden, disagreeable resolution, leaned across the table and spoke in a low voice.

"I—" he began, and was silent again.

"What? What?"

"I— Ah! *Ullah Karim!*"

Mohammed Yar was evidently embarrassed; just as evidently sorry for his host, terribly sorry. Then, as if obeying an overwhelming inner force, he picked up Krelekian's flabby hand where it rested twitching and nervous among the brass-encased coffee-cups, held it high, and examined it intently, as on his first visit.

"Zado!" he murmured, in a low, choked voice. "Zado—dear, dear friend—"

He was silent. He dropped the trembling hand as if it were red-glowing charcoal. He rose very hurriedly and rushed through the shop, out to the sidewalk, Krelekian close on his heels and clutching his arm.

"No, no!" whispered Mohammed Yar, still in that same choked voice. "Do not ask me. Perhaps I am mistaken—and if I am mistaken and should tell you, you would never forgive me! Perhaps I am mistaken. I must be mistaken . . . yes, yes . . . I *know* I am mistaken!"—and he ran down the street, never heeding the Armenian's protests to come back, to explain.

Perhaps it was a coincidence that late that same evening the Kurd, helping the Arab doctor, received a special-delivery letter with the mark of a West Side downtown post-office; a letter perfumed with attar of geranium and saying in Arabic that "the sword of worry and despair has entered the buffalo's soul."

Perhaps it was coincidence that during the next four weeks, while spring burst into the full flower of summer, while Washington and West and Rector Streets began to shimmer with a great, brittle heat that danced about the heaped wares of the Armenian shops with cutting rays, that touched the ramshackle, drab houses and the dust-choked gutters with points of glittering gold, that steeped the open doors of the stores with black splotches like bottomless hollows and wove over everything a crooked, checkered pattern of intolerable orange and crimson—that during four long weeks Mohammed Yar attended strictly to his duties as Doctor El-Touati's factotum and never once found time to call on Zado Krelekian.

Perhaps it was an accident that, when finally he did go to the other's house, he kept himself at a little, well-marked distance and, with clumsy intent, did not see Zado's outstretched hand.

Lastly, it was perhaps by accident that when, after a sharp pause and struggle, he did shake the other's hand, that same hand was suddenly withdrawn with a little cry of pain.

"Something scratched my palm," said Zado Krelekian.

Apologetically the Kurd pointed at the sharp edge of his cuff.

"I am sorry," he smiled, at the same time rapidly dropping into his side pocket a little crystal-tipped needle.

That day it was not the Kurd who inquired after the Armenian's health, but the latter who spoke of it voluntarily, hectically, the words tumbling out of his

mouth as if he had to speak them or choke, as if trying to roll an immense burden of grief and worry
from his stout chest.

"I am not well," he said. "I perspire at night.
My body itches. I have fever. I am not well—not
well at all!"

"Summer," gently suggested Mohammed Yar.
"The fever of summer."

"No, no! It is not that. I tell you I am sick—and
at times I am afraid. Tell me, Mohammed Yar, you
who study with a great Arab doctor—what do you
think?"

The other shook his head.

"I do not know," he replied. "The last time I saw
you I was afraid that you—" He looked up with sudden resolution. "Here is my address," he continued,
giving Zado a slip of paper. "If—I say, if—a tiny
white rash should break out on your hand to-night,
perhaps to-morrow morning, let me know at once.
But tell nobody else—under no considerations whatsoever!" he emphasized in a whisper.

"Why not?"

"Because— Never mind. You will know in time
—if the rash should appear—though Allah grant in his
mercy and understanding that it may not appear!
Allah grant it!" he repeated with pious unction as he
left the shop.

But late that night there was less unction and more
sincerity in his exclamation of "Allah is great indeed!
He is the One, All-Knowing!" when he opened the
telegram he had just received and read its contents to
El-Touati.

"It is done," he said, "and I am off."

At the door he turned.

"Tell me, Haakim," he asked, "are you sure there
is no danger?   Remember I have sworn a most solemn
oath never to take toll with steel or blood or pain for
what happened that day, back home in Khinis, between
him and me!"

"Rest assured," laughed the Arab.   "Your oath is
inviolate.   There will be neither blood nor pain—except perhaps a pain of the mind, which"—he shrugged
his shoulders—"is beyond the probing of human ken,
being entirely a matter of Fate, thus sealed to
us."

"There will also be pain on Aziza's crimson lips
when I crush them with the strength and the desire
of mine own lips!" replied the Kurd from the thresh-
hold.

It was hours later, in the little back room of Zado
Krelekian's shop, that Mohammed Yar put his hand
gently on the Armenian's shoulder.

"Heart of my heart," he said, and his voice was
as soft as the spring breeze, "it is the decree of Fate—
Fate, which comes out of the dark like a blind camel,
with no warning, no jingling of bells; Fate, which is
about the necks of all of us, be we Armenians or
Kurds, Christians or Moslems, like a strangling lash.
Long life may yet be yours. But—" He made a
sweeping gesture.

"Is it—hopeless?"

"Yes.   As hopeless as when Khizr hides his shiny
face."

"But—what can I do?   What—?"

"Nothing!   I spoke to my Haakim, El-Touati.   He
does not know you personally.   But I told him about
you, of the fact that you and I, Armenian and Kurd,

Christian and Moslem, enemies once, became friends in this strange land of America. And he says even as I say: you must shut yourself up where none may see you except I, your very good friend. For these Americans fear—*it!*" Again his hand pressed gently the other's heaving, trembling shoulder. "If you go to an American doctor, if you tell anybody, they will make a report to their health police and send you away to a desolate spot, far away from the land of the living, from everybody, from all your friends—even from me, heart of my heart! It is the law of this land. It is so written in their books. But, doing what I tell you, you will also be shut up, but you will be near your shop—you can take the little house next door, which you own—near Aziza, near—me! And I will take care of you. I—I am your friend, and, being your friend, I am not afraid of—*it!* I, I myself, will bring you food and drink and tobacco and books and papers. But nobody must know, lest the health police find out and send you to the desolate spot!"

"How can we do it?"

"I shall spread a lie, skillfully, hoping that Allah may forgive me the lie because of the friendship which causes it. I will tell your countrymen that a great sorrow, a crushing melancholia, has overtaken you. I shall bring a paper to that effect from the Arab Haakim."

"But," cried Zado Krelekian hysterically, "my shop—my business—my wife?"

"Zado"—there was gentle reproof in the Kurd's accents—"do you not trust me? Have I not been a friend to you? Has ever thought of revenge entered my heart? Zado—heart of my heart—I shall take care of everything for you, because of the respect, the friendship, the love, I bear you!"

And he walked softly out of the shop while Zado Krelekian looked at his hand, at the little white rash that had broken out where the crystal-tipped needle had pricked the skin.

"Leper!" he whispered under his breath. "Leper! Oh, my God!"

And it is thus that Zado Krelekian is cooped up in the back room of his house, with windows nailed down and curtains tightly closed both summer and winter, with fear stewing forever in his brain.

It is thus that Mohammed Yar, once a ragged, thin-mouthed, hook-nosed Kurd tribesman, dresses to-day in the height of fashion and lords it gloriously over Krelekian's Armenian clerks, spending Krelekian's money.

It is thus that, when the mood or the passion takes him, he crushes Aziza in his great, muscular arms and kisses her on the pouting, crimson lips.

Always he smiles when he kisses her. And always he gives thanks to Allah. Always he snaps his fingers derisively in the direction of the closed shutters behind which Zado Krelekian shivers.

Always when, as a good Moslem, he says his morning and evening prayers, he adds:.

"I am glad, O Allah, O All-Knowing One, that I kept my oath—that I did not take toll of Zado Krelekian, neither with steel nor bullet, neither with whip nor fist!"

THE STRENGTH OF THE LITTLE THIN THREAD

IBRAHIM FADLALLAH shrugged his shoulders:

"You do not understand, my friend. You cannot get it through your head that it is impossible to destroy caste and to create fraternity by Act of Parliament. Allah—you can't even do it in your own country."

"But modern progress—the telegraph—the democracy of the railway carriage—" interrupted the American.

"You can compel a Brahmin to sit in the same office and to ride in the same railway compartment with a man of low caste, but you can never force him to eat with him or to give him his daughter in marriage. You spoke of those who are educated abroad—and even they, my friend, when they return to Hind, drift back into caste and the ways of caste. For there is a little thread—oh, such a tiny, thin little thread—which binds them to their own land, their own kin, their own caste. And it seems that they have not the strength to break it—this little thread.

"Ah, yes! Let me tell you something which occurred last year—a true tale—and please do not forget the thread, the little thread—

"Now the whole thing was like a play in one of your theaters—it was staged, dear one, and well staged. The scene was the great hall in which meets the caste

146

tribunal of a certain Brahmin clan.   Imagine, if you
please, a huge quadrangle, impressively bare but for a
low dais at one end, covered with a few Bengali shawls
and an antelope skin or two—ah!—and then the dramatic atmosphere.   Not the atmosphere of death—oh,
no!—much worse than death, much worse.   For what
is death compared to the loss of caste?   And that afternoon they were going to try a man who had polluted his blood, who had sinned a great sin, a great sin
more heinous than the killing of cows—not a sin according to your code of laws—but then they were men
of a different race, and their sins are not your sins—
eh?—and mayhap their virtues may not be your
virtues.

"On the dais sat his Holiness Srimat Muniswamappa Rama-Swami, and on either side of him stood
anxious disciples who looked with awe at his thin,
clean-shaven lips and fanned his holy old poll with
silver-handled yak tails.   Near him sat the pleader and
a few Brahmin grandees, whom he was in the habit of
consulting in cases of importance.   At a respectful
distance were the men of the clan : they filed in slowly,
prostrating themselves in turn before the Swami and
uttering the name of the presiding deity with trembling
lips, while his Holiness smiled a contemplative smile,
and while his fingers counted the beads on his rosary.

"The proceeding opened with a sermon pronounced
by the Swami.   First, he praised Ganesa, Sarasvati,
and half a dozen other assorted deities, and then with
a great abundance of detail and many long-winded
quotations he set forth the duties of the twice-born.
He told them that a Brahmin should not break up
clods of earth nor tear up the grass under his feet;
that he should not look at the setting sun, the rising

sun, the sun in eclipse, the image of the sun in a pool
of water; that he should not point at the stars with
fingers of irreverence; that he should not sleep with
his head turned toward the north or west; that he
should abstain from cutting his nails with his teeth,
from using the same toothstick more than once, from
eating off plates used by others, and from wearing sandals worn by strangers—and a thousand such foolish
injunctions.

"The assembly was politely bored, but the Swami
enjoyed himself hugely. For it gave him an opportunity to show his great learning and his wonderful
memory, and then, like most holy men, he loved to
lay stress on the outward emblems of his faith. He
illustrated his sermon by relating several horrid examples, chiefly that of a wicked barber who had shaved
a Brahmin with a razor which had been polluted by
the shadow of a low-caste falling on it. Finally, he
commented on the advent of modernity and expounded
with more lengthy and tiresome quotations how the
devils of progress, skepticism, irreverence, and anarchy
were making headway amongst the twice-born, how
the young Brahmins were making their names a name
of scorn in the present world and spoiling their chances
for the future world.

"Then he whispered a word to the pleader, who
called up the case of Chaganti Samashiva Rao, a young
Brahmin accused of having sullied his caste by marry-
ing an infidel.

"There was a commotion at the door, and then Rao
appeared, struggling furiously in the arms of half a
dozen muscular youngsters. The pleader explained
that Rao had studied in Boston and that he had brought
home with him a girl, a native of the land of the

foreigners and a Christian, whom he had married according to the laws of the Americans. He had thus polluted himself, his father, his mother, his cow, and his caste. Here the pleader was silent for a few moments to let the atrocity of the crime soak into all hearts, and then he asked the assembly for a verdict. And the assembly shouted like one man: 'Let him lose caste. Drive him out. Drive him out.'

"But Rao rose and declared he was going to make a speech. He said he would tell the old fossils, including his Holiness Srimat Muniswamappa Rama-Swami, what he thought of them. There were roars of: 'Throw him out!' 'Stop his unclean mouth!' and angry hands were raised. But his Holiness smiled a thin, mocking smile and bade the assembly be quiet and listen to what the defendant would have to say for himself.

"Rao acknowledged this permission with a sarcastic bow of gratitude, pulled out his cuffs—he wore English clothes—and proceeded to shock the grave assembly greatly by declaring that he did not give a 'whoop in Hades'—such was the expression he used, he being a perfect English scholar—for all the Brahmins, all the Swamis, and all the caste tribunals in the length and breadth of Hindustan. He had been brought into court by force, he indignantly complained, and he absolutely denied the power and the right of the assembly to punish him. For he had lived several years in America, had become an American citizen, and had voluntarily thrown away his caste as he would a pair of worn-out sandals.

"His Holiness interrupted him, saying that he would now pass sentence on him. But Rao exclaimed: 'Sentence—the devil—you've neither the right nor the might to sentence me.' The Swami, never heeding the interruption, continued with a calm and even voice: 'I sentence you to the living death of the outcast until such time as you expiate your crime, acknowledge your errors, and regain your caste status, which you forfeit to-day, through the regular methods as laid down in the holy books. Your friends and relatives will assemble on the first unlucky day of next week, and will offer, as if to your manes, a libation in a pot of water which a slave girl shall dash against the walls of your house, and all who take part in this ceremony shall be regarded as impure for three days. Your friends and relatives shall not be permitted to accept your hospitality, nor shall you be allowed to share theirs. Your touch shall be pollution unspeakable. Your children shall be outcasts and shall not marry anybody but Mangs and Mahars. Your own father and mother shall be forbidden your house under the risk of losing caste. Neither your barber, your tailor, your cook, nor your washerwoman shall work for you. Nobody shall assist you in any way, not even at the funeral of a member of your household. You shall be debarred access to the temples—'

"Here Rao, who had mocked and laughed during all this sentence, cried: 'Save your breath, oh holy one, for indeed all this tommyrot can never affect me. As to hospitality, I don't care to invite those old fossils of Brahmins into my house, nor could I ever bring myself to set foot in theirs and listen to their tiresome dissertations about the Veda and the Upanishads; besides, I've plenty of European friends. As to my children being outcasts, know, revered uncle, that I have none, and that if ever I should have any they will be Americans like myself and marry like myself. As

to my father and mother being forbidden my house—
well, they're both dead. As to my being debarred
access to your temples—by the great God Shiva—I
never go there anyway—'

"His Holiness waited until Rao had finished, and
then he said, with the same inscrutable smile playing
about the corners of his thin lips: 'I furthermore
sentence you to have torn from your body the sacred
thread of your caste, though'—here he smiled again
—'I hardly believe that you, who have voluntarily
given up your caste and who mock at everything connected with it, can by any chance still have the thread
about your person.'

"Here Rao made a wild dash in the direction of the
door, but he was stopped by many willing hands.
There was a short and furious struggle, his clothes
were torn—and, my friend, it appeared that he, the
scoffer, the atheist, the expatriate, who had renounced
India, who had thrown much filth at caste, who had
become an American, a free-thinker, and a scoffer at
superstitions—still wore next his heart the thin thread,
the holy thread of his caste—the holiest, the most intimate, the most exclusive, the most secret, the most
important emblem of the caste which he affected to
despise—"

Ibrahim was silent, and the American asked: "Well
—what happened?"

The Egyptian lit a cigarette and continued:

"Oh, the usual thing. Rao did penance, he feasted
the priests, he went through the regular process of
ceremonious purification—"

"But what about the girl?"

"His wife? Oh—he sent her back to her own
country—" Ibrahim gave a dry little laugh. "Yes,

my friend, you assuredly understand India. You can reform the world with your progress, your modernity, your splendid democracy—you wonderful Anglo-Saxons. Only it appears that there is a little thread—Allah, what a tiny little thread!—which brings to naught all your wonderful civilization, your liberty, your democracy. Ah, such a tiny little thread, my friend—"

GRAFTER AND MASTER GRAFTER

It is said that, compared to the cunning of the fakir, the Holy Man of Hindustan, even an Armenian, a trustee, a banker, a widow, a demon, and a female cobra during the Grishna Season, are only lisping, prattling babes.

Listen, then, to the tale of Harar Lal, the babu, the banker, the giver of many nautch parties, the sufferer from that envied disease of the idle rich, diabetes; and of Krishna Chucker-jee, the fakir, the Holy Man, the ash-smeared darling of the many gods.

Harar Lal, the babu, was the big man of the village. His earrings were of jade. His face was shiny with ghee. His wife was fat and very beautiful; none of your lean, panther-like women she, but a proper woman, with the walk of the king-goose and the waist of the she-elephant. A most proper woman indeed! Three times he had been to Bombay; and he had brought back marvelous devil-things; clocks which clucked like moor-birds, boxes which had songs and voices in their bowels, resplendent and beautiful ornaments with the magic legend "Made in Birmingham."

He was a banker. And Fate endowed him with such a miraculous skill in the making-out of accounts that a man to whom he had loaned fifty rupees might go on making monthly payments of twenty rupees each for three years without reducing his debt by a single anna. Great are the virtues of Compound Interest! And, indeed, his books proved beyond the shadow of a doubt that the debt, instead of being reduced, would grow with each successive payment, until in the end of a few years the original loan of fifty rupees had become half a *lakh*. He would then give thanks to Shiva, the great god, and to the just laws of the English.

For look you:

During the lawless old Moghul days, the days when the Moslem dogs ruled to the South of the Passes, a quick, crooked dagger-thrust would have ended the babu's earthly career. But the British Raj, the guardian angel of the poor and the pitiful, had established the just laws of Europe in this land of oppression. Thus Harar Lal carried on his business in security, under the shadow of the law, even as they do in England and in America.

There was nothing he would not lend money on, from a nautch girl's blue beads to an unborn calf, from an acre of indigo plants to ten yards of muslin turban cloth; provided the papers were drawn up in proper form and witnessed by a notary public.

And so in good years, when abundant rain watered the smiling fields, when the crops were green and bounteous, the fish swarming in the river, and the trees heavy with fruit, he would reap a goodish share of the gifts of the gods, and—everything being so rich and plentiful—he would naturally increase the interest on loans a little, just a little; while in bad years, when black famine stalked through the fields, when the sun burnt as do the eternal fires in the seventh hall of perdition, when the smoky yellow haze rose from the ground and suffocated the parching crops, when the fish perished of thirst in the drying streams, when the land was dying of hunger, and the call to prayer gave way to the maddening chant of despair— when his heart, his poor, tortured heart—bled with the pity of it all, even then he would prosper exceedingly. For behold: he was a Hindu, a babu, a follower of the praised god who is Shiva, charitable to a fault and quite unlike the Armenian pigs who suck the heart-blood of the unhappy land to the west; again he would loosen the strings of his compassionate purse and advance thousands of rupees to the men of the village. Never would he accept more than three hundred and twelve per cent a month, and he would be content, as only security, with a mortgage on every bullock and goat, every cartwheel and fishing-net, every tree and well in the blessed village.

His eyes filled with tears of gratitude when he beheld the righteous growth of his treasures. I said that he prospered—and, indeed, there was never cartwheel tired, there was never net anchored, tree planted or grain sown but he received his fair share of the profits.

He was the Corporation of the Village.

It was when the juice was being collected from the heads of the opium poppies, that three wandering fakirs, a guru and two disciples, strayed into the village. They were very dirty, and thus very holy. They demanded food, drink, shelter and cowdung fuel from a wretched peasant who lived on the outskirts of the village. Money? No. They had none. They were fakirs, followers of the many gods, very holy, also very dirty. They had no money. Not a single rupee.

"But do not let that worry you," said the guru. "To-night I shall pray to Shiva. *He* will repay you."

So the poor peasant gave rice and ghee and sweet-meats and oil and onions and sugar and tamarinds to the three holy vampires who had never done a stroke of honest work in their lives. They did not have to. For they were of a most thorough and most astounding dirtiness and ditto holiness. They lived thus on the superstitions of the land of Hind; and they lived exceedingly well. They also gave thanks to Shiva, the great god and to the just laws of the English.

For look you:

During the lawless old Moghul days, the days when the Moslem dogs ruled to the South of the Passes, a sharp sword would have quickly removed the heads of the three fakirs. But then the British Raj has established the just laws of Europe in this land of oppression; the laws which preach tolerance and equal rights for all religions and sects. And so these religious parasites had gripped their fangs in the bowels of the land's prosperity, even as in England and in America.

The holy men asked the news of the village, carefully scanning the scraps of bazaar talk; and they learned about Harar Lal, the babu, and they evinced great interest.

The next morning the three were gone. But they had left ample payment for their entertainment. For in the shade of a great babul tree stood a brand-new idol, a Mahadeo which was so exceedingly ugly and bestial and obscene that it was certain to bring prosperity to the village, especially to the peasant who had been the host of the three so dirty, the three so holy men.

Soon its fame spread. Little chaplets of flowers were offered to the holy emblem of creation, and thin-lipped, weary-eyed men and patient, onyx-eyed women sent up many pathetic prayers to the grinning, staring, sensual idol. And the idol prospered. It shone with plentiful libations of ghee, and was more ugly and more holy than ever. The very babul tree did homage to it. For a gorgeous loofah creeper which for many hot and many cold weathers had used the tree for support and nourishment sent down strong shoots and encircled with its sweet-smelling, lascivious flowers the neck and the arms of the Mahadeo.

The babu saw it. He considered it. He was angry. For here was something in the village which could not be assisted with a mortgage at a reasonable rate of interest. Mahadeos are gods. Gods do not need money; only the fakirs, the Holy Men who serve the gods, need money.

Let it be understood that Harar Lal had no intention of fooling with the Mahadeo. He was a Hindu. He was deeply religious. He would sooner have killed his fat and beautiful wife than kill a cow.

Then, one day, the babu discovered how he could make the god pay without defiling his caste, without committing an irreligious act. On the contrary, he would do great honor to the Mahadeo. All he had to do, he thought, was to buy the plot of land which housed the idol. Of course the peasant would not desecrate the god by removing it from the shade of the babul tree which he had chosen for his abode. So he would buy a plot of land and would then acquire a reputation for sanctity by erecting a temple over it. He would spread the tale of the Mahadeo through the countryside. He would advertise in the *Bande Mahrattam* and other native papers; perhaps even in the English press, the Bombay *Times*, the *Englishman*,

the *Pioneer*. There would be many offerings laid at
the feet of the god. He would be the owner of the
temple. He had a brother-in-law who was a Brahmin
priest. Together they would collect the offerings. The
plan was simple.

But the owner of the land absolutely refused to part
with it. Neither cajolings nor threats were of the
slightest avail.

"No, no!" exclaimed the superstitious *ryot*. "No,
by Karma! I will not part with what the gods have
sent me. The Mahadeo has brought luck to my
house. Three weeks ago my wife gave birth to twin
sons. And though she drank buttermilk, she did not
die. Behold what a powerful Mahadeo he is! Also
be pleased to observe his face. How ugly, how bestial,
how obscene! No, there was never Mahadeo like
mine."

About this time one of the three fakirs, Krishna
Chucker-jee by name, came again to the village. He
was dirtier and holier than ever. Again he visited the
house of the peasant. Again he asked for food and
drink and cowdung fuel. Gladly the peasant gave.
He kissed the Holy Man's feet.

Then he told him about the babu's offer.

"Five times Harar Lal has asked me to sell him the
plot of land which houses the Mahadeo. Five times
I have refused. And each time the babu forecloses
on some of my land. What shall I do, O Holy Man?"

The fakir blessed the peasant. He praised him for
his devotion. He told him that in a month he would
receive the answer to his question. But in the mean-
time he was not to breathe a word to anybody about
his, the fakir's, second visit. Also he needn't worry

about the mortgages. Everything would be straightened out.

"See, my friend," he concluded. "For fifteen years neither water nor soap nor scissors have defiled my body. Daily I grow and gain in holiness and filth. Tell me, have you ever seen so much holiness, so much filth, before?"

"No, beloved one of the gods," stammered the peasant.

"Then trust in me. Everything will be straightened out. Even to-night I shall cover my body with ashes and cowdung. Have faith . . . and the gods will be good to you. Praised be the many gods!"

The fakir left, again swearing the peasant to secrecy.

Three days afterwards the babu was on the furthest confines of the village, surveying with grim interest the crops on which he held mortgages, when five fakirs appeared suddenly before him.

They were naked. Their beards and hair were matted. Their lean bodies were covered with dirt and perspiration. Their finger nails had grown into long, twisted, fantastic curves and knots. Even at two miles, with a fair wind, your nose would have convinced you of their exceeding holiness.

So the babu bowed before them.

"Salaam, O babu-jee," exclaimed the oldest and dirtiest of the five. "I have a message for thee."

"Salaam, O Harar Lal," rejoined the other four in the heavy, impressive manner of a Greek tragedy chorus. "We have a message for thee."

The babu was surprised that they knew his name, and he asked them how they knew it.

And Krishna Chucker-jee, the guru, the oldest of the five, answered:

"We know many things, O babu-jee. We are Holy Men, beloved of the gods. Behold our filth! We know that at the age of fifteen thou didst leave thy home in Shahjahanabad, and that thou hadst only five rupees in thy waistband. We know that the gods smiled on thee, and that thou didst prosper exceedingly. All is known concerning thee. And now the gods have ordered us five to travel many miles because they wish to build a temple in thy village to the Mahadeo. Thus the gods send thee message through us."

"Be pleased to deliver it," said the babu, amazed at their intimate knowledge of his affairs.

But Krishna Chucker-jee replied in a dignified and haughty manner:

"Patience, O babu-jee. Patience! For remember that patience is the key of relief, and that nothing comes to an end except the beard of the beardless. Patience, then!"

He squatted on the ground. He rolled up his eyes in a thoroughly disgusting and very bewildering manner. His disciples crowded around him.

"Hush!" they admonished the banker. "Hush, O babu-jee! The guru is now communing with the deity, with Shiva." And they gave a well-trained shudder, in which the babu joined involuntarily.

Suddenly the guru gave a great sigh. He jumped up. His eyes assumed once more their normal, beady focus. He scratched his long, matted hair with his claw-like hands. Then he addressed the babu in gentle tones.

"Shiva has whispered to me. At the appointed hour

everything shall be made most clear. But first it is necessary that thou, O babu-jee, shouldst give us food for twelve days. At the end of the twelve days my four chelas shall go away. Eight days more I shall abide with thee, and then the message shall be given to thee. For the gods are pleased with thee, and they have heard of thy pious desires in the matter of the Mahadeo."

Here he winked furiously at the peasant who happened to pass by and who was watching the scene with open mouth and staring eyes.

The jubilant babu did as he was bidden. For to his Eastern mind there was nothing incredible in such an occurrence.

For twelve days the guru and his four chelas were the guests of the babu. Then they departed. Only Krishna Chucker-jee remained in the house of the banker.

The guru had an earnest talk with his host. He told him that during the eight days which intervened between that day and the delivery of the message he must prepare himself and purify his mind and soul by deeds of charity, ceremonious visits to the Mahadeo, and complicated devotional exercises.

He could rest assured that every rupee given away in charity would be returned a hundredfold to him.

"Wherefore hold not thy hand," said the ascetic at the end of his pious exhortation.

Strictly the babu obeyed the instructions of the Holy One. He tore up mortgages and he distributed food and coins to the gaping villagers.

Eight long days passed. On the morning of the ninth day, Krishna Chucker-jee ordered the babu to fetch a new earthenware jar, two cubits of khassa cloth and a seer of attah flour. And now he would see how everything that he had given away in charity would be restored by the gods a hundredfold.

As a token he told him to bring a rupee, and, taking it from the babu, he asked him to prostrate himself on the ground and to say certain lengthy passages from the Kata Upanishad, while he himself wrapped the rupee in the cloth, placed it in the pot, emptied the attah flour a-top, and then closed the mouth of the jar with a piece of khassa cloth which was sealed with the babu's own signet-ring. Then he told the babu to hide the jar somewhere in the open country.

The next day the jar was brought back. Nobody had tampered with it. The seal was intact. But, miraculous to relate, when the cloth was removed and the jar opened, there were two rupees wrapped in the cloth instead of one.

Three times the ceremony was repeated, with the same prostrations and prayers on the babu's part, while the guru sealed the jar. And finally the rupee had grown to be eight.

"Thou art beloved by the gods," said Krishna Chucker-jee. "Thy deeds of charity smell sweet in their holy nostrils. Again I admonish thee: hold not thy hand!"

And the babu did as he was bid. He held not his hand. He tore up all the other mortgages he had and returned many acres of land to the original owners, the peasants of the village.

"The period of probation has passed," said the guru.

Followed a day of prayer and fasting, and on the next morning the babu was told by Krishna Chucker-jee to bring an extra large jar and to fetch all his

currency notes, all his gold and silver coins, his own
jewels and those of his beautiful, fat wife.

"Fill the jar with them," said the guru. "But leave
sufficient room on top so that the gods can double
them."

The babu did as he was told. He was jubilant.
Then Chucker-jee asked him to prostrate himself and
to recite an especially long passage from the Kata
Upanishad. Meanwhile he himself closed and sealed
the jar.

Devotional exercises over, he directed Harar Lal to
carry away the jar to a spot twenty times as far as
the one which had contained the jar with the one
rupee, and to guard it until the following dawn.

"Cease not to pray for a single minute," continued
the Holy Man. "Let none approach thee or speak to
thee. Do not fall asleep. Fast until thou comest here
again. Obey strictly, so as not to kindle divine anger."

The babu obeyed. He took the jar and carried it
a long distance into the country. He watched it. He
allowed nobody to approach. He prayed incessantly.
But, finally, worn out with his fastings and his
prayers, he fell asleep.

The sun was high in the heavens and the shadows
pointing northward when he awoke. Terror gripped
his heart when he thought that he might have angered
the Mahadeo by failing in his vigil. He seized the
jar in alarm. He examined it carefully. But the
seals were intact. Nobody had tampered with his
treasures. So he felt relieved. Again he watched
and prayed.

Finally he could not stand the suspense any longer.
He picked up the jar and returned to the house.

The fakir was not there. He searched through house

and garden. But there was no sign of the Holy Man.

He called loudly:

"Guru-jee . . .   O guru-jee!"

But no answer came.   Then he inquired of the villagers, but none had seen the Holy One.

Then he thought that perhaps the guru had set out in search of him and would return sooner or later. And he waited a long time till finally anxiety and hunger got the better of his fear.   He ate, and then he opened the jar with the proper ceremonies . . .

But the gods had not doubled his riches.   In fact, they had removed them altogether and had put in their place three large and heavy bricks.

The babu sat down and wept.   That was the end of all things.   To call in the police to aid him against the gods would be a futility.   He visited the babul tree and looked at the Mahadeo.   And it seemed to him that the Mahadeo was solemnly winking at him.

And a great fury seized him by the throat.   He cursed the deities of his native land.

And six months later the *Christian Messenger* printed the glorious news that another pagan, this time a high-class Brahmin, a charitable native Indian banker, after giving away all his wealth in charities to the village where he lived, and tearing up all the mortgages he owned, had been converted to the True Faith; and had even risked his life and been severely beaten because in his righteous new zeal he had endeavored to break a horrid and grinning Mahadeo idol which stood in the shade of a great babul tree at the confines of the village.

THE LOGICAL TALE OF THE FOUR CAMELS

In Sidi-el-Abas it was spring, white spring, and the pale peace of perfumed dawn.

We were smoking and dreaming, too indolent to speak, each waiting for his neighbor to open the trickling stream of soft, lazy conversation. At last, Ibrahim Fadlallah, the Egyptian, turned to the young Englishman and said:

"Soon, oh my dear, you will return to your own country, so listen to the moral tale I am about to tell, so that you can take back to your own people one lesson, one small lesson which will teach you how to use the manly virtues of honor, self-restraint, and piety—all accomplishments in which you unbelievers are sadly deficient. Give me a cigarette, oh my beloved. Ah, thanks; and now listen to what happened in Ouadi-Halfa between Ayesha Zemzem, the Sheik Seif Ed-din, and Hasaballah Abdelkader, a young Bedouin gentleman, who is very close to my heart.

"The Sheik was a most venerable man, deeply versed in the winding paths of sectarian theology— he had even studied the Sunna—and of a transcendent wisdom which his disciples declared to be greater than that of all the other Sheiks.

"But even in your own country it may be that

sanctity of the mind and grace of the dust created body do not always match. Indeed, the Sheik's beard was scanty and of a mottled color; he was not over-clean, especially when you consider that as a most holy man he was supposed to be most rigorous in his daily ablutions. He had grown fat and bulky with years of good living; for tell me, should not a holy man live well so that he may reach a ripe old age, and that many growing generations of disciples may drink the clear drops of honeyed piety which fall from his lips?

"Besides, to compensate for the many piastres he spent on himself, he tightened the strings of his purse when it came to paying for the wants of his large household. He said it was his duty to train his sons and the mothers of his sons in the shining virtue of abstemiousness, asking them to repeat daily the words in the book of the Koran: 'Over-indulgence is a most vile abomination in the eyes of Allah.'

"His first two wives had grown gray, and, his old heart yearning for the untaught shyness of youth, he had taken as the third, Ayesha Zemzem, the daughter of the morning. My dear, do not ask me to describe her many charms. My chaste vocabulary could never do her justice. Besides, do you not know that our women go decently veiled before strangers? Thus who am I to know what I am not allowed to see?

"Suffice it to say that she was a precious casket filled with the arts of coquetry, that she was tall and slender as the free cypress, that her forehead was as the moon on the seventh day and her black eyes taverns of sweetest wine. But the heart of woman acknowledges no law, respects no master except the one she appoints herself, and so it was that Ayesha had no love for the Sheik in spite of his white sanctity, and though he knew the Koran and all the commentaries by heart.

"And then one day she saw Hasaballah, and her veil dropping by chance, he saw her.

"Hasaballah had but lately returned from that famed asylum of learning and splendor, that abode of the Commander of the Faithful, the noble town of Stamboul. He had come back dressed in robes of state, and when he donned his peach-colored coat embroidered with cunning Persian designs in silver and gold, the men in the bazaar looked up from their work and exclaimed: 'Look at him who with his splendor shames the light of the mid-day sun.'

"He was indeed a true Osmanli for all his Bedouin blood, and the soft fall of his large Turkish trousers, which met at the ankle, the majestic lines of his silken burnous, the bold cut of his famed peach-colored coat, were the despair of all the leading tailors in Ouadi-Halfa and the envy of all the young bloods. His speech was a string of pearls on a thread of gold. He walked lithely, with a jaunty step, swaying from side to side. He was like a fresh-sprung hyacinth and the master of many hearts.

"I said that Ayesha saw him and her veil was lowered; and you, oh my dear, you know the heart of man, and you also know what many women shall always desire. You will not be shocked when I tell you that on the very same night you could have seen Hasaballah leaning against the wall in the shadow of the screened balcony which protruded from the Sheik's harem; and there he warbled certain appropriate lines which I had taught him. Indeed, I had used them myself with great effect on a former occasion.

" 'I am a beggar and I love a Queen.
'Tis thee, beloved, upon whose braided locks
The fez lies as a rose-leaf on the brook;
'Tis thee whose breath is sweetest ambergris,
Whose orbs are dewdrops which the lilies wear.'

"Claptrap! Oh, I don't know. You should have heard Hasaballah's own effort. He was going to address her as 'blood of my soul,' but I thought it altogether too extravagant. The time to woo a woman is when you first see her, and the way to woo her is the old-fashioned way. Flatteries never grow old, and I always use the time-honored similes.

"I tell her that she is as beautiful as the pale moon, that her walk is the walk of the king-goose, that the corners of her mouth touch her pink ears, that she has the waist of a lion, and that her voice is sweeter than the song of the Kokila-bird.

"But permit me to continue my tale.

"Two hours later Hasaballah and Ayesha knocked at my gate, and, touching my knee, asked me for hospitality and protection, which I granted them, having always been known as the friend of the oppressed and the persecuted. And early the following morning the Sheik came to my house, and I received him with open arms as the honored guest of my *divan*.

"After partaking of coffee and pipe he said:

" 'Ibrahim, last night when I went to the women's quarter to join my female household in their midnight prayer, the weeping slaves told me that Ayesha had run away. Great was my grief and fervent my prayers, and when sleep at last closed my swollen eyelids I saw in my dreams the angels Gabriel and Michael descend from heaven. They took me on their shining wings into the seventh hall of Paradise, and there I saw the Messenger Mohammed (on whom be praises) sitting on a throne of pearls and emeralds, and judging men and jinn.

" 'And the Prophet (peace on him) said to me: "Go thou in the morning to the house of my beloved and obedient servant Ibrahim Fadlallah, where thou shalt find Ayesha, and with her a certain good-for-nought young scoundrel, whom thou shouldst carry before the Kadi and have punished with many lashes." Thus, O Ibrahim, obeying the commands of the blessed Prophet (on whom peace), I ask you to give up to me Ayesha and Hasaballah, that I may kill the woman and have the man much beaten, according to the wise and merciful law of the Koran.'

"And I replied: 'O most pious Sheik, your tale is strange indeed, though amply corroborated by what I am about to relate. For last night, after the fugitives had asked me for protection, I also prayed fervently to Allah (indeed He has no equal), and in my dreams the angels Gabriel and Michael carried me on widespread wings into the seventh hall of Paradise, even into the presence of the Messenger Mohammed (on whom be benedictions).

"And the Prophet (deep peace on him) turned to me and said:

" 'Ibrahim, the pious and learned Sheik Seif Ed-din has just left the abode of the righteous to return to his earthly home. I gave him certain orders, but after he left I reconsidered my decision. When he visits you in the morning, tell him it is my wish that he should leave Hasaballah undisturbed in the possession of the woman he has stolen, and should accept two camels in payment of her.'

"The Sheik pondered awhile, and replied:

" 'Verily it says in the most holy book of the Koran that Allah loveth those who observe justice, and that the wicked who turn their backs on the decisions of the Prophet (on whom peace) are infidels who shall hereafter be boiled in large cauldrons of very hot oil. Now tell me, Ibrahim, are you sure that last night the Prophet (peace on him) did not say that I should accept four camels, and not two, in payment of the bitter loss inflicted on my honor and dignity? Indeed, for four camels Hasaballah may keep the woman, provided the animals be swift-footed and of a fair pedigree. Upon those two points I must insist.'

"Then, oh my eyes! I thought that bargaining is the habit of Jews and Armenians, and I sent word to Hasaballah to give four camels to the Sheik. And everybody was happy, everybody's honor was satisfied, and there was but little scandal and no foulmouthed gossip to hurt the woman's reputation.

"I have told you how we Moslems, being the wisest of mankind, settle affairs of honor and love. Tell me, do you not think that our way is better than your crude Christian method of airing such matters in a public court of law, and of announcing to a jeering world the little details of harem life and of love misplaced?"

After a moment's reflection the Englishman replied:

"I must say, since you ask me, that I consider yours a disgraceful way of bargaining for a few camels where the shame of a misled woman and the honor of an outraged husband are in the balance. In my country, as you say, the whole affair would have been aired in court and considered from every possible point of view, thus giving the respondent, the petitioner, and the co-respondent equally fair chances.   The judge finally, according to our strict though humane law, would have pronounced a divorce decree in favor of the Sheik, and would have sentenced Hasaballah to pay to the Sheik a heavy fine—a fine of many hundreds of pounds."

And Ibrahim interrupted quickly:

"But, beloved one, you have no camels in your country."

THE TWO-HANDED SWORD

He judged each act of the passing days by three pictures in the back cells of his brain. These pictures never weakened, never receded; neither during his meals, which he shared with the other students at Frau Grosser's *pension* in the Dahlmannstrasse, nor during his hours of study and research spent over glass tubes and crucibles and bottles and retorts in the Royal Prussian Chemical Laboratory overlooking Unter den Linden, with Professor Kreutzer's grating, sarcastic voice at his left ear, the rumbling basso of the professor's German assistants at his right.

There was one picture which showed him the island of Kiushu rising from the cloudy gray of the China Sea, black-green with cedar and scarlet with autumn maple, and the pink snow of cherry fluffing April and early May; the island which stood to him for princely Satsuma, and Satsuma—since he was a samurai, permitted to wear two swords, the *daito* and the *shoto*— for the whole of Japan.

There was the picture of his grandfather, the Marquis Takagawa—his father had gone down fighting his ship against the Russians under Makarov—who in his youth had drawn the sword for the Shogun against the Mikado in the train of Saigo, the rebel chief, who had finally made his peace with his sovereign lord and had given honorable oath that he would lay the lives, the courage, and the brains of his descendants for all time to come on the altar of Nippon to atone for the sin of his hot youth.

There was, thirdly, the memory of his old tutor, Komoto, a bonze of the Nichiren sect who had made *senaji* pilgrimages to the thousand shrines, who had taught him the Chinese classics from the Diamond Sutra to the King-Kong-King, later on the wisdom of Ogawa and Kimazawa and the *bushi no ichi-gon*— the lessons of Bushido, the lore of the two-handed sword, the ancient code of Nippon chivalry.

"The spiritual light of the essential being is pure," Komoto had said to the marquis when the governors of the cadet school at Nagasaki had decided that the young samurai's body was too weak, his eyes too short-sighted, his blood too thin to stand the rigorous military training of modern Japan. "It is not affected by the will of man. It is written in the book of Kung Tzeu that not only the body but also the brain can raise a levy of shields against the enemy."

"Yes," the marquis had replied; for he, too, was versed in the Chinese classics. "Ships that sail the ocean, drifting clouds, the waning moon, shores that are washed away—these are symbolic of change. These, and the body. But the human mind is essential, absolute, changeless, and everlasting. O Takamori-san!" He had turned to his grandson. "You will go to Europe and learn from the foreigners, with your brain, since your body is too weak to carry the burden of the two-handed sword. You will learn with boldness, with patience, and with infinite trouble. You will learn not for reward and merit, not for yourself, but for Nippon. Every grain of wisdom and knowledge that falls from the table of the foreigners you will pick up and store away for the needs of the

Rising Sun. You will learn—and learn. But you will learn honorably. For you are a samurai, O Taka-mori-san!"

And so the young samurai took ship for Europe. He was accompanied by Kaguchi, an old family servant, short, squat, flat-nosed, dark of skin and long of arm. A low-caste he was who had sunk his personality in that of the family whom his ancestors had been serving for generations, who had never considered his personal honor but only that of his master's clan which to him stood for the whole of Nippon.

If Takagawa Takamori had been small among the short, sturdy daimios of Kiushu, he seemed wizened and diminutive among the long-limbed, well-fleshed men of Prussia and Mecklenburg, and Saxony who crowded the chemical laboratory of Professor Kreutzer. Gentlemen according to the stiff, angular, ramrod German code, they recognized that the little parchment-skinned, spectacled Asian was a gentleman according to his own code, and so, while they pitied him after the manner of big blond men, lusty of tongue, hard of thirst and greedy of meat, they sympathized with him. They even liked him; and they tried to help him when they saw his narrow-lidded, myopic eyes squint over tomes and long-necked glass retorts in a desperate attempt to assimilate in six short semesters the chemical knowledge which Europe had garnered in the course of twice a hundred years.

Professor Kreutzer, who had Semitic blood in his veins and was thus in the habit of leaping at a subject from a flying start and handling it with consciously dramatic swiftness, was frequently exasperated at Takagawa's slowness of approach and comprehension. On the other hand, his German training and traditions made him appreciate and admire the student's Asiatic tenacity of purpose, his steel-riveted thoroughness and efficiency which made it impossible for him to forget a fact which he had once mastered and stored away. Perhaps his method of learning was parrotlike. Perhaps his memory was mechanical, automatic, the fruit of his early schooling when, with the mountain wind blowing icy through the flimsy shoji walls, he had knelt in front of Komoto and had laboriously learned by heart long passages from the Yuen-Chioh and the erudite commentaries of Lao-tse. Whatever the basic cause, whatever his method, the result was peculiar—and startling to his fellow students. Given a certain discussion, a certain argument which sent his German class-mates scuttling for library and reference books, the young samurai seemed to turn on a special spigot in his brain and give forth the desired information like a sparkling stream.

"Sie sind ja so'n echter Wunderknabe, Sie Miniatur gelbe Gefahr!" (for that's what he called him: a "miniature yellow peril") the professor would exclaim; and he would give him a resounding slap on the back which would cause the little wizened body to shake and smart.

But, sensing the kindliness beneath rough words and rougher gesture, Takagawa would bow old-fashionedly, with his palms touching his knees, and suck in his breath noisily.

He was learning—learning honorably; and at night, when he returned to his rooms in the *pension,* he would go over the garnered wisdom of the day together with Kaguchi, his old servant. Word for word he would repeat to him what he had learned, until the latter, whose brain was as that of his master—persistent, parrotlike, mechanical—could reel off the chemical formulæ with the ease and fluency of an ancient professor gray in the craft. He had no idea what the barbarous foreign sounds meant. But they amused him. Also he was proud that his young master understood their meaning—his young master who stood to him for Kiushu and the whole of Nippon.

Summer of the year 1914 found Takagawa still at work under Professor Kreutzer, together with half a dozen German students who like himself were using the Long Vacations for a postgraduate course in special chemical research, and a Prussian officer, a Lieutenant Baron Horst von Eschingen, who on his arrival was introduced by the professor as "a *rara avis* indeed —pardon me, baron!" with a lop-sided, sardonic grin— "a brass-buttoned, much-gallooned, spurred, and booted East-Elbian Junker who is graciously willing to descend into the forum of sheepskin and learned dust and stinking chemicals, and imbibe knowledge at the feet of as humble a personage as myself."

The German students laughed boisterously, while the baron smiled. For it was well known throughout the empire that Professor Kreutzer was a *Liberaler* who disliked bureaucratic authority, sneered at the military, and was negligent of imperial favor.

From the first Takagawa felt a strong liking and even kinship for Baron von Eschingen. He understood him. The man, tall, lean, powerful, red-faced, ponderous of gesture and raucous of speech, was nevertheless a samurai like himself. There was no doubt of it. It showed in his stiff punctiliousness and also in his way of learning—rather of accepting teaching. For the professor, who welcomed the opportunity of bullying with impunity a member of the hated ruling

classes, took a delight in deviling the baron's soul, in
baiting him, in putting to him sudden questions hard
to solve and pouncing on him when the answer did
not come swift enough, with such remarks as: "Of
course, *lieber Herr Leutnant,* what can I expect? This
is not a hollow square, nor a firing squad, nor anything connected with martingale or rattling scabbard.
This is science—the humble work of the proletariat—
and, by God, it needs the humble brain of the proletariat to understand it."

Another time—the baron was specializing in poisonous gases and their effect on the human body—the
professor burst out with: "I can't get it through my
head why you find it so terribly difficult to master the
principles of gas. I have always thought that the
army is making a specialty of—gas bags!"

Von Eschingen would bite his mustache and blush.
But he would not reply to the other's taunts and gibes;
and Takagawa knew that the baron, too, was learning; learning honorably; nor because of reward and
merit.

They worked side by side through the warm, soft
July afternoons—while the sun blazed his golden pano-
ply across a cloudless sky and the scent of the linden
trees, drifting in through the open windows, cried
them out to field and garden—cramming their minds
with the methodical devices of exact science, staining
their hands with sharp acids and crystals, with the professor wielding his pedagogic whip, criticizing, sneering, mercilessly driving. More than once, when Kreutzer's back was turned, Takagawa would help the
baron, whisper him word or chemical formula from
the fund of his tenacious Oriental brain, and then the
two would laugh like naughty schoolboys, the German

with short, staccato bursts of merriment, the Japanese discreetly, putting his hand over his mouth.

Finally one afternoon as they were leaving the laboratory together and were about to go their separate ways at the corner of the Dorotheenstrasse, Takagawa bowed ceremoniously before the officer and, painfully translating in his mind from the Chinese book of etiquette into Japanese and thence into the harsh vagaries of the foreign tongue, begged him to tie the strings of his traveling cloak and deign to set his honorable feet in the miserable dwelling of Takagawa Takamori, there to partake of mean food and entirely worthless hospitality.

Baron von Eschingen smiled, showing his fine, white teeth, clicked his heels, and accepted; and the following evening found the curious couple in Takagawa's room: the former in all the pale-blue and silver glory of his regimentals, the latter, having shed his European clothes, wrapped in a cotton crêpe robe embroidered on the left shoulder with a single pink chrysanthemum, queer and hieratic—the *mon*, the coat of arms of his clan.

To tell the truth, the baron had brought with him a healthy, meat-craving German appetite, and he felt disappointed when all his host offered him was a plate of paper-thin rice wafers and some very pale, very tasteless tea served in black celadon cups. His disappointment changed to embarrassment when the Japanese, before filling the cups, went through a lengthy ceremony, paying exaggerated compliments in halting German, extolling his guest's nobility, and laying stress on his own frightful worthlessness.

"And the funny little beggar did it with all the dignity of a hidalgo," the baron said the next morning to a major in his regiment who had spent some years as military attaché in Japan. "Positively seemed to enjoy it."

The major laughed. "Why," he replied, "you ought to feel highly honored. For that Jap paid you no end of a compliment. He has initiated you into the *cha-no-yu,* the honorable ceremony of tea sipping, thus showing you that he considers you his equal."

"His—his equal?" flared up the other, who, away from the laboratory, was inclined to be touchy on points of family and etiquette.

"To be sure. Didn't you say his name is Takagawa Takamori?"

"Yes."

"Well—the Takagawas are big guns in their own land. They don't make 'em any bigger. They are relatives of the Mikado, cousins to all the feudal houses of Satsuma, descendants of the gods, and what not—"

It was not altogether snobbishness which caused the German to cultivate the little Asiatic after that. He really liked him. At the end of a few weeks they were friends—strangely assorted friends who had not much in common except chemistry, who had not much to talk about except acids and poisonous gases. But they respected each other, and many a sunny afternoon found them strolling side by side through the crowded thoroughfares of Berlin, the baron swinging along with his long, even step, the tip of his scabbard smartly bumping against the asphalt, while Takagawa tripped along very much like a small, owlish child, peering up at the big man through the concave lenses of his spectacles.

Only once did the samurai mention the reasons

which had brought him to Europe. They were passing the Pariser Platz at the time, and stopped and turned to look at the half company of Grenadiers of the Guard who were marching through the Brandenburger Thor to change the castle watch, shoulders squared, rifles at the carry, blue-clad legs shooting forth at right angles, toes well down, the spotless metal on spiked helmet and collar and belt mirroring the afternoon sun, while the drum major shook his horse-tailed bell tree and a mounted captain jerked out words of command:

"*Achtung! Augen—links! Vorwärts! Links an! Links an! Marsch!*"

Takagawa pointed a lean, brown finger.

"The scabbard of my blue steel spear is the liver of my enemy," he quoted softly, translating from the Japanese. "I carry the red life on my finger tips; I have taken the vow of a hero!" and when the baron looked down, uncomprehending, asking astonishedly: "Hero? Hero?" the other gave a little, crooked smile.

"The mind too fights when the body is too weak to carry the burden of the two-handed sword," he explained. "The mind too can be a hero. Mine is!" he added, with utter simplicity. "For my body aches for the touch of steel, while I force my mind to drink the learning of books. My mind bends under the strain of it. But I do it—for Japan."

The baron's hand descended on his friend's lean shoulder.

"Yes," he said. "I understand, old boy. I have an older brother. No good for the King's coat—lost a leg when he was a kid. Family shot him into the Foreign Ministry. Works like a slave. But, *auf Ehrenwort,* he hates it, the poor old beggar!"—and, seeing a drop of moisture in the other's oblique eyes, he went on hurriedly: "Now, as to that gas—that new one Kreutzer is driveling about—with some unearthly, jaw-breaking Greek name and that fine, juicy stink to it—do you remember how—" And a moment later they were deep once more in the discussion of poison gases.

July swooned into August and, overnight, it seemed, the idyl of peace was spattered out by a brushful of blood. Excitement struck Berlin like a crested wave. People cheered. People laughed. People wept. A conjurer's wand swung from Spandau to Köpenick, thence east to Posen, and north and northwest in a semicircle, touching Kiel, Hamburg, Cologne, and Mayence. A forest of flags sprang up. Soldiers marched in never-ending coils down the streets, horse and foot, foot again, and the low, dramatic rumbling of the guns. They crowded the railway stations from Lehrter Bahnhof to Friedrichstrasse Bahnhof. They entrained, cheered, were cheered, leaned from carriage windows, floppy, unstarched fatigue caps set jauntily on close-cropped heads, singing sentimental songs:

Lebt wohl, ihr Frauen und ihr Mädchen,
Und schafft euch einen And'ren an. . . .

The cars pulled away, bearing crudely chalked legends on their brown sides—"This car for Paris!" "This car for Brussels!" "This car for Calais!"— and, twenty-four hours later, the world was startled from stupid, fattening sleep through the news that Belgium had been invaded by the gray-green hordes, led by generals who had figured out each chance of victory and achievement with logarithmic, infallible cunning, and that already the Kaiser had ordered the menu which should be served him when he entered Paris.

The wave of war struck the laboratory and the *pension* in the Dahlmannstrasse together with the rest of Berlin.

People assumed new duties, new garb, new language, new dignity—and new psychology. The old Germany was gone. A new Germany had arisen—a colossus, a huge, crunching animal of a country, straddling Europe on massive legs, head thrown back, shoulders flung wide; proud, defiant! And sullen!

Takagawa did not understand. He had come to Berlin to learn honorably. He was not familiar with European politics, and Belgium was only a geographical term to him.

War? Of course! War! It meant honor and strength and sacrifice. But—

There was Hans Grosser, the only son of Frau Grosser, the comfortable, stout Silesian widow who kept the *pension*. Long, lean, pimply, clumsy, an underpaid clerk in the Dresdner Bank, he had been heretofore the butt of his mother's boarders. When at the end of the meal the *Kompottschale,* filled with stewed fruit, was passed down the table, he was the last to help himself, and then apologetically. The day after war was declared he came to dinner—his last dinner before leaving for the front—in gray-green, with a narrow gold braid on his buckram-stiffened collar, gold insignia on his epaulet, a straight saber dragging behind his clicking spurs like a steel-forged tail. Overnight the negligible clerk had become *Herr Leutnant*— second lieutenant in the reserves, detailed to the 124th Infantry. The butt had become the potential hero.

He was listened to, bowed to. He was the first to dip the battered silver spoon into the *Kompottschale*.

Dinner over, cigars and cigarettes lit, he held court, leaning over the piano in all his gray-green glory. He received congratulations which he accepted with a yawn. But when Takagawa bowed to him, saying something very kindly and very stiltified in his awkward German, Grosser looked him up and down as he might some exotic and nauseating beetle, and it was clear that the other boarders approved of his strange conduct.

It was the same in the laboratory. When he entered the students who were already there turned stony eyes upon him.

"Good morning, gentlemen," he said. A harsh, rasping sound, something between a cough and a snort, was the reply.

Only the professor seemed unchanged.

"Good morning, miniature yellow peril!" he said, while the German students formed into a group near the window whence they could see the soldiers file down Unter den Linden, with the hollow tramp-tramp-tramp of drilled feet, the brasses braying out their insolent call.

They seemed silent and grave and stolid, though at times given to unreasonable, hectic fits of temper. They talked excitedly among themselves about *"Weltpolitik,"* about *"Unser Platz in der Sonne"* and *"Deutsche Ideale."* Every once in a while one of them would whisper something about *"die Engländer,"* pronouncing the word as if it were a dread talisman. Another would pick up the word: *"die Engländer,"* with a tense, minatory hiss. Then again they would all talk together, excitedly; and once Takagawa, busy with a brass crucible and a handful of pink crystals, could hear: "Japan—the situation in the Far East—Kiauchau—"

Baron von Eschingen, usually punctual to the minute, did not make an appearance at the laboratory that morning.

"Getting ready for the wholesale butchery," the professor explained to Takagawa in an undertone. "Sharpening his cleaver and putting a few extra teeth in his meat saw, I've no doubt."

Takagawa felt disappointed. He would have liked to say good-by to his friend, ceremoniously. For he remembered how his father had gone forth at the outbreak of the Russo-Japanese War. He had only been a small child at the time, but he recollected everything: how his mother and grandmother had bowed low and had spoken unctuously of *naijo*, of inner help; how the little girls of the household had brought their *kai-ken* dirks to be blessed by the departing warrior; how Komoto had quoted long passages from the *Po-ro-po-lo-mi*, reënforcing them with even lengthier quotations from the *Fuh-ko;* how his father had taken him to his arms with the true *bushi no nasaké*, the true tenderness of a warrior, and how immediately after his father had left the women had put on plain white linen robes, without hems, as the ancient rites prescribe for widows.

"You—you don't think he'll come back here before he leaves for the front?" he asked the professor.

"Certainly," laughed the other. "He isn't through yet with these!" indicating a wizardly array of tubes and pipes whence acrid, sulphurous fumes were rising to be caught, yellow, cloudy, whirling, in a bulb-shaped retort which hung from the ceiling.

"But—he is a samurai, a soldier!" stammered Takagawa. "What have these—these gases to do with—"

"With war?" Kreutzer gave a cracked laugh. "Don't you know?"

"I know the ingredients. I know how the gas is produced."

"Oh, you do; do you?"

"Yes."

And Takagawa, turning on the right spigot in his fact-gathering brain, reeled off the correct formula in all its intricacies.

The professor laughed again. "And you mean to say," he asked in the same sibilant undertone, "that you have no idea what the gas is for—that you have no idea why Baron von Eschingen has honored us these six weeks with his spurred and booted presence?"

"Why—no!"

Kreutzer slapped his knees. "Blessed innocence!" he chuckled. "Blessed, spectacled, yellow-skinned, Asiatic innocence! It is— Well, never mind!"

He turned to the German students who were still talking excitedly among themselves.

"Silentium!" he thundered. "War is all very well, gentlemen. But we are not here to kill or to remake the map of Europe. We are here to learn about—" And then a lengthy Greek word and the hush of the classroom.

The baron, who had shed his pale-blue and silver regimentals for a uniform of gray-green, came in toward the end of the lesson. He spoke courteously to the students, who instinctively stood at attention, shook hands with Takagawa with his usual friendliness, and drew the professor into a corner where he engaged him in a low, heated conversation.

"I won't do it!" Takagawa could hear Kreutzer's angry hiss. "The lesson is over. I insist on my academic freedom! I am a free burgess of the university. I—" and the baron's cutting reply: "This is war, *Herr Professor!* I am here by orders of the Ministry of War. I order you to—"

Takagawa smiled. Here was the real samurai speaking; and he was still smiling ecstatically when, a moment later, the professor turned to the class.

"Go downstairs, *meine Herren,*" he said. "I have a private lesson to give to—to"—he shot out the word venomously—"to our army dunce! To our saber-rattling gray-green hope! To our so intelligent East-Elbian Junker! To—"

"Shut up!" came the baron's harsh voice. "Don't you dare, you damned—" At once he controlled himself. He forced himself to smile. "I am sorry, gentlemen," he said, "to disturb you and to interfere with your lessons in any way. But I have some private business with the professor. War—you know—the necessities of war—"

"Yes—yes—"

"*Natürlich!*"

"*Selbstverständlich!*"

"*Sie haben ganz Recht, Herr Leutnant!*" came the chorus of assent, and the students left the laboratory together with Takagawa, who went last.

"Wait for me downstairs, old boy," the baron called after him as he was about to close the door.

Arrived in the street, without civil words or touching their hats, the German students turned to the left to take their "second breakfast" at the Café Victoria, while Takagawa paced up and down in front of the building to wait for his friend.

Troops were still marching in never-ending files, like a long, coiling snake with innumerable, bobbing heads, and crowds of people were packing the sidewalks in a dense mass, from the Brandenburger Thor to beyond the Schloss.

They whirled about Takagawa. A few noticed him—only a few, since he was so small—but these few glared at him. They halted momentarily, mumbling: "A Japanese!"

"Ein Ausländer!" ("A foreigner!")

There was sullen, brooding hatred in the word where, only yesterday, it had held kindliness and hospitality and tolerance.

Takagawa stepped back into a doorway. Not that he was afraid. He did not know the meaning of the complicated emotion called fear, since he was a samurai. But something intangible, something nauseating and hateful, seemed to float up from the crowd, like a veil in the meeting of winds—the air, the people, the music, everything, suddenly shot through with peculiar, disturbing, prismatic diffractions.

He was glad when the baron's tall form came from the laboratory building.

"Sorry I kept you waiting," said the officer, slipping his white-gloved hand through the other's arm. "I've only a minute for you at that. Got to rush back to headquarters, you know. But—a word to the wise —is your passport in order?"

"Yes. Why?"

The baron did not seem to hear the last question. He took a visiting card from his pocketbook and scribbled a few rapid words. "Here you are," he said, giving the card to Takagawa. "Take this to my friend Police Captain von Wilmowitz, at the Presidency of

Police—you know—near the Spittelmarkt. He'll see to it that you get away all right before it's too late— you, and your old servant, Kaguchi—"

"Get away? Too late? You mean that—"

"That you'd better wipe your feet on the outer door-mat of the German Empire. Get out of the country, in other words. Go to Holland, Switzerland—any-where."

"Why?"

"War!" came the baron's laconic reply.

"Yes, but Japan and Germany are not at war!"

The baron had put back his pocketbook and was buttoning his tunic. "I know," he said. "But Eng-land declared war against us three hours ago, and Japan is England's ally. Hurry up. Do what I tell you. I'll drop in on you to-night or to-morrow and see how you're making out." He turned and came back again.

"By the way," he went on, "be careful about any pa-pers you take along. Destroy them. Your chemistry notebooks—the notes you made during class. There's that poison gas, for instance." He was silent, hesi-tated, and continued: "I'm sorry about that, Taka-gawa. Puts both you and me in a devilishly embar-rassing position. You see, I had no idea—honestly— that war was due when the powers that be detailed me on that chemistry course. I thought it was all a tre-mendous bluff. Otherwise I would never have dreamt of working side by side with you, comparing notes on these poison-gas experiments, and all that. Well"—he shrugged his shoulders—"what's the use of crying over spilt milk? Burn your notebooks—chiefly those dealing with the gas." And he was off.

Takagawa looked after him, uncomprehending. The

poison gas! Here it was again. The same mysterious allusion. First Professor Kreutzer had spoken of it, and now the baron.

But what did they mean? What did it signify?

Finally, obeying the suggestion of the dusty laboratory windows looking down on him from their stone frames, Takagawa reëntered the building and went straight to Professor Kreutzer's lecture room.

He found the latter seated at his desk, his chin cupped in his hands, his haggard face flushed and congested. The man seemed to be laboring under an excitement which played on every quivering nerve of his body; the hand supporting the lean chin showed the high-swelling veins, and trembled.

He looked up as Takagawa entered, and broke into a harsh bellow of laughter. "Come back, have you, you stunted yellow peril!"

"Yes. I want to ask you about—about the gas."

Again the professor laughed boisterously.

"The gas!" he cried. "The poison gas! To be sure! Not quite as innocent as you made yourself out to be a while back, are you? Well, by God, I'll tell you about the poison gas! Got a remarkable sort of brain, haven't you? Retentive faculty abnormally developed—don't need written notes or any other sort of asses' bridge, eh? Just as good! Couldn't take anything written out of Germany. But your brain—your tenacious Oriental brain—they can't put that to the acid test! All right! Listen to me!"

Professor Kreutzer did not stop to dissect himself or his motives. He obeyed, not a feeling, a sudden impulse, but a pathological mood which was the growth of forty years. For forty years he had hated autocratic, imperial Germany. For forty years he had battled with his puny strength against militarism. Now the steel-clad beast had won. The shadow of war had fallen over the land. His gods lay shattered about him.

Forty years of ill-suppressed hatred—brought to a head, half an hour earlier, by Baron von Eschingen's curt command: "This is war, *Herr Professor*. I am here by orders of the Ministry of War. I order you to—"

That uniformed, gold-braided jackanapes to order him, a scientist, a thinker!

Kreutzer swore wickedly under his breath. He turned to the Japanese, and talked to him at length, going with minute care over the whole process of making poison gas, from the first innocuous-looking pink crystal to the final choking cloudy yellow fumes. He made Takagawa repeat it, step by step, formula by formula. Finally he declared himself satisfied. "You know it now, don't you?" he asked.

"Yes, sir."

"You'll never forget it?"

"No, sir."

"All right. You have what you came here to get. In one respect at least you know as much as the German War Office. Go back to Japan—as soon as you can." He returned to his desk and picked up a book.

Takagawa went after him. *"Herr Professor!"* he said timidly.

"Well? What is it now?"

"I—I—" the samurai hesitated. "I know the gas. I know how it is produced, how it is projected, how it affects the human body. I understand all that. But what is it for?"

"You—you mean to say you don't know?"

The professor twirled in his chair, utter incredulity in his accents. Then, reading the question in Takagawa's oblique eyes, sensing that the man was asking in perfect good faith, in perfect innocence, he rose, took him by the arm, and led him to the window. He pointed. Afternoon had melted into a soft evening of glowing violet with a pale moon growing faintly in the north. The linden trees stood stiff and motionless as if forged out of a dark-green metal. But still the soldiers tramped. Still there was the glitter of rifle barrel and sword tip and lance point. Still crowds packed the sidewalks, cheering. The professor made a great gesture. It was more than a mere waving of hand and arm. It seemed like an incident which cut through the air like a tragic shadow.

"They are going out to kill—with bullet and steel. But gas, too, can kill—poison gas, projected from iron tanks on an unsuspecting, unprepared enemy! It can win a battle, a campaign, a war! It can change the course of world history! It can ram imperial Germany's slavery down the throat of a free world! Poison gas—it is a weapon—the newest, most wicked, most effective weapon!" The professor was getting slightly hysterical. "Take it back with you to Japan —to France, to England—anywhere! Fight us with our own weapons! Fight us—and give us freedom— freedom!" And, with an inarticulate cry, he pushed the Japanese out of doors.

Takagawa walked down the Dorotheenstrasse like a man in a dream. His feelings were tossed together into too violent confusion for immediate disentanglement. "You will learn, not for reward and merit, not for yourself, but for Japan!" his grandfather, the old marquis, had told him. And he had learned a great secret—for Japan. And Japan would need it. For, passing the newspaper kiosk at the corner of the Wilhelmstrasse, he had glanced at the headlines of the evening edition of the *"Vossische Zeitung"*:

"Japan Stands by England. Sends Ultimatum. War Inevitable!"

War inevitable—and he was a samurai, a man entitled to wield the two-handed sword, though his body was too weak to carry the burden of it.

What of it? The professor had told him that poison gas, too, was a weapon, the most modern, most effective weapon in the world; and he had its formula tucked snugly away in his brain.

The poison gas! It was his sword! But first he must get out of the country. He hailed a taxicab and drove straight to the Presidency of Police. A crowd of foreigners of all nationalities—anxious, nervous, shouting, gesticulating—was surging in the lower entrance hall of the square, baroque building. But the baron's card proved a talisman, and in less than half an hour Takagawa had seen Police Captain von Wilmowitz, had had his passport viséed and had received permission for himself and his servant Kaguchi to leave Berlin for Lake Constance on the following day.

Captain von Wilmowitz repeated the baron's warning: "Take nothing written out of Germany. Neither yourself nor your servant. They'll examine you both thoroughly at the Swiss frontier. Be careful," and Takagawa had hidden a smile.

Let them search his person, his clothes, his baggage. They would not be able to search his brain. He started figuring rapidly. He would go to Switzerland, thence via Paris to London. The Japanese ambassador there was a second cousin of his. He would give him the precious formula, and then—

He returned to the *pension* in the Dahlmannstrasse, settled his bill, and ordered Kaguchi to pack. Notebook after notebook he burned, and as he worked he was conscious of a feeling of power. There was no actual presentiment, no psychic preliminaries. It simply was there, this feeling of power, as if it had always been there. He was a samurai, and his was the two-handed sword—a two-handed sword forged in a stinking, bulb-shaped glass retort and shooting forth yellow, choking, sulphurous fumes.

In the next room a half dozen Germans were smoking and drinking and singing. He could hear Hans Grosser's excited voice, and now and then a snatch of song, sentimental, patriotic, boastful, and he thought that he too would soon again hear the songs of his fatherland, back in the island of Kiushu, in the rocky feudal stronghold of the Takagawas. The bards would be there singing the old heroic epics; the *uguisus* would warble the old melodies. Komoto would be there, and he himself, and his grandfather, the marquis.

"You will learn honorably!" his grandfather had told him. And he had learned. He was bringing back the fruit of it to Nippon.

He turned to Kaguchi with a laugh.

"I have learned, Kaguchi, eh?"

"Yes," replied the old servant, "you have learned indeed, O Takamori-san!"

"And"—he said it half to himself—"I have learned honorably."

Honorably?

He repeated the word with a mental question mark
at the end of it.

Had he learned—honorably?

He stood suddenly quite still. An ashen pallor
spread to his very lips. He dropped the coat which
he was folding. Doubt floated upon him imperceptibly, like the shadow of a leaf through summer dusk.
Something reached out and touched his soul, leaving
the chill of an indescribable uneasiness, and indescribable shame.

"Honorably!" He whispered the word.

He sat down near the window, looking out into
the street. Night had fallen with a trailing cloak of
gray and lavender. The tall, stuccoed apartment
houses on the Kurfürstendamm, a block away, rose
above the line of street lamps like a smudge of sooty
black beyond a glittering yellow band. Still people
were cheering, soldiers tramping.

Kaguchi spoke to him. But he did not hear. He
stared unseeing.

He said to himself that he had come to Germany,
to Berlin, as a guest, to partake of the fruit of wisdom and knowledge. Richly the foreigners, the Germans, had spread the table for him. Generously they
had bidden him eat. And he had dipped his hands
wrist-deep into the bowl and had eaten his fill in a
friend's house, giving thanks according to the law of
hospitality.

Then war had come. Belgium, France, England,
Russia—and to-morrow Japan. To-morrow the
standard of the Rising Sun would unfurl. To-
morrow the trumpets would blow through the streets
of Nagasaki. Peasants and merchants and samurai
would rush to arms.

And he was a samurai; and he had a weapon, a weapon of Germany's own forging—the formula for the poison gas, safely tucked away in his brain.

They had taught him in good faith.   And he had learned.   Nor would he be able to forget.

Professor Kreutzer?   He did not count.   He was a traitor.   But his friend, Baron von Eschingen, the Prussian samurai who had worked side by side with him, who had even helped him get away?

Takagawa walked up and down.   His labored, sibilant breathing sounded terribly distinct.   From the next room there still came excited voices, the clink of beer steins, maudlin singing:

Von allen den Mädchen so blink und so blank . . .

winding up in a tremendous hiccup.   But he did not hear.   In his brain something seemed to flame upward, illuminating all his thoughts.

They were very clear.   He could not stay here, in the land of the enemy, while Nippon was girding her loins.   Nor could he go home.   For home he was a samurai, entitled to wield the two-handed sword. And he carried that sword in his brain, the formula for the poison gas.   He would be forced—forced by himself, forced by his love of country—to give it to Nippon, and thus he would break the law of hospitality, his own honor.

He had learned the formula honorably.   But there was no way of using it honorably.

A great, tearing sob rose in his throat.   Then he heard a voice at his elbow: "O Takamori-san!"

He turned.   "Yes, Kaguchi?"—and, suddenly, the

answer to the riddle came to him. He looked at the old servant.

"You love me, Kaguchi?" he asked.

"My heart is between your hands!"

"You trust me?"

Kaguchi drew himself up.

"You are a samurai, O Takamori-san. The sword of Kiushu is unsullied."

"And unsullied it shall remain! And so," he added incongruously, "you will speak after me the foreign words which I shall now teach you, syllable for syllable, intonation for intonation"; and, step by step, formula by formula, he taught Kaguchi the meaningless German words.

For hours he worked with him until the old man reeled off the strange sounds without hitch or error.

"You know now?" he asked him finally, even as the professor had asked him earlier in the afternoon.

"Yes."

"You'll never forget it?"

"No."

Takamori Takagawa smiled.

"Kaguchi," he said, "you will go from here to London, using this passport." He gave him the official paper which Herr von Wilmowitz had viséed. "In London you will seek out the ambassador of Nippon, who is my cousin. You will tell him word for word what I have just taught you, adding that it is the formula of a poison gas and that this gas is mightier than the two-handed sword and will, perhaps, win the war for Nippon and her allies. You will furthermore tell him—and let this message be transmitted by him to my respected grandfather—that I learned this formula honorably, but that I could not

take it back with me to Nippon without sullying the
law of hospitality, since the foreigners taught me in
good faith. I myself, being thus caught between the
dagger of my honor and the dagger of my country,
have tried to make a compromise with fate. Honorably I tried to do my duty by Nippon, honorably I
tried to keep the law of hospitality untainted. I do
not know if I have succeeded. Thus—" he made a
gesture, and was silent.

Kaguchi bowed. His rugged old face was motionless. But he understood—and approved.

"You! Ah—" the word choked him.

"Yes." Takamori inclined his head. He used the
old Chinese simile which his tutor had taught him.
"I shall ascend the dragon."

He put his hand on Kaguchi's shoulder. "Come
back here in half an hour," he said. "Fold my hands
as the ancient customs demand. Then notify my
friend, the German samurai. He will help you get
over the frontier—with the formula safe in your
brain."

And the servant bowed and left the room without
another word.

The young samurai smiled slowly. An old quota-
tion came back to him: "I will open the seat of my
soul with a dagger of pain and show you how it
fares with it. See for yourself whether it is polluted
or clean."

He walked across the room, opened the mirror
wardrobe, and took from the top shelf a dirk—a splendid, ancient blade in a lacquer case, whose guard was
of wrought iron shaped like a chrysanthemum. Then
he took off his European clothes and put on a voluminous white hemless robe with long, trailing sleeves.

Very slowly he knelt. Carefully, according to the rites, he tucked the sleeves under his knees, to prevent himself falling backward, since a samurai should die falling forward. He took the dirk from the scabbard.

The next moment it had disappeared beneath the flowing draperies. He made a hardly perceptible movement. One corner of his mouth was slightly twisted, the first sign of great suffering heroically borne. His right leg was bent back, his left knee too. Then he drew the dirk slowly across to his right side and gave a cut upward.

Crimson stained his white robe. His eyes, glazed, staring, held a question—a question, a doubt to the last. Had he acted honorably? Had he—?

He fell forward. . . .

It was thus that Baron von Eschingen, ushered in by Kaguchi, found him.

"Hara-kiri!" he said, drawing a sheet across the dead man's face; and then, quite suddenly: "Yes—yes. I understand—honorable little beggar!"

BLACK POPPIES

DELICATELY, with nervous, agile fingers he kneaded the brown poppy cube against the tiny bowl of his pipe, then dropped it into the open furnace of the lamp and watched the flame change it gradually into amber and gold.

The opium boiled, sizzled, dissolved, evaporated. The fragrant, opalescent smoke rolled in sluggish clouds over the mats, and Yung Han-Rai, having emptied the pipe at one long-drawn inhalation, leaned back, both shoulders pressed well down on the square, hard, leather pillows, so as better to inflate his chest and keep his lungs filled all the longer with the fumes of the kindly drug.

The noises of the outer world seemed very far away. There was just a memory of street cries lifting their hungry, starved arms; just a memory of whispering river wind chasing the night clouds that clawed at the moon with cool, slim fingers of white and silver.

A slow smile overspread Yung Han-Rai's placid, butter-yellow features. He stared at the rolling opium clouds. They seemed filled with a roaring sunset of colors, fox-brown and steel-blue and purple; like the colors of his past dreams moving and blazing before him, changing into his future dreams.

That evening he had smoked thirty-seven pipes,

each pipe an excellent and powerful mixture of Yu-
nan and Benares poppy-juice.

Earlier in the evening he had used a precious pipe
of rose crystal with a yellow jade mouthpiece and
three black silk tassels, which his older brother had
given him years earlier, during the Eighth Moon fes-
tival in honor of Huo Shen, the god of fire. It was
a charming pipe, the mouthpiece carved minutely with
all the divinities of the Taoist heaven, from Lao Tzu
himself to the Spiritual Exalted One; from the Pearly
Emperor to the Ancient Original; from the Western
Royal Mother to the god of the T'ai Shan, the Eastern Peak, who watches the rock-strewn coast of the
Yellow Sea against the invasions of the outer
barbarian.

Yung Han-Rai liked this pipe. But he did not
love it.

He loved his old bamboo pipe, quite plain, without tassels or ornaments. Once it had been white
as ivory. But to-day it was blackish-brown, with a
thousand and ten thousand smokes. It was fragrant
with a thousand and ten thousand exquisite memories.
Yung Han-Rai had used it during the latter part of
the evening, and was using it now.

He called it his pipe of August Permanence, while
he called the other his pipe of Delightful Vice, comparing the first to a wife grown gnarled and wrinkled
and berry-brown in her lord's service, and the second
to a courtezan, whom one caresses, pays and—forgets.

He smoked three more pipes, one after the other,
in rapid succession.

The immaterial substance of his inner self had
floated away on the gray wings of smoke. His soul
reached to his former life, his longings, his loneliness,

and his failure. It was failure no longer. He would find that old life fair and satisfying. He might even find the lesser gods.

The opium sizzled with a reedy, fluting song. There was no other sound. Even the whispering wind had died; the street cries had guttered out like spent candles.

He smoked. . . .

Then came to him the vision.

He saw very little now except the house itself, and, of the house, veiled through the opalescent saraband of the poppy fumes, he saw really only the three violet lanterns above the door.

He had seen the house so often, remembered it so well. It was part of his dreams, thus part of his real life. He had always loved it, with an almost physical, sensuous love. It was like a fretted, chiseled ingot, with a pagoda roof that shimmered in every mysterious blending of blue and green and purple, like the plumage of a gigantic peacock, or the shootings of countless dragonflies.

Too, he had always loved the three lamps below the carved, deep-brown pagoda beam. They were of a glorious, glowing violet, faintly dusted with gold; and, depending from them, fluttered long streamers of pottery-red satin, with inscriptions from the Chinese classics in archaic Mandarin hieroglyphics.

These inscriptions changed every night; they seemed to blend with his own changing moods. That was their greatest charm.

Last night he had been in a poetic mood, and the silken strips had lisped some of Han Yu's lilting lines, about "moonlight flooding the inner gallery, where the japonica stammers with silvered petals." To-night the drift of his mind inclined toward the philosophical, and he read on the fluttering streamers three quotations from the Kung-Yuan Chang.

The first was: "Is virtue a thing remote?" The second: "I wish to be virtuous!" The third: "Lo and behold—virtue is at hand!"

He loved the entrance hall of the house, with the floor completely hidden under a shimmering mass of Kien-Lun brocades that were like moon-beams on running water, and, square in the center, an ancient Ming rug of imperial yellow stamped with black bats as a sign of good luck. These, with the three small tables of ebony and dull-red lacquer supporting an incense burner, an ivory vase for the hot wine, and a squat, earthen pot filled with a profusion of feathery parrot-tulips in exotic shades, and, in the far corner, a huge, fantastic tiger in old crackle-glaze porcelain—all these, made for him a little world in themselves.

He loved the stilted, never-changing ceremonial of Pekinese politeness with which the master of the house —somehow, because of the whirling clouds of poppy smoke that veiled the room, he had never been able to see his features distinctly—greeted him, night after night. He would receive his caller on the threshold, bowing with clasped hands, and saying:

"Please deign to enter first."

Whereat Yung Han-Rai would bow still lower.

"How could I dare to, O wise and older brother?" he would retort, sucking in his breath, and quoting an appropriate line from the *Book of Ceremonies and Exterior Demonstrations*, which proved that the manner is the heart's mirror.

Then, night after night, after another request by his host, he himself still protesting his unworthiness, he would enter as he was bidden and be asked to "deign to choose a mat," on the west side of the room, as a special mark of honor. And a soft-footed servant in a crimson, dragon-embroidered tunic and a cap with a turquoise button would bring two jade cups; cups not of the garish green *iao* jade which foreigners like, but of the white and transparent *iu* jade that the rites reserve for princes, viceroys, Manchus, ministers, and distinguished literati.

He himself was a literatus.

Had he not, many years ago, competing against ninety-seven picked youths from all the provinces of the Middle Kingdom, passed first in the examination at the Palace of August and Happy Education, and obtained the eminent degree of San Tsoi? Had not the Dowager Empress, in person, thereon congratulated him? Had not his mother been thanked publicly for having given birth to such a talented son? And his prize poem—was it not being quoted to this day by white-bearded priests, sipping their jasmine-flavored tea in the flaunting gardens of Pekin's Lama monastery?

He remembered how the poem began:

> "Day reddens in the wake of night,
> But the days of our life return not.
> Sweet-scented orchids blot out the path,
> But they die in the drift of waters,
> And their flowers are blotted out,
> But their perfume . . ."

Yes. He himself was a literatus. But he would again protest his unworthiness.

"I shall drink if you wish me to, O wise and older

brother," he would say. "But from a wooden cup with no ornaments," he would add.

And then, according to the proper rules of conduct prescribed by the ancients, the master of the house would insist three times, and he would drink the hot, spiced wine from the jade cup.

It was so to-night.

He entered, exchanged the customary Pekinese civilities, sipped his cup of wine, and smiled at his host who smiled back.

"Will you smoke?" asked the latter.

"Gladly."

"A pipe of jade, or a pipe of tortoise-shell with five yellow tassels?"

"Either would be too flattering for me. Are you not my brother, very wise and very old? And am I not the unworthy and very little one? Let me, I beseech you, smoke my old bamboo."

"Your lips will endow even an old bamboo with harmonious beauty far more precious than all the precious metals of the Mountains of the Moon," his host replied courteously, and bowed.

He filled both pipes. The folds of smoke joined over the lamp whose flame was hidden by a filagree screen of butterflies in green enamel.

"The opium will clear the clouds from our brains," continued the master of the house slowly. "It will purify our judgments, make our hearts more sensitive to beauty, and take away the tyrannical sensations of actual life—the sources, these, of all vulgar mistakes. Will you smoke again?"

"With pleasure."

Both men drew in the acrid fumes with all the strength of their lungs.

Yung Han-Rai smiled dreamily.

"Did not Hoang Ti, the Yellow Emperor himself, once remark that. . . .?"

The sentence died unfinished on his lips.

They smoked in silence for nearly half an hour. The room was filling with scented fog. Already the objects scattered about had lost their outline, and the silken stuffs on the walls and the floor gleamed less brilliantly.

Yung Han-Rai felt a confused sensation of the marrow of his bones and his muscles, some of which seemed to soften and almost to melt away, while others seemed to strengthen and grow greatly, while his subconscious brain seemed endowed with a new and intense vitality. He no longer noticed the weight of his body pressing on the mat; rather he became conscious of a tremendous intellectual and ethical power.

Hidden things became clear to him. The soul within his soul came to the surface with a flaming rush of speed. He felt himself part of nature—a direct expression of cosmic life. The currents of the earth pulsed in his veins with a puissant and mysterious rhythm.

High on the wall he saw a soft glow. It was an ancient gilt-wood statue representing Han Chung-le, the greatest of the Taoist immortals, who was supposed to have found the elixir of life.

Yung Han-Rai smiled at him familiarly, even slightly ironically.

After all, the thought came to him, he and Han Chung-le were brothers, immortal both.

He smoked again.

The poppy tasted sweet as summer rain. . . .

After a lapse of time, hours, days, weeks—he knew

not, he became conscious that the master of the house was addressing him. The voice was soft, like the far piping of a reed.

"I have considered everything," the voice said. "I have thought well. I have thought left and thought right. There exists no doubt that my daughter, the Plum Blossom, will greatly appreciate your many and honorable qualities. She, on the other hand, will make you a delightful wife. Her eyes are like sunbeams filtering their gold through the shadows of the pine woods. The mating-songs of all the birds are echoed in the harmony of her voice. Too, she is a vessel filled with all the domestic virtues. She is strong and high-breasted. She will bear you as many men-children as there are hairs in my queue."

"Your too-indulgent lips have pronounced words full of the most delicate beauty," replied Yung Han-Rai. "Alas, it grieves me, but I cannot accept. I am the very little and unimportant one. My ancestry is wretched, my manners deplorable, and my learning less than the shadow of nothing at all. The honor would be too great, O wise and older brother."

"It is my own justly despised family which will be exquisitely honored," replied the other, rising, and bowing deeply with clasped hands. "Let there—I humbly implore you—be a marriage between you and the Plum Blossom. You will make an excellent son-in-law, virtuous, learned, a respecter of the ancient traditions of Ming and Sung."

Yung Han-Rai was about to speak, to protest once more, as the proper ceremonial demanded, his utter unworthiness. His lips had already formed the carefully chosen words when, very suddenly, he was silent. He became nervous, uneasy, frightened. Cold beads of perspiration trickled slowly down his nose.

He bent forward; listened.

That noise. What was it?

Something from the outside world, the unreal world of facts, seemed to brush in on unclean, sardonic wings, to disturb the perfect peace of the house, to break and shiver the poppy-heavy air.

Cries of the street, in an uncouth, foreign language:

"Yer gotta travel the straight an' narrow if yer want me t' stick t' yer, get me?"

"Gee, kid! Listen t' me! I ain't never spoke a woid to th' guy, I tells yer honest!"

"Well—looka here. . . ."

The voices drifted away. Came other noises. The hooting of the Elevated, around the corner on Chatham Square. The steely roar of a motor exhaust.

Motor? Elevated? Chatham Square?

What was it, Yung asked himself? What did the words signify?

Streets—noises—foreigners—coarse-haired barbarians. . . .

No, no—by the Excellent Lord Buddha!

They were only the figments of his dreams; dreams which he had often, day after day; dreams which he hated and feared—

Dreams which he must kill!

With shaking fingers he reached for the opium jar. He kneaded the brown cube. He roasted it, filled his pipe, and smoked.

And, at once, the poppy ghosts drew swiftly down about him on silver-gray wings, building around him a wall of fragant, gossamer clouds, suffusing the soul within his soul with the wild loveliness of a forgotten existence.

With a wealth of deep, radiant conviction, this former existence, blending with his life of might-have-been, poured into his brain. His brain inflamed his heart. His thoughts softened; they trembled like a wavering line of music in a night-blue wind of spring. The fringe of his inner consciousness stretched far and out, away to the stars and the high winds, into a great and sweet freedom.

He smoked again.

He became conscious of something like a rain of summer flowers. The feet of his soul were walking down the path of some tremendous, dazzling verity. The facts of the outer world touched him no longer with their hard, cutting edges. These facts were untrue; they were not; they were only the lying thoughts of the lying, lesser gods.

The poppy fumes whirled up, wreathing everything in floating vapors. They darkened the air with a solid, bloating shadow. The room disappeared. Disappeared his host.

He saw again the outside of the house, the tilted, pagoda roof shimmering like a gigantic peacock; saw again the three violet lanterns above the door.

He was now walking away from the house, but he turned and saw that the inscriptions on the three fluttering streamers had changed once more.

The first read: "Love—like moon-born clouds casting their tremulous shadows over stairs of rose-red jade!" The second: "Love—like little ghosts of May-time ruffling the river of heart's desire!" The third: "Love—like a hidden lute softly lilting behind a silken alcove!"

So he strolled away, beneath a vaulted night, subtly perfumed, secret, mystical, netted in delicate silver mist, and the soft starlight drifting down through budding boughs into budding earth, and the dreams in his soul moving thick and soft ahead of him; and he felt, deep within him, as the Lord Gautama Buddha must have felt on the day of creation, when his golden smile first dawned on chaos and the love in his heart released the forces of nature.

And the opium clouds drove the night to the west, and the broad, level wedge of day streamed out of the east; and the strength of the young sun came, stemming the morning mists.

The air was a rapidly whirling wheel of gleaming dust, shedding crimson and purple sparks; a brook went gurgling past, sparkling like a flow of emeralds, there was a staccato breeze flickering over the sun-spotted fields like the wind of a Manchu lady's gaily-flirted fan; and the voice of his heart's desire whispered through the green roll of creation, and he saw, etched against the distance, the Pavilion of Exquisite Love that rose slowly from a garden of great black poppies, curved fantastically into an upper story framed by balconies, then raced away with spires and turrets and tinkling silver bells to a bright, pigeon-blue sky.

So he smoked again.

The fragrant fumes of his pipe, with the light of the lamp playing upon them, laid a shining ribbon of gold from his heart to the pavilion.

His feet stepped softly upon it. He reached the pavilion, and entered.

The Plum Blossom was sitting erect on a chair of ebony and lacquer encrusted with rose-quartz, and the sweep of his heart's desire came down upon Yung Han-Rai like a gentle, silvered miracle.

"Hayah! my bridegroom!" she said, rising, and bowing low.

"Hayah! my bride!" he replied, and kowtowed three times.

He trembled a little. In his blood he felt pulsing the whole earth with her myriad expressions of life and the making of life, as if dancing to the primal rhythm of all creation.

He looked at her.

He saw her very clearly. The poppy smoke had faded into memory.

Her face was like a tiny, ivory flower, beneath the great wedding-crown of paper-thin gold leaves, with emeralds like drops of frozen green fire, with carved balls of moonstone swinging from the lobes of her ears. The finger nails of her right hand were very long, and encased by pointed filagrees of lapis lazuli studded with seed pearls.

She wore a long gown, that was like a current of glossy silver, embroidered with trailing powder-blue clouds and peach blossoms and, along the bottom of the skirt, a golden dragon in whose head shimmered the seven mystic jewels. The jacket, with its loose sleeves of plum-color encircled by bands of coral lotus buds, was tight and short, of apple-green satin embroidered with sprays of *yulan* magnolias and guelder roses, loped with fretted buttons of white jade; while her slippers were of porcelain, of the one called *Ting-yao*, which is fifth in rank among all perfect porcelains, thin as a paper of rice, fragile as the wings of the silk-moth, melodious as the stone *khing* when gently struck by a soft hand, violet as a summer's night and with an over-glaze like the amber bloom of grapes.

Again he kowtowed.

She was very close to him. Nothing separated them except the delicate threshold between dream and fact. Beyond that threshold there was peace, there was love, there was the eternal thrill of fulfillment, there was an end of those yearnings, of the loneliness and the pains of actual life that had bruised his soul these many years.

So he smoked again. He enveloped himself in a thick, strongly-scented poppy cloud, and he stepped a little beyond the threshold, and knelt at her feet.

"I love you, Plum Blossom," he said. "I love you, O very small Blossom of the Plum Tree!"—and he reached for the *kin*, the Chinese lute, which was at her elbow on a pillow of yellow satin embrodiered with an iridescent rain of pearls.

His fingers caressed the instrument. They brushed over the cords.

The ancient Tartar melody winged up in minor, wailing harmonies, like the fluting of long-limbed rice birds flying against the dead-gold of the autumn sky; and he sang:

"I love you. You are in my heart. You are in my soul. You are in the soul within my soul, where the world has not been spotted by dirt and lies, but is pure as the laughter of little children; where there are no fetters of the flesh nor galls of earthly restraint; where the winds roam in the pathless skies of outer creation, with none but the Buddha's will to check their vagabond waywardness. . . ."

Gently his fingers trembled across the strings of the lute. The accompaniment rippled in white tone-waves, silver-flecked; it quivered on a high note, spreading a network of infinitely delicate tone filaments, then brushed out with an abandon of throbbing cadences, like tiny, drifting ghosts of spring tinkling their girdle gems of fretted jade.

"I love you," he sang. "Daily my love for you echoes through the vaulted halls of my dreams, my life; echoes in smiles and tears and hopes of fulfillment. Daily the thought of you comes to me with flute songs and flowers. Daily I launch the boat of my desire on the lilied pond of your soul. Daily I seek you in the whirling smoke of the poppies. . . ."

He paused.

Skillfully, between thumb and second finger, he twanged the third string. The note trembled as on the brink of an abyss. It sobbed like a flame in the meeting of winds. Then it blew clear into a high rush of ecstasy, and he sang again:

"Daily I have sought you in the whirling smoke of the poppies. Hayah, my bride! And to-day I have found you—found you."

Again he paused.

An overpowering desire tore across him burningly. In a back cell of his brain, he caught the whispered fragment of some enormous truth; saw, with the eyes of his body, the opium fumes pointing with dreamy, blue fingers; saw, with the eyes of his soul, the Plum Blossom's starry little face.

"To-day I have found you," he sang; and again he twanged the third cord between thumb and second finger.

It trembled. The clear note rose, then broke a little. And he bent over the lute and pulled the cord taut.

It sobbed protestingly. There was a tiny snap. Then, suddenly, the cord broke, with a jarring ring.

"To-day I have found you," he sang; and his voice broke; vanished in the whirling fog of the poppies.

He felt a curious, sweet pain. An immense shutter seemed to drop across his mind with a speed of lightning. There was a momentary break in his consciousness, a sense of vague, yet abrupt dislocation, of infinite, rather helpless regret, and the door opened—

"Looka here, yer darned Chink hop-head!" came a rough voice.

Bill Devoy, detective of Second Branch and on the Pell Street beat of sewer gas and opium and yellow man and white, stepped inside. He sniffed, turned up the gas jet, then crossed to the window and opened it wide.

"Gosh! Wot a smell!"

He looked about the room, dusty, grimy, bare of all furnishings except the narrow, wooden bunk where Yung Han-Rai lay stretched out, the bamboo pipe in his stiff fingers, and the small taboret with the smoker's paraphernalia which stood beside the bunk.

He touched the Chinese on the shoulder with his heavy hand.

"Looka here, Yung," he said. "I don't wanta pinch yer. Ye're a decent lad. I'm only gonna talk t' yer like a Dutch uncle, see? Yer gotta cut out the poppy, get me? Wottahell! Look at yerself! Look at this room! Doity and grimy, and not a stick o' furniture! Ain't yer ashamed o' yerself? Wottya mean—soakin' yerself in th' black smoke every night, wastin' every cent yer earn on hop? Ain't yer got no sense at all, yer poor Chink? And they tells me yer useter be a gent, back home in Chinkieland—a real gent, eddycated and of a swell family! Wottya mean, yer poor, weak-spined fish?"

Again he touched the other on the shoulder. He bent down a little more closely. Then a hush came into his voice, as he saw the wistful smile on the yellow, wrinkled old face of the dead man.

"Gee!" he whispered. "Oh, Gee!"

THE PERFECT WAY

HERE, where Pell Street jutted out from the Bowery, there was not even a trace of the patina of antiquity, that bitter and morose grace which clings about old houses like the ghosts of dead flowers. There was nothing here except the marks of the present—hard, gray, scabbed, already rotting before having lived overmuch.

The noises of the street seethed in frothy, brutal streaks: the snarling whine of Russian Jews bartering over infinitesimal values; the high, clipped tenor of metallic, Italian vernaculars; the gliding sing-song of Chinese coolies; and only occasionally an English word, sharp and lonely and nostalgic. There was the rumbling overtone of the Elevated around the corner on Chatham Square; the sardonic hooting of a four-ton motor dray; the ineffectual tinkle-tinkle of a peddler's bell. Rain came and joined in the symphony; spluttering in the leaky eaves-troughs, dripping through the huddled, greasy alleys, mumbling angrily in the brown, clogged gutters.

And Yu Ching sat there by the window and stared with cold, black eyes into the cold, wet evening, neither seeing nor hearing. Behind him shadows coiled, blotchy, inchoate, purplish-black, with just a fitful dancing of elfin high-lights on a teakwood screen, its tight, lemon silk embroidered with japonica, fluttering their silvered petals, and on a small crystal statue of Confucius that squatted amid the smoking incense sticks.

The corner lamp flared up, mean and yellow. The light stabbed in and mirrored on the finger-nails of his pudgy right hand. The hand was very still. Still was the man's face—large, hairless, butter-colored.

The rain spluttered and stammered. The street cries belched defiantly. The peace in Yu Ching's heart was perfect, exquisite.

Momentarily, there came to him fleeting memories of the days when his own life, too, had been an integral and not unimportant part of that cosmic Pell Street energy, when he had been a shrewd and respected merchant, who had contributed his share of wisdom and gossip to the evening gatherings of his countrymen in the liquor store of the Chin Sor Company—the "Place of Sweet Desire and Heavenly Entertainment."

Came memories of his wife, Marie Na Liu, sweet with lissom, unformed sweetness of sixteen years, tiny and soft and high-breasted, with the golden hair of a Danish mother and the creamy, waxen skin, the sloe-black eyes of a Chinese father.

Across the poetry of her youth had lain the stony drag and smother, the subtle violence, the perfumed dirt of the bastard Pell Street world. She had been like a rainbow bubble floating on the stinking puddles of Chinatown vice. But he had loved her dearly. His love for her had burned away the caked, black cinders, the dross and the dirt.

Her love for him—? There were classic, scholarly traditions in his clan; one of his ancestors had been a poet of no mean repute in the days of the *Ta Tsing*

Kwoh, the "Great-Pure Kingdom"; and so Yu Ching had compared Marie Na Liu's love to a dewdrop on a willow spray, a flaunting of fairy pennons, and the sound of a silver bell in the green mists of twilight— smiling, with kindly intent, at the last simile; for he had been forty-seven years of age and she sixteen when he had married her, quite respectably, with a narrow gold ring, a bouquet of cabbagy, wired roses, a proper, monumental wedding cake, a slightly shocked Baptist clergyman mumbling the words of the blessed ritual, and at the organ a yellow, half-caste boy introducing wailing Cantonese dissonances into the *"Voice that breathed o'er Eden."*

Down at the "Place of Sweet Desire and Heavenly Entertainment," the comment had been brutally unflattering.

"You are old, and she is young!" had said Nag Hong Fah, the paunchy restaurant proprietor, fluttering his paper fan. *"Hayah!* On the egg combating with the stone, the yolk came out, O wise and older brother!"

"The ass went seeking for horns—and lost its ears!" Yung Lung, the wholesale grocer, had darkly suggested.

And Yu Ch'ang, the priest of the joss temple, had added with pontifical unction:

"When I see the sun and the moon delivered up by the eclipse to the hands of the demons; when I perceive the bonds that fasten an elephant; and when I behold a wise man surrendering—ah—to the foolish abominations of the flesh, the thought forces itself upon me: 'How mighty is the power of evil!'"

Thus, at the time of their marriage, had run the

gliding, malicious gossip of Chinatown. But when, quite casually, Yu Ching had repeated it to his wife, who was busying herself amongst the cook pots of their neat little Pell Street flat, she had given him a rapid kiss.

"You sh'd worry, yer fat old sweetness!" she had laughed. "Them Chinks is just plain jealous. You treat me on th' level—and I'll retoin the compliment, see? Besides, I'm stuck on yer snoozly old phiz! I ain't goin' t'waste no time huntin' for thrills, as long as ye're true to me! I'm a good Christian—I am—"

"And I am a good Buddhist, Plum Blossom!"

"Hell's bells—wot's the difference, sweetness?"

They had been happy. And to-day he had forgotten her. He had completely forgotten her; and he knew —subconsciously, for he never reflected on the subject —that she had been faithful to him; that never, either by word or deed, had she caused him to lose faith; that she had lived up, straight and clean, to the words of the ritual: love, honor, obey.

He knew—subconsciously—that he had broken her heart when he walked out of her life, three years ago.

Very impersonally, he wondered what had become of her. Then he cut off the wondering thought. He smiled. He said to himself that she, too, had been an illusion, a mirroring of shadows in the dun dusk of his soul.

She did not matter.

Why—he put his fingers together, delicately, tip against tip—nothing mattered. . . .

Outside, more lights sprang up against the violet of the sky, spotting the gloom. The noises grew as, with night, grew and heaved the dark-smoldering passions of the city. A pint pocket flask dropped, smashed against a stone. A foul curse was answered by throaty, malign laughter. Came the tail-end of a gutter song; a shouted, obscene joke, old already when the world was young; more curses and laughter; a sailor's sodden, maudlin mouthings; a woman's gurgling contralto:

"Aw—chase yerself! Wottya mean, yer big stiff?"

The drama of the city. The comedy. The vital, writhing entrails. Life, clouting, breathing, fighting eternally.

But Yu Ching did not see, nor hear. His heart was as pure as the laughter of little children, as pure as a gong of white jade. There was hardly a trace of the outer world, dimly, on the rim of his consciousness.

His soul had reached the end of its pilgrimage. Calm, serene, passionless like the Buddha, it sat enthroned beyond the good and the evil.

"All forms are only temporary!"—there was the one great truth.

He smiled. Mechanically, his thin lips formed the words of the Buddha's Twenty-Third Admonition:

"Of all attachments unto objects of desire, the strongest is the attachment to form. He who cannot overcome this desire, for him to enter the Perfect Way of Salvation is impossible. . . ."

The rain had ceased. A great slow wind walked braggingly through the skies. The Elevated, a block away, rushed like the surge of the sea. The Bowery leered up with a mawkish, tawdry face.

The noises of the street blended and clashed, blended and clashed. A thousand people came and went, people of all races, all faiths—gulping down life in greedy mouthfuls.

And still the peace in Yu Ching's heart was perfect and exquisite. Still he smiled. Still, mechanically, his lips mumbled the words of the Buddha:

"By day shineth the sun. By night shineth the moon. Shineth also the warrior in harness of war. But the Buddha, at all times by day and by night, shineth ever the same, illuminating the world, calm, passionless, serene—"

The end of his soul's pilgrimage. . . .

And presently—to-day, to-morrow, next year, ten years from now—his body would die, and his spirit would leap the dragon gate, would blend its secret essence with the eternal essence of the Buddha's soul. . . . And what else mattered?

He bent his head.

"Fire and night and day art Thou," he whispered, "and the fortnight of waxing moon—and the months of the sun's northern circuit—"

The end of his pilgrimage!

And the beginning had been hard. For he had loved Marie Na Liu. He had not wanted to harm her.

But the Voice had spoken to him in the night, asking him to arise and throw off the shackles of desire, the fetters of the flesh; to forget the illusions; telling him that, whatever meritorious results might be attained by prayers and sacrifices, by austerities and gifts, there was no sacrifice to be compared with that of a man's own heart. Such a sacrifice was the excellent sanctifier—exhaustless in result.

"Sure," had said Bill Devoy, a detective of Second Branch and detailed to the Pell Street beat of opium and sewer gas and yellow man and white; he had

caught on to the gossip in the course of a murder in-
vestigation that had nothing whatsoever to do with the
pilgrimage of Yu Ching's soul—"that Chink's got religion—wot *he* calls religion. I don't know if a yaller
Billy Sunday's come down to Pell and Mott, but I
do know as that there Yu Ching's hittin' the trail to
salvation—as them Chinks hit it—sittin' all day like
a bump on a log, just smilin', and never sayin' a damn
word. Meditatin' they calls it. Gee! He gives me
the creeps, he does—"

At first, Marie Na Liu had laughed.

"Say—wottya mean, sweetness?" she had asked.
"Leave me? Goin' t'leave—*me?*" Then her voice had
risen a hectic octave. "Is there another skoit? For if
there is—say—"

"No, Plum Blossom. There is no other woman—
never will be. Woman is an illusion—"

"Wottya handin' me?"

"The flesh is an illusion. There is just my soul—
the Buddha has spoken to me in the night—"

"You've been eatin' Welsh rabbit again—down to
the Dutchman's! You know it never agrees with yer!"

"No, no!"

He had smiled, gently and patiently. Gently and
patiently, he had tried to explain to her, had tried to
make her understand.

"But—sweetness—listen t'me! Yer can't leave me
—oh, yer can't. . . ."

She had argued, cajoled, threatened. But nothing
she could say had made any impression on him. It had
seemed to her, suddenly, as if she had never really
known this man; this man with whom she had lived in
the close physical and mental intimacy of married life
in a little, box-like flat. She had felt—looking at him,

serene, passionless, calm—as if an alien life, an alien existence, was enfolding him; enfolding him away from her, in an incomprehensible and unhuman quietude.

He had seemed to her far away—so far away—and her narrow, white hands had stretched out. helplessly, appealingly; had touched the crinkly, dark-blue silk of his blouse.

"Aw—come on, sweetness"

Again he had tried to explain; and, finally, while she had not seen the tremendous and elemental force, ancient and racial, that was driving him on to his decision, she had understood the result.

He was going to leave her! Yu Ching, her man, was going to leave her!

"Aw—Gee!"

She had cursed. Then her gutter flow of words had floundered in the eddy of her hurt love and pride and vanity, her sheer amazement.

"Ye're goin' to—? Ye're really, rtally goin' to—?"

"I must. The Buddha has spoken to me. I must break the shackles of the flesh, the ropes of illusion— *ahee!*—the ropes of sand! It is a most meritorious act."

"Meritorious, is it?" Swiftly her passion had turned into an icy sneer. "Meritorious, is it—to break a goil's heart? To trample on her—and spit on her— to—?"

He had sighed, a little wearily.

"I shall leave you suitably provided for. I shall only take along a couple of thousand dollars. All the rest is yours—the money—the business—everything."

"Money? Business? Who cares?" She had come close to him, smiling up at him, piteously, with her broad, crimson, generous mouth, the black, somber orbit of her eyes dimmed with tears. "I don't want money! I want you, sweetness! You, you, you! Aw—Gee—don't yer see?"

But he had not moved; had patiently continued smiling. And then she had understood that she might as well plead with some immense and stony sending of fate, and her passion had leaped out in a splattering stream of abuse:

"Yer damned Chink! Ye'll pay fer this—say— ye'll pay fer this some day! Aw—yer damned, yaller hop-head of a Chink!"

She had laughed hysterically, her soft little oval of a face twisted into a terrible grimace.

"I hate yer! I despise yer! Clear outa here! I don't wanta ever see yer ugly mug again! Clear out! I hate yer—yer damned, fat Chink!"

And so he had left her.

So he had left Pell Street, its warm, tame conveniences, its pleasant, snug reek, its zest and tang of shrewd barter and shrewd gossip, his friends, his Tong, his life as he had known it and savored it these many years.

So he had gone on pilgrimage, seeking for release from illusion, from attachment to objects of desire, seeking the Buddha's Perfect Way, wandering here and there, even returning to China where he made the *sengaji* circuit of the thousand and three blessed shrines.

In lonely wayside temples he had sat, talking to gentle priests about the faith and the hope that were his, thinking ever of release from fleshly bondage, turning his eyes toward the mazed depths of his soul, and meditating on the mysterious way which is Life. And

when at times the air had been heavy with the musk
of remembrance and regret, of passion and longing,
when his subconscious fancy had peopled his brain cells
with pictures of his former existence—Pell Street, his
friends sipping their tea and smoking their crimson-
tasseled pipes in the "Place of Sweet Desire and Heavenly Entertainment," Marie Na Liu, her white smile
flashing through the purple night—he had done penance, submitting to the supreme physical ordeals, gradually subduing his body and his mind.

Thus, finally, he had found peace, perfect, exquisite;
and then somehow, he never knew why or how—"that,
too, was Fate," he used to say afterwards, "I but followed the way of my Fate. Who can avoid what is
written on the forehead in the hour of birth?"—he
had returned to New York, and so he sat there by
the window and looked out upon the shrill Babel of
the Pell Street night—calm, serene, passionless.

Just below the window, an elderly Chinese was ar-
guing with a countryman, quoting the polished and
curiously insincere phrases of Mandarin sages, in a
stammering falsetto:

"Pa nien jou chi—i tien jou ki—"

A policeman whistled shrilly. A barrel-organ
creaked a nostalgic, Sicilian melody. . . .

Yu Ching neither saw nor heard.

These people—what did they matter? They were
only cosmic atoms whirling aimlessly in the wind of
desire, like formless swarming snatches of dreams.
No! Nothing mattered, nothing was real, except the
soul.

He smiled, and whispered praises to the Buddha,
and then, suddenly, yet imperceptibly, like the shadow
of a leaf through summer dusk, he felt that he was not

alone in the room, that eyes were staring at him.

He turned, just a little startled.

The door was open.

From the fluttering gas jet in the outer hall, a wedge of light streamed in. Sharply outlined in its bluish-green rays, Marie Na Liu stood there, her face pale and drawn. She stood silent and motionless, but as though charged with some kind of elemental force that was inexhaustible.

Yu Ching twisted in his chair. For a moment, something reached out and touched his soul, leaving the chill of an indescribable uneasiness. For a moment, he thought of his former life; thought of it in terms of a new life, a future life; it opened before him, holding immense and measureless perspectives.

Then, with slow deliberation, he turned his back upon his wife.

"O Buddha!" he mumbled. "All forms are only temporary—illusions of the flesh! Thou knowest! I know!"

Outside, the wind shrieked. The Elevated cars blundered along their steely spider's web, like weary creatures seeking shelter.

"Say! Yu Ching! Listen t'me!"

He did not turn.

"Buddha!" he prayed. "Permit me to withdraw my senses wholly into meditation!"

"Looka here!" came Marie Na Liu's voice, strident and challenging.

She closed the door and stepped into the room. He could hear the rustle of her garments, could smell a faint perfume.

He bent his head on his chest; tried to conquer his senses.

"I wanta talk t'yer!"

He did not move; did not speak.

Peace, perfect, exquisite—there was the secret of life, the way of salvation. He had reached it once, had felt it once; like the stillness of dawn in a lonely place, like the quiet hush of unseen stars. He had reached it and felt it. He did not want to lose it again. The pilgrimage had been hard, hard.

Deliberately, he gathered his soul into an inner fold of his consciousness.

And then, as from very far off, across illimitable distances, he heard again his wife's voice—low, appealing; presently leaping out extraordinarily strong, with a sweep of utter abandon.

"Bill Devoy—'member the plain-clothes cop?— slips me woid that ye've retoined. And—well. . . ."

"Say! When y' left me, three years ago, I sed to myself I'd never forgive yer—never wanted t'see yer mug again. Told yer I hated yer, didn't I? Gee— I was sure some sore! But," she gave a little throaty, embarrassed laugh, "well—here I am—see?"

Silence. He could hear her breath coming in sibilant, staccato sobs. Again her voice:

"Y'make it hard fer a feller, don't yer? Say! Sweetness! I got my pride—I'm a woman, ain't I?"

Her voice broke a little.

"Sweetness! Aw—Gawd! Why don't yer speak t'me?"

The words wavered, sank, rose again.

"Why don't yer say somethin'? Anything—oh— anything! Just toin and look at me, won't ye? Coise me! Swear at me! Tell me to clear outa here! But —please—speak! Aw—sweetness—won't yer talk t'me—please?"

Yu Ching felt words rising in his throat. He choked them back. All this—Pell Street, the noises of the night, his wife—was an illusion in a sea of illusions. It was not real. It was taking place in an alien world of dreams. There was only his own soul, safe in some inner and secret sanctuary of eternity, where the riot and tumult of external life dared not intrude.

He smiled, very gently.

Somewhere, quite close to him, there was the sweet passion and pain of long, exquisite suffering, some intense yearning. But, surely, it was not in his own body, his own heart. It was just the remote experience of a life which he had once known—which he would never know again.

"All forms are only temporary—only temporary—" he mumbled.

"So yer won't talk t'me—eh?"

The question came with a harsh, vindictive grating, and something beyond fear stole with a freezing touch upon Yu Ching's placid soul. He conquered the feeling, sent it reeling back to the undergrowth of his stilled, half-remembering consciousness.

Came silence.

It seemed eternities until once more Marie Na Liu's harsh words dropped into the great, open void.

"Well—don't talk, if yer don't feel like it! But— ye'll listen t'me, awright, awright, yer damned Chink! Sure Mike! Ye'll listen—"

The voice plunged on, piercing, high-pitched.

"'Member young Nag Gin Lee? Ol' Nag Hong Fah's nephew from Frisco, who came here t' learn the business? Young feller—'member?—more my own age. Swell lookin' guy, and some classy dresser, 'member him? Say, yer damned fat old Chink! D'yer remember him? Yer don't? Well—I do! Yes, sir, I do! And d'yer know why? D'yer wanta know?"

She spoke through her teeth. Her words clicked and broke like dropping icicles.

She rushed up to her husband. She gripped his shoulders with frantic hands. She forced him to turn and look up until she could stare straight into his black, oblique eyes, her own eyes blazing fire and hate.

"Not that ye'll care! Not that ye'll give a damn! But—yer might as well know. Me and young Nag— me and him. . . ."

She burst into gurgling, hysterical laughter that shook her whole body.

"Me and him—me and him. . . ."

He rose; trembled.

Marie Na Liu's last words had staggered him like a blow between the eyes.

He tried to control himself.

Peace, perfect, exquisite! The peace of the soul, calm, passionless, serene, in a world of illusions— ropes of illusions—ropes of sand. . . .

His thoughts groped, slipped.

Peace—the Buddha's peace—the end of his soul's pilgrimage. But—and an extraordinary revulsion caught him, flashed upon him like a sheet of black fire—what did it matter—his soul's pilgrimage? What did anything matter, except—

Marie Na Liu!

Golden-haired—sloe-eyed. . . . Her little feet had crushed his heart. . . .

He felt a terrible weakness in his knees, and a catch in his throat. For a tenth part of a second his memory turned back. He thought of a day, a spring day. He had come home rather earlier than usual, had found young Nag sitting across from his wife, close to her. He had heard them laugh as he came up the stairs—had heard mumbled words.

He stood there, a deep sob shaking his massive frame, and Marie Na Liu was still laughing, loudly, hysterically.

"Sure! Me and him—me and him. . . ."

She rushed to the door, opened it, stood no the threshold.

"Me and him—yer poor fish! And yer never knew —yer never guessed!"

Her words came like the lash of a whip. Yu Ching sank back in his chair. He heard the door close.

His wife—and young Nag! His wife—and young Nag!

The words repeated themselves in his thoughts. They expanded and multiplied. They were in his veins, in his bones, in the roots of his hair. They seemed to fill every nook and cranny of his brain.

He looked out of the window. The night had thickened. Mist wreaths pointed with long, bloodless fingers. Above them a heavy cloud-bank lumbered clumsily in the lilt of the wind.

Somebody laughed below the window. Somebody cursed.

Life was down there; passion and desire, love and hate and ambition—life, real life. His own soul, he thought, had dared sublime achievement; it had failed, had plunged him into an abyss.

He slumped in his chair; he cried, with cracked, high-pitched sobs, as strong men cry.

He did not hear the rattling of the door knob. He

did not see the melting and dimming of the bluish-green gas jet in the outer hall, as the door opened and closed again.

But, suddenly, a faint scent of flowers was in his nostrils. Suddenly he felt, close to him, at his knees, a yielding form; heard soft, broken words:

"Aw—sweetness! Don't yer believe wot I sed! I lied! Honest t' Gawd, I lied! Yer know I lied—don't yer—don't yer, sweetness?"

And his arms folded about her, and she nestled like a tired bird.

Then he smiled, very gently, very patiently.

"Peace," he whispered. "Ah—peace—perfect, exquisite. . . ."

TAO

It was now the custom of Li Ping-Yeng, the wealthy retired banker, to sit near the open window and look up at the sky, which seemed always to be packed with dirty clouds, or down into Pell Street, toward the corner, where it streams into the Bowery in frothy, brutal, yellow-and-white streaks. Occasionally, huddled snug and warm in a fold of his loose sleeve, a diminutive, flat-faced Pekinese spaniel, with convex, nostalgic eyes and a sniffy button of a nose, would give a weak and rather ineffectual bark. Then, startled, yet smiling, Li Ping-Yeng would rise and go down-stairs to the Great Shanghai Chop Suey Palace in search of food.

To do this, he had to cross his apartment.

Fretted with shifting lights, it lay in dim, scented splendor. Underfoot stretched a thick-napped dragon rug of tawny orange and taupe, picked out with rose-red and brown. Age-darkened tulip-wood furniture faded into the corners, where the shadows drooped and coiled. The door of the outer hall was hidden by a great, ebony-framed screen of pale lotus silk embroidered with conventionalized figures, black and purple and maroon, that represented the "Hei-song-che-choo," the "Genii of the Ink," household gods of the literati; while here and there, on table and taboret and étagère, were priceless pieces of Chinese porcelain, blue-and-white Ming and Kang-he beakers in aubergine and oxen-blood, crackled *clair-de-lune* of the dynasty of Sung, peachblow celadon, Corean Fo dogs and Fong-hoang emblems in ash-gray and apple-green.

This was the room, these were the treasures, which years ago he had prepared with loving, meticulous care for the coming of his bride.

She had come, stepping mincingly in tiny bound feet, "skimming," had said an impromptu Pell Street poet who had cut his rice gin with too much heady whompee juice, "over the tops of golden lilies, like Yao Niang, the iron-capped Manchu prince's famous concubine."

But almost immediately—the tragedy had not loomed very large in the morning news, starting with a crude head-line of "Woman Killed in Street by Car on Wrong Side," and winding up with "The Chauffeur, Edward H. Connor, of No. 1267 East 157th Street, was held at the West 68th Street Station on a charge of homicide"—her body had passed into the eternal twilight, her soul had leaped the dragon gate to join the souls of her ancestors.

And to-day Li Ping-Yeng, in the lees of life, was indifferent to the splendors of Ming and Sung, of broidered silks and carved tulip-wood. To-day there was only the searching for his personal *tao*, his inner consciousness removed from the lying shackles of love and hate, the drab fastening of form and substance and reality.

Daily, as he sat by the window, he approached nearer to that center of cosmic life where outward activity counts for less than the shadow of nothing. Daily he felt the tide rise in his secret self, trying to blend with the essence of eternity. Daily, beyond the dirty clouds of lower Manhattan, beyond the Pell Street reek of sewer-gas and opium and yellow man and white, he caught a little more firmly at the fringe of final fulfillment.

Food? Yes. There was still the lying reality called body which needed food and drink and occasionally a crimson-tasseled pipe filled with a sizzling, amber cube of first-chop opium. Also, there was the little Pekinese spaniel that had once belonged to his bride,—"*Su Chang*," "Reverential and Sedate," was its ludicrous name,—and it cared nothing for *tao* and cosmic eternity, but a great deal for sugar and chicken bones and bread steeped in lukewarm milk.

"*Woo-ooff!*" said "Reverential and Sedate."

And so, startled, yet smiling, Li Ping-Yeng went down-stairs to the Great Shanghai Chop Suey Palace, exchanged courtly greetings with the obese proprietor, Mr. Nag Hong Fah, and ordered a heaped bowl for the spaniel, and for himself a platter of rice, a pinch of soey cheese, a slice of preserved ginger stem, and a pot of tea.

Twenty minutes later he was back in his chair near the window, scrutinizing sky and street.

Unseeing, meaningless scrutiny; for it was only the conscious, thus worthless, part of his brain which perceived, and reacted to, the details of what he saw: the lemon tints of the street lamps leaping meanly out of the trailing, sooty dusk and centering on a vivid oblong of scarlet and gold where Yung Long, the wholesale grocer, flung his sign-board to the winds and proclaimed thereon in archaic Mandarin script that "Trade revolves like a Wheel"; an automobile-load of tourists gloating self-righteously over the bland, shuffling Mongol's base infinitudes; a whisky-soaked nondescript moving along with hound-like stoop and flopping, ragged clothes, his face turned blindly to the stars and a childlike smile curling his lips; or, perhaps, hugging the blotchy shadows of a postern, the tiny figure of Wuh Wang, the wife of Li Hsü, the hatchet-man, courting a particularly shocking fate by talking, face close against face, to a youth, with a checked suit and no forehead to speak of, whose native habitat was around the corner, on the Bowery.

Also voices brushed up, splintered through the open window, the stammering, gurgling staccato of felt-slippered Cantonese, suggestive of a primitive utterance going back to the days before speech had evolved; the metallic snap and crackle of Sicilians and Calabrians talking dramatically about the price of garlic and olive-oil; the jovial brogue of Bill Devoy, detective of Second Branch, telling a licenseless peddler to "beat it"; the unbearable, guttural, belching whine of Russian Hebrews, the Pell Street symphony, with the blazing roar of the elevated thumping a dissonant counterpoint in the distance.

Li Ping-Yeng saw, he heard, but only with the conscious, the worthless part of his brain; while the real part, the subconscious, was occupied with the realization of himself which he must master in order to reach the excellent and august wisdom of *tao*—the search of his inner soul, beyond the good and the evil, which, belike, he had muddied by his too great love for his wife.

This *tao* was still too dim for him to see face to face. It was still beyond the touch and feel of definite thought. Its very possibility faded elusively when he tried to bring it to a focus. Yet he knew well what had been the basis of it. He had learned it by the bitterest test of which the human heart is capable

—the negative test; the test of suffering and unfulfilled desire; the test of acrid memory. "Memory," he would say to himself, over and over again, patiently, defiantly, almost belligerently, when the thought of his wife's narrow, pleasurable hands rose flush with the tide of his regrets and, by the same token, caused his *tao* once more to dim and fade—"memory, which is of the dirt-clouted body, and not of the soul."

Yet in the matter of acrid memory and unfulfilled desire Miss Edith Rutter, the social-settlement investigator who specialized in the gliding vagaries of the Mongol mind as exemplified in Pell Street, had brought back at the time an entirely different tale, an entirely different interpretation of Chinese philosophy, too.

But be it remembered that philosophy is somewhat affected by surroundings, and that Miss Rutter had been on a visit to an aunt of hers in Albany, balancing a Jasper ware tea-cup and cake-plate on a scrawny, black-taffeta-covered knee, and, about her, tired, threadbare furnishings that harped back to the days of rep curtains, horsehair *chaise-longues,* wax fruit, shell ornaments, banjo clocks, pictures of unlikely children playing with improbable dogs, cases of polished cornelian, levant-bound sets of Ouida, and unflinching, uncompromising Protestant Christianity.

"My dear," she had said to Aunt Eliza Jane, "the more I see of these Chinamen, the less I understand them. This man I told you about, Mr. Li Ping-Yeng —oh, a most charming, cultured gentleman, I assure you, with such grand manners!—I saw him a few minutes after they brought home the poor crushed little body of his young bride, his two days' bride, and, my dear,—would you believe it possible?—there wasn't a tear in his eyes, his hands didn't even tremble. And when I spoke to him, tactful, gentle, consoling words, what do you imagine he replied?"

"I've no idea."

"He smiled! Yes, indeed, *smiled!* And he said something—I forget the exact words—about his having, perhaps, loved too much, his having perhaps been untrue to his inner self. I can't understand their philosophy. It is—oh—so inhuman!" She had puzzled. "How *can* anybody love *too* much? What *can* he have meant by his 'inner self'?"

"Pah! heathens!" Aunt Eliza Jane had commented resolutely. "Have another cup of tea?"

Thus the judgment of the whites; and it was further crystallized in detective Bill Devoy's rather more brutal: "Say, them Chinks has got about as much feelings as a snake has hips. No noives—no noives at all, see?" and Mr. Brian Neill, the Bowery saloon-keeper's succinct: "Sure, Mike. I hates all them yeller swine. They gives me the bloody creeps."

Still, it is a moot point who is right, the Oriental, to whom love is less a sweeping passion than the result of a delicate, personal balancing on the scales of fate, or the Occidental, to whom love is a hectic, unthinking ecstasy, though, given his racial inhibitions, often canopied in the gilt buckram of stiffly emotional sex-romanticism.

At all events, even the humblest, earthliest coolie between Pell and Mott had understood when, the day after his wife's death, Li Ping-Yeng had turned to the assembled company in the back room of the Great Shanghai Chop Suey Palace, which was for yellow men only and bore the euphonic appellation, "The Honorable Pavilion of Tranquil Longevity," and had said:

"The ancients are right. One must preserve a proper

balance in all emotions. The man who, being selfish, loves too much, is even as the one who cooks the dregs of wretched rice over a sandalwood fire in a pot of lapis lazuli, or as one who uses a golden plow in preparation for cultivating weeds, or as one who cuts down a precious camphor-grove to fence in a field of coarse millet. Such a man is the enemy of his own *tao*. It is most proper that such a man should be punished."

After a pause he had added:

"I am such a man, brothers. I have been punished. I tied my soul and my heart to a woman's jeweled ear-rings. The ear-rings broke. The woman died. Died my heart and my soul. And now, where shall I find them again? Where shall I go to seek for my *tao?*"

There had come a thick pall of silence, with only the angry sizzling of opium cubes as lean, yellow hands held them above the openings of the tiny lamps; a sucking of boiling-hot tea sipped by compressed lips; somewhere, outside, on the street, a cloudy, gurgling trickle of obscene abuse, presently fading into the memory of sounds.

The men sighed heavily. Coolies they were, the sweepings of the Canton gutters and river-banks, cooks, waiters, grocers, petty traders; yet men of an ancient race, behind whom stretched forty centuries of civilization and culture and philosophy, in solemn, graven rows. Thus they were patient, slightly hard, not easily embarrassed, submimely unselfconscious, tolerant, permitting each man to look after his own fate, be it good or evil. Anti-social, an American would have called them, and he would have been wrong.

Li Ping-Yeng had bared his naked, quivering soul to their gaze. He was their friend; they respected him. He was a rich man, an educated man. Yet Li

Ping-Yeng's life was his own to make or to mar.
Sympathy? Yes; but not the arrogant indelicacy of
help offered, of advice proffered.

Thus they had thought, all except Yu Ch'ang, the
priest of the joss-temple.

For many years, since he made his frugal living by
catering to the spiritual weal of Pell Street, it had been
the latter's custom, when he foregathered with his
countrymen, to gain face for himself and his sacerdotal
caste by talking with nagging, pontifical unction about
things religious and sectarian. But, being a hedge-
priest, self-appointed, who had received only scanty
training in the wisdom of the "three precious ones,"
the Buddha past, the Buddha present, and the Buddha
future, he had found it hard to uphold his end when
tackled by Li Ping-Yeng, the banker, the literatus,
anent the contents of such abstruse books of theological learning as the "Park of Narratives," "Ku-liang's
Commentaries," or the "Diamond Sutra."

Now, with the other baring his bleeding soul, he
had seen a chance of settling the score, of causing
him to lose a great deal of face.

"Little brother," he had purred, "I am a man of
religion, a humble seeker after truth, whose knowledge
is not to be compared with yours; yet have I thought
much. I have thought left and thought right. Often
in the past have we differed, you and I, on minor
matters of philosophy and ceremonial. May I, the
very useless one, address words of advice to you, the
great literatus?"

"Please do."

"Ah! Then let me reply with the words of Confucius, that he who puts too much worth on worthless
things, such as the love of woman, the love of the

flesh, is like the wolf and the hare, leaving the direction of his steps to low passions. To lead such a man into the august ways of *tao* is as futile as tethering an elephant with the fiber of the young lotus, as futile as the attempt to cut a diamond with a piece of wood, as futile as trying to sweeten the salt sea with a drop of honey, or to squeeze oil from sand. Ah, ahee!" He had spread out his fingers like the sticks of a fan and had looked about him with brutal triumph.

The other's features, as yellow as old parchment, indifferent, dull, almost sleepy, had curled in a queer, slow smile. He was smoking his fourth pipe, a pipe of carved silver, with a green-amber mouthpiece and black tassels. The room had gradually filled with scented fog. The objects scattered about had lost their outlines, and the embroidered stuffs on the walls had gleamed less brilliantly. Only the big, violet-shaded lanterns on the ceiling had continued to give some light, since poppy vapors are slow to rise and float nearer the ground.

"You are wrong, wise priest," he had replied.

"Wrong?"

"Yes. For there is one who *can* tether the elephant with the fiber of the young lotus, who can cut a diamond with a piece of soft wood, sweeten the salt sea with a drop of honey, and squeeze oil from sand."

"Who?" Yu Ch'ang had asked, smiling crookedly at the grave assembly of Chinese who sat there, sucking in their breath through thin lips, their faces like carved ivory masks.

Li Ping-Yeng had made a great gesture.

"The Excellent Buddha," he had replied, in low, even, passionless, monotonous accents that were in curious, almost inhuman, contrast to the sublime, sweeping faith in his choice of words. "The Omniscient Gautama! The All-Seeing Tathagata! The Jewel in the Lotus! The most perfectly awakened Blessed One who meditates in heaven on His seven-stepped throne!"

And again the grave assembly of Chinese had sat very still, sucking in their breath, staring at their neat, slippered feet from underneath heavy, hooded eyelids, intent, by the token of their austere racial simplicity, on effacing their personalities from the focus of alien conflict; and then, like many a priest of many a creed before him, Yu Ch'ang, sensing the silent indifference of his countrymen and interpreting it as a reproach to his hierarchical caste, had let his rage get the better of his professional, sacerdotal hypocrisy.

"The Buddha? Here? In Pell Street?" he had exclaimed. He had laughed hoarsely, meanly. "Find Him, the Excellent One, the Perfect One, in Pell Street? Look for the shining glory of His face—here —in the soot and grease and slippery slime of Pell Street? Search, belike, for fish on top of the mountain, and for horns on the head of the cat! Bah!" He had spat out the word, had risen, crossed over to the window, thrown it wide, and pointed to the west, where a great, slow wind was stalking through the sky, picking up fluttering rags of cloud. "Go! Find Him, the Buddha, in the stinking, rotten heaven of Pell Street! Go, go—by all means! And, perhaps, when you have found Him, you will also have found your *tao*, fool!"

"I shall try," had come Li Ping-Yeng's reply. "Yes; most decidedly shall I try." He had walked to the door. There he had turned. "Little brother," he had said to the priest over his shoulder, without malice

or hurt or bitterness, "and why should I not find Him
even in the Pell Street gutters? Why should I not
find my *tao* even in the stinking, rotten heaven that
vaults above Pell Street? Tell me. Is not my soul
still my soul? Is not the diamond still a diamond,
even after it has fallen into the dung-heap?"

And he had stepped out into the night, staring up
at the purple-black sky, his coat flung wide apart, his
lean, yellow hands raised high, indifferent to the rain
that had begun to come down in flickering sheets.

"Say, John, wot's the matter? Been hittin' the old
pipe too much? Look out! One o' these fine days I'll
raid that joint o' yours," had come detective Bill
Devoy's genial brogue from a door-way where he had
taken refuge against the elements.

Li Ping-Yeng had not heard, had not replied; except
to talk to himself, perhaps to the heaven, perhaps to
the Buddha, in staccato Mongol monosyllables, which,
had Bill Devoy been able to understand, would have
convinced him more than ever that that there Chink
was a sure-enough hop-head:

"Permit me to cross the torrent of grief, O Buddha,
as, even now, I am crossing the stream of passion!
Give me a stout raft to gain the other side of blessed-
ness! Show me the way, O King!"

Back in the honorable Pavilion of Tranquil Longevity, slant eye had looked meaningly into slant
eye.

"Ah, perhaps indeed he will find his *tao*," Yung
Long, the wholesale grocer, had breathed gently; and
then to Yu Ch'ang, who had again broken into harsh,
mean cackling, said:

"Your mouth is like a running tap, O very great and
very uncouth cockroach!"

"Aye, a tap spouting filthy water." This was from Nag Sen Yat, the opium merchant.

"A tap which, presently, I shall stop with my fist," said Nag Hop Fat, the soothsayer, winding up the pleasant round of Oriental metaphor.

Thus was displayed, then, the serene, if negative, sympathy of the Pell Street confraternity, further demonstrated by its denizens leaving Li Ping-Yeng hereafter severely alone and by replying to all questions and remarks of outsiders with the usual formula of the Mongol when he does not wish to commit himself: "No savvy!"

"I feel so terribly sorry for him,"—this from Miss Edith Rutter,—"Is there really nothing I can do to—"

"No savvy."

"Looka here,"—from Bill Devoy,—"you tell that brother-Chink o' yourn, that there Li Ping-Yeng, to stop hittin' the black smoke, or I'll pinch him on spec, see?"

"No savvy."

"Listen!"—from the old Spanish woman who kept the second-hand store around the corner, on the Bowery,—"What do you think he's going to do with all the truck he bought for his wife? I'd like to buy the lot. Now, if you want to earn a commission—"

"No savvy."

"Is he goin' t' try holy matrimony again, or near-matrimony?"—from Mr. Brian Neill, the saloon-keeper, who occasionally added to his income by unsavory deals between the yellow and the white,—"For, if he wants another goil, there's a peacherino of a red-headed good-looker that blows into my back parlor once in a while and that don't mind Chinks as long's they got the kale—"

"No savvy."

And even to the emissary of a very great Wall Street bank that in the past had handled certain flourishing Manila and Canton and Hankow accounts for the Pell Street banker, and who, unable to locate him personally and being slightly familiar with Chinese customs, had sought out the head of the latter's masonic lodge and had asked him why Li Ping-Yeng had retired from business, and if, at all events, he wouldn't help them with the unraveling of a knotty financial tangle in far Shen-si. Even there was the same singsong answer:

"No savvy," exasperatingly, stonily repeated.

"No savvy, no savvy."

For two days after his wife's tragic death Li Ping-Yeng, to quote his own words, had given up vigorously threshing mere straw, by which term he meant all the every-day, negligible realities of life.

He had begun by selling his various business interests; nor, since he was a prosy Mongol whose brain functioned with the automatic precision of a photographic shutter and was nowise affected by whatever was going on in his soul, had he made a bad deal. On the contrary, he had bargained shrewdly down to the last fraction of a cent.

Then, prudently, deliberately, the patient and materialistic Oriental even in matters of the spirit, he had swept his mind clear of everything except the search for his *tao*, the search for his salvation. This *tao* was to him a concrete thing, to be concretely achieved, since it was to link him, intimately and strongly, not with, as would have been the case had he been a Christian, an esoteric principle, a more or less recondite, theological dogma, but with a precious and beneficent in-a giant rush of splendor and, greatly, blessedly, overwhelm him and destroy his clogging, individual entity.

But how was this to be attained? Had he been a Hindu ascetic, or even a member of certain Christian sects, he would have flagellated his body, would have gone through the ordeal of physical pain. But, a Mongol, thus stolidly unromantic and rational, almost torpidly sane, he had done nothing of the sort. On the contrary, he had continued to take good care of himself. True, he had begun to eat less, but not purposely; simply because his appetite had decreased. And his real reason for keeping his wife's Pekinese spaniel tucked in his sleeve was because "Reverential and Sedate" reminded him when it was time for luncheon or dinner, hours he might otherwise have forgotten.

The idea of suicide had never entered his reckoning, since he held the belief of half Asia, that suicide destroys the body and not the soul; that it is only a crude and slightly amateurish interruption of the present life, leaving the thread of it still more raveled and tangled and knotted for the next life, and yet the next.

He had passed over the obvious solution of devoting himself to charity, to the weal of others, as it had seemed to him but another instance of weak and selfish vanity, fully as weak and selfish as the love of woman; and the solace of religion he had dismissed with the same ready, smiling ease. Religion, to him, was not an idea, but a stout, rectangular entity, a great force and principle, that did its appointed duty not because people believed in it, but because it *was*. The Buddha would help him, if it be so incumbent by fate upon

the Buddha, regardless, if he prayed to him or not, if
he memorized the sacred scriptures, if he burned
sweet-scented Hunshuh incense-sticks before the gilt
altar or not. For the Buddha, too, was tied firmly to
the Wheel of Things. The Buddha, too, had to do his
appointed task. Thus, Li Ping-Yeng had decided,
prayers would be a waste of time, since they could not
influence the Excellent One one way or the other.

How, then, could he acquire sufficient merit so as
to reach his *tao*, beyond the good and the evil?

Of course, first of all, mainly, by tearing from his
body and heart even the last root of the liana of desire,
of love, of regret for his wife; by again and again
denying, impugning, destroying the thought of her,
though, again and again, it would rise to the nostrils
of his remembrance, with a stalely sweet scent like the
ghost of dead lotus-blossoms.

She was on the shadow side of the forever. Her
soul, he would repeat to himself, incessantly, defiantly,
belligerently, had leaped the dragon gate. Broken
were the fetters that had held him a captive to the
tinkle-tinkle-tinkle of her jeweled ear-rings. A mere
picture she was, painted on the screen of eternity, im-
personal, immensely aloof, passed from the unrealities
of the earth life to the realities of the further cosmos.
He must banish the thought of her, must forget her.

And he did forget her, again and again, with the
effort, the pain of forgetting choking his heart.

Sitting by the window, his subconscious mind cen-
tered on his *tao*, his salvation, the blessed destruction
of his individual entity, "Reverential and Sedate" huddled in a fold of his loose sleeve, scrutinizing street
and sky with unseeing eyes, he would forget her
through the long, greasy days, while the reek of Pell

Street rose up to the tortured clouds with a mingled aroma of sweat and blood and opium and suffering, while the strident clamor of Pell Street blended with the distant clamor of the Broadway mart.

He would forget her through the long, dim evenings, while the sun died in a gossamer veil of gold and mauve, and the moon cut out of the ether, bloated and anemic and sentimental, and the night vaulted to a purple canopy, pricked with chilly, indifferent stars.

He would sit there, silent, motionless, and forget, while the stars died, and the moon and the night, and the sky flushed to the opal of young morning, and again came day and the sun and the reek and the maze and the soot and the clamors of Pell Street.

Forgetting, always forgetting; forgetting his love, forgetting the tiny bound feet of the Plum Blossom, the Lotus Bud, the Crimson Butterfly. Her little, little feet! Ahee! He had made his heart a carpet for her little, little feet.

Forgetting, reaching up to his *tao* with groping soul; and then again the thought of his dead wife, again his *tao* slipping back; again the travail of forgetting, to be forever repeated.

And so one day he died; and it was Wuh Wang, the little, onyx-eyed, flighty wife of Li Hsü, the hatchet-man, who, perhaps, speaking to Tzu Mo, the daughter of Yu Ch'ang, the priest, grasped a fragment of the truth.

"Say, kid," she slurred in the Pell Street jargon, "that there Li Ping-Yeng wot's kicked the bucket th' other day, well, you know wot them Chinks said—how he was always trying to get next to that—now—*tao* of his by trying to forget his wife. Well, mebbe he was all wrong. Mebbe his *tao* wasn't forgetting at all. Mebbe it was just his love for her, his always thinking of her, his *not* forgetting her—that was his real *tao*."

"Mebbe," replied Tzu Mo. "I should worry!"

THE END

www.ingramcontent.com/pod-product-compliance
Lightning Source LLC
Chambersburg PA
CBHW050503260626
47157CB00004B/1170